MW01275368

NIGHT SPELL

NIGHT SPELL

LUCINDA BETTS

APHRODISIA

KENSINGTON BOOKS

http://www.kensingtonbooks.com

APHRODISIA BOOKS are published by

Kensington Publishing Corp.
850 Third Avenue
New York, NY 10022

All Kensington Titles, Imprints, and Distributed Lines are available at special quantity discounts for bulk purchases for sales promotions, premiums, fund-raising, and educational or institutional use.

Special book excerpts or customized printings can also be created to fit specific needs. For details, write or phone the office of the Kensington special sales manager: Kensington Publishing Corp., 850 Third Avenue, New York, NY 10022, attn: Special Sales Department, Phone: 1-800-221-2647.

ISBN: 0-7582-1469-3

First Trade Paperback Printing: October 2006

10 9 8 7 6 5 4 3 2 1

Printed in the United States of America

For SKK, who delivers the perfect combination of pleasure and pain.
For WTT, who fills my dreams with magic.

Contents

My Captor

1

Still tangled in ribbons of dreams, my consciousness fought to focus. Surreal images rose to the surface. Powerful hands grabbing my wrist. A handsome face. A strange scent and muscular thighs. Were there . . . sultans? Harems?

No. There weren't. Just dreams, I realized, breathing easier. Dream images.

I squinted my eyes toward the alarm clock, but seeing nothing, I gave up trying. Still too early.

I closed my eyes and snuggled back into my bed, sifting through the dream memories, trying to remember. I dreamed . . . I'd been kidnapped. A Sultan wanted me, and a gorgeous mercenary had stolen me. How exotic.

I vaguely remembered a story I'd heard on NPR about a Romanian or Hungarian woman escaping after being kidnapped and used as a sex slave. Marquis de Sade's Justine had been kidnapped and did a stint in a basement with stinky monks. The kidnapped Romanian from the radio had been kept in a dingy hotel room filled with fat, bald men with bad breath.

The watery memory I had of my dream was much more

glamorous. I hadn't been Romanian, and I hadn't been in a basement. There were billowing tents and silken cords and beautiful flowing genie pants.

With a little more ease, I opened my eyes and squinted at my clock. Retinas still not stretching, pupils still not dilating, I saw nothing. Still too early.

Closing my eyes, I sieved through my memories for more juicy tidbits. I clearly remembered checking into the Morgan, a four-star luxury hotel in Manhattan. I was going to stay for three days as part of a well-earned vacation.

I remembered a black-and-white marbled floor and cool art deco furnishings. A good-looking doorman bought me dewy pink tulips from the adjacent drugstore. At the time I thought the move was too polished, but I love tulips and was charmed nonetheless.

I dreamed I bought a coke at the bar, bypassing room service to check out the patrons. I'd found no one interesting and had taken the coke to my room.

But that part wasn't a dream. I really was on vacation. I really was at the Morgan.

What time was it?

Forcing my eyes to open and focus, I looked around me . . . and blinked.

A sea of green silk billowed above me. The scent of hot dust filled the air. Was I in a tent? I turned my head. A big post stood in the center of the fluttering green silk. Was that flap opposite me a door?

I tried to focus on my surroundings, and became increasingly aware of a growing pressure in the back of my head. It hurt. A lot.

Closing my eyes felt like the right thing to do, and as I drifted into sleep, a rational part of my brain told me that the world would make more sense when I woke.

I hoped it was right.

* * *

Sleep lifted slowly from my eyes. From the soft comfort of my bed I admired the hues floating above me.

Sunlight filtered through the emerald-colored walls, filling the space with bright silhouettes of leaves, fingers of tree branches. A slight breeze lifted the fabric, billowing it with a soft whisper. Dappled colors surrounded me, beautiful underwater colors.

Then I realized. This was not the Morgan. I was in a tent!

My heart pounded like a crazed antelope leaping over the plains, and I tried to sit. I couldn't. Fighting panic, I realized— my hands were tied behind my back.

I opened my mouth to scream, but my brain warned against it. *Don't tell anyone you're awake*, it urged. I blinked again, acknowledging that it was right, this time.

Closing my eyes, I took a deep breath.

A deep melodic voice interrupted my meditation. "Good," he said, the tone slow, rich, seductive. Otherworldly. "You indicate some ability to control yourself. You show promise."

I tried to scream, but the sound refused to budge from my lungs. I fought the paralysis. And lost. I just . . . couldn't scream. Panic pounded through my veins.

"The Sultan will be extremely pleased with your control," he said.

I tried again. My lungs worked! This time I did scream. So much for control. I screamed for help. I screamed for mercy. I screamed obscenities that weren't nearly as creative as I might have hoped given the situation. Finally, I screamed to a God I wasn't sure existed.

The result of my screaming didn't make me any more religious. No golden chariots appeared at my rescue. No sword-bearing angels came to avenge me. Instead, the implacable voice of the man standing in the doorway responded in an almost gentle fashion.

"Now is the time for screaming and lack of control," he said. "Scream all you like—today. No one can hear you except me. Mariah is deaf, and if she could hear, she would not help you." His sensual voice had a husky, mocking quality that sent a shiver down my spine.

Unearthly. Elegant. Did Pierce Brosnan have a younger brother with a habit of kidnapping women? My captor seemed vaguely familiar, like I'd met him in a dream. A feathered memory tickled the back of my mind. There was something . . .

My captor approached me, almost floating in his gracefulness, and he moved to touch my head. Panic swelled, filling me with an overpowering desire to escape this tent. Now. Regardless of the guy's looks, I hadn't signed up for this, and nothing about the situation in which I found myself was consensual.

I pulled away from him wanting all of my strength, but as if in a dream, I was as weak as a child. In slow motion, I tugged my wrists, feeling like I struggled through a sea of molasses. I was so slow, so weak. What was wrong with me?

Drugs . . . it must be drugs, whatever he'd used to steal me from the Morgan Hotel. Telazol? Ketamine? I could barely move, despite my will to run. My bonds held.

I shouted again, but it didn't sound like my voice. Kathleen Battle's voice fell from my lips, singing a passionate scene of anger and rage. Birds took wing from the branches above my tent.

"I would recommend that you cease shouting by nightfall. Why let the lions and hyenas know where you are?" His calm tone ridiculed me.

He touched my head again, despite my noisy writhings. His hand unnerved me, burning into my skin even through my hair.

He paused at the tent's flap and said, looking me in the eyes, "Mariah will be here shortly to see to your needs. When you calm yourself enough to think of escape, be aware that you are several hundred kilometers from the nearest town, and the people of that town do not speak English."

I'd been screaming and struggling through his brief soliloquy, and I was nearly frozen in panic. My mind absorbed only a few words: "lions," "several hundred kilometers," "no English." I'd also heard the word "escape." Until then, I hadn't accepted that my situation warranted escape.

Terror rose through my throat.

All parts of my brain agreed upon the next course of action: I cried. I cried until I fell asleep.

But even as sobs ripped themselves from my chest and sleep crept up on me, I realized that a man as good looking as my captor would not need to kidnap anyone, not for himself anyway.

With a few kind words, he'd have the attention of most women I knew. Maybe even me. Images of his dark hair coupled with fair skin, aqua-blue eyes and sharp features danced across my imagination. His easy competence was the sort that generated trust in people.

When he wasn't kidnapping women.

I slid into consciousness again. My mind fought to find the Morgan, but the old woman made it impossible. She silently sponged warm, fragrant water over me. Was the fragrance lavender?

I struggled violently to sit up in bed, yanking on my ties. My wrists and ankles burned under the cords, and my feet longed to run.

But the old woman held up a hand. Like magic, I stopped. Panic drained away, leaving dreamy lethargy in its place.

I stared at her a minute, wondering at the power in her hand. She looked like drawings of Baba Yaga from the fairy tales I'd read as a child, wizened and brown. Wrinkled raisin eyes peered from her sunken face.

I still felt fuzzy headed, like if I tried hard enough I could detach myself from my body and view myself from above. I thought I'd woken in a bed, but now I found myself tied to a chair, hard and unyielding.

Heat permeated the air and the mat-covered ground beneath my feet. The intense heat didn't feel like New York, and the dust didn't smell like Manhattan. My captor mentioned lions. Hadn't he?

Lions. I rolled the word around my consciousness. *Lions.*

Like leaves across a late-summer pond, the word floated through my mind.

Where did lions live? My mind's eye played pictures of big cats roiling over some dusty land.

But a country's name wasn't coming with the picture of the landscape. Someplace in Africa. They were gone in India, weren't they?

I'd watched enough nature shows to know the answer to this question. Rest would bring the answer.

Closing my eyes, I let the old woman do her job. Cool, fragrant water trickled over my brow. Her strong hands massaged warm oil into my calves, into my arms.

When she finished, she held a drink for me. Cool lemony water. So refreshing.

She untied my hands slowly, letting my wrists memorize the texture of the silky binds. After the tie slithered off, she held it up for me to see. *Do not try to escape,* her expression said. *I am trusting you.*

An aromatic stew appeared on the table near the door flap. It must have been there all along. The scent of fresh tomatoes and Indian herbs filled the tent. Naan bread appeared at its side. I ate it, and I enjoyed it.

The old woman was a witch. The lethargy she'd cast on me was something I couldn't swim past. My feet were bound, true, but escape no longer beckoned me.

Where would I go? Was I really in some exotic land miles— no, kilometers—from nowhere?

I finished the stew, using the bread to suck up every last morsel. The old woman—Mariah, I reminded myself—nodded in approval.

She knelt at my feet with a grace surprising in an old woman. With deliberate movements, with slow and exaggerated hands, she untied the silky cords binding my feet. She stood, and with the elegance of a movie star, she held the tent flap open, and gestured for me to leave my green nest.

I did.

Looking at the landscape, I felt like I'd been sucked into the television and delivered to Discovery-channel land. Dry savannah lay all around me. Thick baobab trees peppered the hills. A river trickled below us.

The air smelled amazing. Had I ever before smelled air free of exhaust? And the heat; it defied description. I'd never been to the Southwest. Could anywhere in the United States be this hot?

Mariah gently nudged me toward a small building. I realized it was a bathroom, an outhouse. I then realized that my clothing were not my own.

Someone had dressed me in a sunflower-colored dress. Finely woven cotton fit tightly across my breasts and stomach, loose and flowing around my legs. Ignoring the achingly blue sky and the strange scent of the dust, I quickly undid the buttons over my breasts and looked down.

My no-nonsense underwear were gone. Now, a leopard-print bra pushed my breasts high, made them look full and tempting. My pink nipples peeked out the top. A tiny triangle covered my pubis, also leopard print. Tiny black strings ran over my hips, up the back of my ass.

I stumbled into the outhouse in a cloud of yellow cotton. As I closed the door behind me, names of countries that had lions and that looked like this on television started to filter to the top of my brain—Tanzania, Kenya, South Africa.

Toto, I said to myself, *we're not in Kansas anymore*. But I guess Oz did have lions. If I found myself talking to a tin man, I'd have to question my sanity. The world felt strange—monkeys might fly across the cloudless blue sky.

When I came out of the outhouse, the panoramic view shocked me, took my breath away. I scanned the horizon seeing nothing unnatural, nothing made by human hand. A wide trickling river. Scrubby trees clinging to the shoreline. Huge boulders scattered over the landscape.

Not a house. Not a road. Not an electric pole in sight.

And Mariah was gone. But her witchy magic wasn't. I felt compelled to sit on a boulder. To sit and watch.

In bare feet, I climbed to the top of the big rock. A bright blue lizard with a peach-colored throat scampered away. A bottle-green snake gave me an apologetic look and slithered into the shade. Overhead, a bird of prey cried, sounding like my heart.

And then the old witch returned. With a crook of her gnarled index finger, Mariah indicated I should return to my tent. She wasn't a servant—she was Baba Yaga. Her chicken-legged home lurked just on the other side of one of these boulders. I knew it.

So when Baba Yaga called, I went willingly, filled with that strange lassitude.

I knew I couldn't escape on foot. Where were my shoes? I'd need a car—or a camel. Did they have camels in East Africa?

My knees felt weak. From travel? From fear? I couldn't say. From the witch's spell.

My vision felt strange, wavelike and uncertain. If I blinked I might see a purple sky, blue and yellow striped zebras, a river running in flamboyant orange.

Jet lag, I told myself. *Drugs.*

I went to my bed in my emerald nest, and I did not object when Mariah fastened the silky cords around my wrists and ankles.

I would have objected to the blindfold, but in my complacency and confusion, she tied it over my eyes before I knew what she was doing.

Mariah was a witch. Black magic was her paintbrush. I was her canvas.

Then she brushed my hair while I lay tied, and I relaxed, despite my captivity. The mattress beneath me felt like a cloud, like a slow-rolling wave crossing the Caribbean on a sultry day.

The blindfold brought a strange comfort. In the purple blackness, silvery stars danced before my eyes. Gold ones shot past my view.

Maybe the blindfold meant they were going to transport me someplace, and perhaps that someplace would be more amenable to escape. Maybe they realized that they had the wrong girl and they were bringing me home. If they were going to kill me, I thought, they would have done it by now.

Maybe I'd just wake up in my own pillowy bed, in my sea of blue blankets with sun streaming through my white eyelet curtains. Set on a timer, my coffee would just start dripping into the pot, filling my apartment with its delicious scent. I know I must have been smiling as I drifted off to sleep.

I thought fates worse than death were literary exaggerations.

"You no doubt have many questions, and I will answer none of them."

His voice seemed to come from a distant place, and it rung with a fantastic vibration—like he was both behind me and miles away. And his words did not reassure me, although I didn't say as much. If I appeared implacable maybe he'd leave me alone.

"I'm going to give you some rules. They are simple and basic. You will obey them." With my captor in the room, the blindfold was no longer comforting. Where was he? What was he doing? Panic threatened to overwhelm me. I couldn't imagine feeling more vulnerable.

"Who are you?" I demanded, doing my best to sound imperious. "My father will pay you, if it's ransom you're after."

"I like your attitude," he responded in a voice as rich as dark chocolate. If a magician could special order a voice, he'd want this one. "But I will not answer any of your questions." I wondered just how much Dad could afford. This guy seemed like he had very expensive tastes.

I heard him pause as he approached me, and then he said, "Here are the rules."

I waited, hoping for something like, "Say 'please,' and you can go home."

"I will not penetrate you until you beg for it."

At this, I started fighting my bonds in earnest. My dreamlike weakness of the previous day was gone. My wrists jerked and flailed, yanking the ties until they were as taut as my muscles.

"Penetrate" could have several meanings, none of which sounded good. "Are you crazy?" I screamed. "Get away from me!" I tried to rub my blindfold off with my shoulder. Was he getting closer? The blindfold stubbornly held. Damn Mariah and her knot-tying skills.

"Don't be afraid. I will not enter you until you ask—until you beg. And you will. Even then I will not harm you."

In my experience, people say, "I'm not going to hurt you" just before they hurt you. What doctor tells a patient that the injection will hurt like a son of a bitch?

I screamed wildly.

When he caressed the arch of my foot I screamed again, kicking my tied feet maniacally. Unperturbed, he waited until I stopped. My throat was beginning to ache. While continuing his caress up my ankle, he said, "I will touch you everywhere, in every imaginable way, but I will not penetrate you until you want it. And you will want it." His voice sounded huskier than I remembered.

I knew then that he used "penetrate" as in "to insert the penis into the vagina or anus of." I'd been—unrealistically—hoping that he'd meant "penetrate" as in "to gain insight."

As his warm palm approached the inside of my thigh, I

found myself hoping for a version of "penetrate" that involved knives and hearts, preferably my knife and his heart.

"One day," he said, "just hearing my voice will make you wet." His thumb just brushed through the thin silk of my panties, just above my clit. I jumped, arching my back to get away from him.

"The leopard spots suit you, my little fighter." He chuckled. "And so do the black strings. How does that feel across your clit?" He shifted the string, and I bucked away, screaming.

Then he said, "My goal is to have you wanting me at the sound of my voice. You've had too much control for too long. It's time for a change." His thumb danced gently across my labia, so accessible in this thong, despite my efforts.

I made some small sound in the back of my throat, realizing the hopelessness of my situation. "Today—now—you can fight me without repercussions. But listen to my rules, for I will not change them." I squirmed away again, but no matter where I moved, his clever hands found a light way to tease. His fingertips found my nipple through the cotton fabric of my dress and bra. The gentle pinch sent a shock through my body. What had I done to deserve this?

"Why are you doing this to me?" I sobbed. "Get away!"

"I demand that you will not fight me. That is my rule." Again, I bucked to no avail, and again he laughed. His thumb insistently pushed against my nipple, and the corresponding thrill that ran through me sparked more than fear. "Don't worry. I know that today you can't help but fight. You won't be punished for any recalcitrance today. But tomorrow and thereafter . . ."

The threat hung in the air, and I thought that he was going to leave it unfinished. His breath warmed my cheek as he whispered in my ear, "Tomorrow and thereafter, you will be punished if you fight me."

I froze with the intensity of his whispered voice, and he left before I could respond.

2

Nighttime was a surreal haze, passed half awake and half asleep. Splashings from the river below dampened my uneasy slumber. I heard a crocodile crying, her tears filling the river. The laughter of hyenas fell from Baba Yaga's lips. Leopards poured from her chicken-legged hut and flooded the baobab's plains.

The heat of the morning washed over me, barely impacting my deep fatigue.

Baba Yaga cackled from the dusty riverbed, and Mariah appeared in my tent with a crooked grin. Her wicked intent filled my blood with fear, urged my feet to flight.

In her thrall, I stood and walked toward her, wanting freedom from her magic. My sunflower-yellow dress, unwrinkled from my uneasy night's sleep, floated around me, bathing me in a golden glow.

Mariah stood me in the tent's center, next to a large, smooth pole that supported the green silken walls. She snapped my loosely bound wrists quickly together and just as quickly yanked a rope.

My hands were now above my head. No escape.

The witch was quick and full of dirty tricks. I made a mental note to hate her. As she tied the blindfold around my eyes, I did my best to thwart her. I failed.

My captor must be strong indeed to command this evil witch. Baba Yaga was sometimes wise and sometimes wicked in my fairy tales, but I never heard of anyone commanding her. Not for any length of time.

"Leave us," he said to her. He couldn't be talking to me, tied as I was.

His entrance woke me in a way the sun couldn't. He woke fear in me, and he woke in me a longing to be free.

My captor woke in me a longing.

His musky man smell filled the tent. I wished I could see him, and I wanted to fight. But pinioned by the witch, fighting wasn't an easy option.

Neither was complacency.

"Please. Don't do this. Let me go home," I said toward the door, struggling to keep my voice level. "What are you going to do?" Somehow, his actions didn't fit my idea of a kidnapping for ransom.

This was weirder.

Had he walked closer to me? "Fight your fear, and master yourself," my captor suggested, sounding like Yoda. Was he teasing me? "You might enjoy yourself."

Maybe, but the life I'd led before this did not equate enjoyment with being tied like this in front of a strange man. I tried a different approach.

"What's your name?" In psychodrama novels, weren't the FBI agents always urging the parents or spouses of the victims to do something to humanize the bad guy?

It didn't work. But then, I don't think it worked in the books or movies either. I guess most creeps aren't amenable to humanization.

"Don't fight me," he replied. His voice came from directly behind me, and I scurried around the pole. "If you can find a way to conquer your fears, I might find a way to let you escape."

He was probably lying. But faint hope was better than none. I planted my feet in the ground and closed my eyes, trying not to fight.

Could I succumb to his touch?

Snick. Snick. Snick. Cold metal of a knife zipped over first one shoulder blade, then the other. My yellow dress slithered off me, ruined. I wanted to cry then. *Snick.* My leopard panties were cut. I felt them slither off, too. *Snick.* My bra opened, baring my breasts. *Snick. Snick.* It, too, fell off.

Naked, bound, and exposed in front of a strange man in some exotic land surrounded by lions, and told not to fight . . . Maybe a Tibetan monk could accept such a fate without a struggle, but I was neither Tibetan nor a monk. His warm palm caressed my naked stomach, and futilely, I began to struggle, dancing around the pole like some crazed Maypole maiden.

I don't know what I expected as a consequence of my actions. Punishment implied violence, didn't it? But instead, he seemed nearly happy.

In a light tone, he said, "Ah, I've made my wishes clear— you are not to struggle, you are not to fight me. You've understood this, and yet you thrash."

He gently touched the underside of my breast and I redoubled my efforts, trying to put the pole between him and me but mostly twisting my arms in the effort.

My bonds held, and they felt like they'd hold for eternity. I yanked and pulled while I danced in circles. He too redoubled his efforts, and he succeeded where I failed. Without my sight, I launched myself right into his arms. Probably he planned it that way.

He captured each of my nipples in a light pinch, and I couldn't move, not without hurting my breasts. I was trapped. Fighting him would really hurt me.

For the moment, I was his. The liquid zing between my thighs was due to shock.

It wasn't pleasure, not at all.

"How will I punish you, you wonder?" His breath was warm against my cheek, and his cock throbbed against my ass. I couldn't place his accent—too neutral. It sounded American but clipped, and his syntax was a little off. Who was this guy?

Suddenly, he wasn't touching me, although I could still hear him breathing in my ear. I could still smell him. The thought of his retribution brought fear of brutality to my mind. Tied, I could do nothing to protect myself. Would he spank me? I froze, stealing myself for pain.

None came.

I realized then that I was well and truly at his mercy. Perhaps my best hope at getting home would come from obeying this, this . . . I didn't even know how to describe him. "Monster" seemed like too strong of a word. Whatever he was, I didn't want him to hurt me. I felt afraid enough as it was.

"Okay," I said, my voice husky from shouting. "I won't fight you. I won't fight you, I promise." As a signal of good faith, I straightened my shoulders, pushing my nipples against his fingertips.

Again, that liquid silk between my thighs.

"Ah," he said in that tone, "but is that a promise you can keep?" Releasing my nipples, his fingers lit across the inside of my thigh, barely touching. I held still, like a gazelle caught in the gaze of a hungry lion. I even held my breath.

He was so close to my clit. Each breath I took felt like fire in my chest, and it sounded as loud as stampeding buffalo. God help me, I was soaking wet.

And then he was gone. Or his fingers were. "You don't need this," he said, and my blindfold was gone.

I could see.

And his dark hair, loose and curling at his shoulders gleamed in the tent's light. His face was beautiful—his features delicately molded, ethereal. The blue of his eyes exactly matched the African skies.

Even his hands . . . His fingers were so long, so white and delicate. A vampire might have fingers like this, but my captor didn't look interested in sucking blood.

"Can you keep your promise?" he repeated. "Answer me."

I nodded.

"Answer me."

I swallowed. "I'll try."

He nodded. "Let's test your ability a bit, shall we?" He captured my nipple in his teeth and slid his tongue across it. I gasped. Maybe I shifted, but I didn't fight.

I wanted to fight. But I didn't.

"Good," he said in response. Did he sound disappointed?

I shifted and my nipple slid of its own accord across his tongue.

"But you shall still be punished," he said. And my captor left.

I wondered briefly whether my punishment involved leaving me tied to a pole. I'd read that cowboys in the Old West used to tie up unruly horses. But that wasn't my fate. My world spun in a swirl of ambers and golds, and Mariah appeared bringing dust from the savannahs with her.

The old woman, staring at me with her raisin eyes, untied my ankles with the same slowness she'd shown before. Freed by her gnarled fingers, the cords fluttered around my ankles like kelp floating in the Indian Ocean, somehow freed from gravity.

"Mariah," I said to Baba Yaga. She looked at me. Was she really deaf? Could she read lips? "Help me escape this place. If we get back to the U.S., you can live with us. My father will hire you. You can be rich and live in New York City." She looked at me blankly. "New York City?" I repeated and nodded with a smile.

She shook her head and continued with her task of brushing my hair, which crackled under her touch. Whether she didn't understand me or didn't care to get me back home, I didn't know. Maybe she didn't like America. She put down her brush and made to leave. "Mariah," I said, and she looked again. "Thank you." Even Baba Yaga might appreciate good manners. Her implacable look gave me no indication of whether or not I was correct.

No one replaced my clothes. No more dress. No more panties.

I was naked except for my sheet. The old woman directed me toward the boulder and then disappeared. I sat.

Strange birds flew overhead, pink as flamingos but the size of egrets. The sun shifted, and they turned into tiny hummingbirds. When I saw their salmon wings against the white clouds, I thought my heart might stop from the beauty of it.

The nights were different.

Then the sky was black as ink, and I could see no lights no matter where I turned my eyes. The stars were shockingly bright and close. I thought I could touch them. I knew I could, but fear of getting burned kept me from trying.

All the constellations were foreign, except maybe the Big Dipper, which was twisted strangely and so close to the horizon. New shapes appeared in the sky, a new one each night: a leopard chasing an antelope, a lioness roaring to the sky, a snake coiled around a tree ripe with fat fruit.

Escape seemed like a faraway dream, scurrying away as quickly as I could breath. How far would I get in a lion-infested wilderness in bare feet and a makeshift toga?

My captor must have had a camel or a magic carpet. He arrived daily as if conjured. Even if he had a car, I could barely imagine pulling into some remote village in a stolen Jeep and a toga. If he rode a camel, my predictions were gloomier. I wasn't sure I could even get onto a camel, toga or otherwise. And how did one steer such a beast?

Yet in some ways, my fear had diminished. Death and violence seemed unlikely. Neither had happened yet, and there had been ample opportunity for both. Also, my captor hadn't lied to me, so I felt inclined to believe him when he said he wouldn't hurt me.

On the other hand, he seemed pretty intent on molesting me.

My stomach grew queasy. Maybe I'd been kidnapped into slavery. But then, why was I here in the middle of nowhere? Ransom? My father, a rich and influential politician, would pay—I felt sure of that.

Maybe my captor was some sort of pervert who was entertaining himself while awaiting the ransom booty. That seemed plausible. And yet . . . and yet his actions seemed so deliberate, as if he had planned to molest me from the beginning. Weren't perverts unable to help themselves? My captor seemed quite in control.

Something about him seemed strangely familiar. Had I seen him at some party? I met so many people at my dad's political soirees. I thought I'd have remembered a face like his, but then again, maybe not. I'd made a lifelong habit of ignoring men, good looking or otherwise, when it came to my personal life.

When I heard, "Hello, Samantha," I knew my punishment was imminent. My captor gave me a slow smile. He looked dangerous, like a pirate or rogue from some historical romance. He looked like a genie, powerful and strong.

"You have me at a disadvantage, sir. I don't know your name."

"I will not answer your question." He walked toward me, leopard like. Without thinking, I tried the silken bonds holding my wrists. They still held. He saw my movement and smiled.

My imagination provided a picture of me tied with my arms above my head, naked. I'm twenty-five and healthy. I run and I ride horses. I have thick blond hair that borders on red, and my legs are long. I'm pretty sure that most men who saw me naked and tied to a pole would want to touch me, but I was filled with self-doubt.

Did he want me, or was it just a job?

Why did I care?

"I didn't ask a question," I replied, purposefully quieting all movement.

"I know that you graduated magna cum laude from Swarthmore, Samantha, but you don't need to get pedantic with me. A question was implied, but I will not provide an answer." He flashed an impudent grin and said, "I won't even imply an answer."

I tried not to feel shocked that he knew where I'd gone to school and how well I'd done. He could have used the Internet, I supposed, but it was still creepy.

"Ask no more questions, or I will consider upping your punishment." I swallowed, and he correctly read my trepidation. "Before we begin today's adventure, you will drink this." He brought a glass of red wine from the table near the tent's flap to my lips. Good but strong, the wine went right to my head. Had he drugged it?

That wouldn't necessarily be a bad thing.

I started to speak, but he touched my lips with his finger. Made bold by the wine, I found myself looking at his face. The intensity of his expression surprised me.

"Shh," he said. "No more words from you. I've said I won't hurt you, and I won't. I've said I won't penetrate you until you beg for it, and you will."

He was at my side, untying me. My captor held my chin in his right hand, and he told me to fold my arms behind my back. The position arched my body, thrusting my breasts out. My breasts—and face—felt painfully naked.

He lifted my hair and shifted it over my left shoulder, away from him. My captor pinched both nipples unrelentingly hard between his finger and thumb, lifting my breasts and letting them fall naturally as he did so.

"Your body is so beautiful," he said. Then a wicked grin crossed his face. "And it will betray you. Have no doubt."

This was humiliating, the way he handled me as if I were nothing but a body.

Despite myself, I was wet.

It could have been worse.

My captor said, "Today I will punish you."

It could have been better.

3

My punishment began. It hardly seemed fair. All I'd done was struggle a bit, and who wouldn't under similar circumstances?

He pushed me back on the bed gently and held my arms above my head. "Samantha, you are remarkably beautiful. Your waist looks like it's sculpted from marble, and your breasts are perfect."

I felt heat rise to my cheeks, and I looked away from him in my shame. No one had seen me like this before. To my further mortification, I felt tears sting my eyes.

"Remember to control yourself. If you were to fight me during a punishment, the consequences may be more than you would like." Believing him, I vowed to remain motionless through whatever sick thing he was about to implement.

My captor retrieved the black silken ties and wrapped them around my wrists. They felt like snakes twining around my hands, around my forearms, and then they bound me to the ebony bedposts.

When he wrapped the tie around my ankle, I watched the snake slither over my shin and then around the arch of my foot.

Just before it took its form as a cord and bound my leg to the bedpost, it turned and laughed at me.

Mariah appeared with a wooden bowl filled with water. Not a drop spilled as she set it on the table. Soap and a straightedge razor filled her hands, and she placed them on the table, too. Where had the table come from? It was covered with intricate carvings of savannah animals: lions and baboons and snakes and impala.

"You may leave us now, Mariah," my captor commanded. Green silk of the tent billowed above me, and she evaporated without a sound. Maybe she could hear.

The straightedge razor grew scales, wicked and silvery. It winked a black button eye at me and crept from the table into my captor's hand. Smiling like it belonged there, it rested in his palm.

Mesmerized, I stared at it. Its steely eyes looked right back at me, bolder than brass. Surely he wasn't about to cut my throat . . .

My captor turned to the table. "Ha!" I wanted to shout to the straightedge. "See? You're going back to where you belong!" But something in its expression stopped me. It seemed to know more than I.

My captor picked up the porous sponge and dipped it in the water. He wrung it, one handed. Damp lavender scent filled the air. He turned back toward me, the razor wickedly smiling at me now. Then he sponged my golden pubic hair until I was drenched. He lathered me with soap.

Finally realizing his intention, I moaned. But it wasn't my voice that filled the tent; it was the sound of a flock of sparrows winging away from a hunting kestrel.

"Be careful not to squirm. I would hate to cut you." His wicked grin matched the wicked blade. I could feel it, the lather in my pubic hair, then the cold scraping of a razor.

Again, I whimpered. Sparrows flew.

"That's a good sound," he said. "Moan some more."

I didn't.

"You must learn to take orders. Obey me in all things. Continue moaning." I complied. He couldn't stop my heart from racing across the savannah.

"That's good," he said in a husky voice. "I apologize for the cold steel, but I want to see all of you." He roughly ran his palm over my breast, and I involuntarily pushed into him. My captor took it as a complement.

"Are you smooth enough?"

No, gleamed the straightedge.

"Yes," I said.

"Let me see." My captor brought his face to my naked pubis. He ran his cheek over me. Almost lovingly.

Let me, gleamed the straightedge.

"That's nice," my captor said, flicking his tongue over the area. His breath was hot. His tongue was wet. I pushed against him, and the pressure sent a secret message to my brain.

When his tongue slid over my clit, the whole world knew the message. I wanted this.

I wanted him.

"Mmm," he responded, desire thickening his voice. "A perfect shave."

The razor gleamed smugly at me as my captor placed it back on the table.

"Now I have an excuse to oil all of your beautiful body every day. We must oil you, or this will itch."

He toweled my shorn area with a gentle touch, and to my embarrassment, he proceeded to oil me. His palms covered every inch of me: my breasts and nipples, my neck, my stomach. His strong fingers oiled the knots of tension in my shoulders and back.

Without bidding, I moaned the entire time, as much from pleasure as from fear.

He didn't complain.

When his hands reached my stomach and pubic area, I realized that my earlier fear had diminished. He hadn't actually hurt me, and I was beginning to trust that he wouldn't.

When the palm of his hand oiled my clitoris, I squirmed. But not away from him. The sparrows landed on a branch and watched as the hawk passed above them, eating none of them. He didn't admonish me this time.

As slow as molten lava making its final descent across the flatlands, his finger traced the nub of my clit. With each spiral around it, galaxies were born in an explosion of stars.

He was going too fast. He wasn't going fast enough.

And then his index finger brushed my anus, caressed that sensitive area. A part of me wanted to mold to his touch like lava binds to the earth, but the intimacy of the touch jarred the spell.

I bucked my whole body. "Get away, you crazy bastard!" I shrieked. I couldn't trust this guy—of course I couldn't. What had I been thinking?

He chuckled and said, "I can see what we have to work on."

He left, the tent flap gently waving in his wake.

The forlorn call of some bird filled the air.

The old witch shooed me out of my tent, though I was naked save a sheet. With now calloused toes, I climbed to the top of my rock, enjoying its heat.

Staring out at the river, I observed two lions on the other side of the rushing brown water. The male, with a big black mane, mounted the female over and over again. Perhaps tired, they'd rest and then start over again.

Watching, I ran my finger over my swollen clit. There was no one to see me. Should I have been filled with self-loathing? It was obvious to me that I would beg for what he had to offer, eventually.

You will, said the turquoise lizard as it puffed out its orange throat.

I mean, come on. After one serious molestation, I was molding to him, becoming his. Did I really think I could withstand more?

I looked down at my fingers as they explored my clit, my labia. This was crazy. I'd never masturbated in my life. I pulled my sticky finger away, and crossed my arms over my breasts.

The lioness howled across the river and the lion thrust into her again and again.

What else did I have to do but think about sex? Maybe that was his point, why he left me alone for such long stretches of time.

As a teenager and college student, I had this romantic idea that I should save myself for my husband. My friends would roll their eyes at me as they headed off to the bedroom for a romp with their boyfriends—and sometimes girlfriends. And I could see their point. I'd read all the feminist stuff, too. But sleeping around could affect my family life pretty dramatically. Any college student, any potential boyfriend with political leanings knew my father, if only by reputation. I always asked myself, Did he want me, or did he want my political connections? If I slept with him, would he try to blackmail my father or me? I didn't want to smear my dad's name. I mean, look what Jeb Bush's daughters did to him, and prescription fraud isn't nearly as risqué as female promiscuity.

My fingertips danced over my hardened nipples. I could smell my musky dampness.

Regardless, between my romantic notions and the danger involved in intimate liaisons, I hadn't had sex yet. I was waiting to meet a nice doctor or scientist, but unfortunately, all the men I found most interesting were lawyers or politicians-in-the-making.

Such thoughts made me think of my folks. Surely my family

had noticed my disappearance by now. The tabloids might already be having a field day. What would they think if I willingly slept with this guy?

But if I had sex with my captor, I wouldn't be promiscuous; I would be a victim. I cupped a breast and tentatively pinched a nipple, more gently than my captor had.

Only I would know the truth if I capitulated. Well, my captor would, too. There was freedom in that.

That gave me an idea. What if I were totally free with him and acted like a complete harlot? He'd implied that my submission would lead to freedom. But still, if I succumbed, that would surely startle him.

It would surprise me, too, but I'd had no shortage of shocks lately.

While I might not completely object to wanton sex with a total stranger, I didn't like what was happening to my name— my father's name—back home. My parents would be sick with worry. I needed to get home.

The last time my captor had left, I'd heard his car drive off, tires crunching over the pebbled drive and sand. Eventual escape would involve something more mundane than a camel. Thank God.

I lay back against the hard granite, warm from the sun, and unabashedly palmed my breasts. Were they as beautiful as he'd said?

With my fear in abeyance, I really could imagine stealing his vehicle and driving away, even in a toga. But I had some practical questions. Where could I get clothing? Not that I'd seen one, but maybe I could steal them off a clothesline. Would there be enough gas to get me to the nearest town? Once I got to whatever capital this country had, could I even find the embassy? Maybe I could call the embassy from whatever town I found. I knew enough ambassadors personally. Maybe I would know the ambassador of this country. That would help keep this entire affair under wraps.

Across the river the pair of lions were sleeping, twined around each other, a look of contentment on both of their faces.

I was not content. I ached for something.

Someone, said the turquoise lizard, correcting me.

My nipples were as hard as the rock under my butt. My thighs were soaked. My clit, engorged. And I was filled with a longing I'd never imagined.

Enough.

I sat up, scowling.

The next time my captor was around, I vowed to see if I could find where he parked the car . . . and where he put the keys.

Maybe or maybe not I'd act like a harlot.

Probably I would.

Good plan, said the turquoise lizard. *Be a harlot*. He turned and mounted a female who'd come to admire his lovely peach throat.

Across the river, the lioness snored her agreement.

The next time my captor came to me, I was asleep. I awoke gently with warm sweet kisses over my neck, across the tops of my breast. They fell like rose petals over my skin.

By the time I realized what he was doing—spreading my legs and attaching some contraption to them—desire had me in her heady grip.

I began to struggle, but his sensual voice said, "Don't make me punish you, Samantha. Relax."

I obeyed, wondering how far his game would go.

I wondered if he could alleviate the burning desire between my thighs, if he could alleviate it without humiliating me.

My captor clicked the final hook of the device, and my

thighs spread wide. I tried to close my knees, but no action on my part could prevent it.

Immobile and helpless, I felt resignation in me grow. He gently tied my hands behind my back so that my breasts thrust out.

That crooked grin crossed his face. And imagining how I looked—thrusting breasts, tied hands, spread thighs—I was sure I knew why.

My captor rubbed oil over my entire body, taking care to appreciate the smoothness of my pubis. He then retrieved a small jar from the table. Was it rouge? He dipped in his thumb and rubbed it over one nipple, and then the other. He rubbed a bit over my clitoris.

Standing back to admire his efforts, he said in a sensual voice, "My God, you look beautiful."

"Why are you doing this?" I asked, more as a matter of formality. I wasn't really expecting an answer, and I didn't get one.

I was able to ignore the caresses at first.

But like silk, his hands traveled over my calves, thighs and stomach. He traveled gently over my sides and teased the bottoms of my breasts.

"A statue of you belongs in the Louvre," I heard him say under his breath.

I did not respond. His strokes created a growing tension that excited me. They held an elusive promise that hovered just out of reach.

What kind of person would I be if I gave in?

I wanted to close my eyes, but I did not. Instead I stared up at him as my body responded to his erotic touch. My response was out of my control.

He saw my desire. "You're hungry, too." His husky acknowledgment flamed my craving. If I could have touched myself, I would have.

Sensing my growing need, he stepped back. I bit my lip to

keep my protest to myself. "I want you to tell me what you feel when I touch you here," he commanded. He brushed my nipple with his thumb. It pebbled, hardened and ready. I lay silently; he could see what I felt. Telling him how much he excited me was too mortifying.

"Answer me," he demanded.

I drew a breath and paused, "Shame," I finally answered. It was only the beginning of the truth.

"Ah, we'll get you over that. But my question is, where do you feel it when I touch you like this?" His thumb pressed harder on my nipple, and the pleasure drew a small moan from me.

"On my nipple," I answered. It was the obvious answer.

"Where else," he demanded, his blue eyes looking at me unwaveringly. Perhaps he saw the stubborn set to my jaw. He changed demands. "Arch your back, and before you think of defying me, remember the punishments. There are greater humiliations than being shaved, and there are greater pleasures."

I arched my back. That alone may have undone me, but he then played with both nipples. Pushing them in, pinching them gently, rolling them between his fingers.

"More."

Obeying him was frighteningly easy. I pushed my breasts toward him, wanting him to touch them, wanting him to nip them, wanting him.

"When I touch your perfect nipple, Samantha, where else do you feel it?"

"In my heart. It's beating faster." I could see his pleasure in my answer. "And between my legs."

"Here?" he asked.

"Higher," I moaned. I had enough control left to not thrust myself against him, but it wasn't a sure thing.

Teasing me, tormenting me, he touched me above my clit, too high for relief. As he well knew.

"No," I mewled. I'm not proud. I mewled. I wanted release like I had wanted nothing before in my life. If I could have moved his hand to the right spot, I would have. I would have plunged his hand between my legs, pressed it against my clitoris until I came. I begged for release, in my mind. Only in my mind. Thankfully, the words didn't come from my mouth.

"Here?" he asked, finally touching my clitoris.

"Yes," I gasped, pushing myself against him, losing control finally.

To no avail. His clever fingers danced away from me, leaving me craving his touch.

Seeing my response, my captor stopped and smiled. "Look how much we'll enjoy each other."

Then he walked out the door.

Some enjoyment.

Lying on my boulder watching the animals, listening to their secrets, I found my fingers more and more often between my thighs.

That afternoon, thick gray clouds gathered on the eastern horizon.

It occurred to me that masturbating might calm me. I might be less willing to answer my captor's call if I could satiate myself.

You need a mate, the lizard said.

I wondered how many orgasms would slake me to the point where I would find my captor uninteresting.

I told myself that I wanted to wait until evening to hide my activities from Mariah, but the truth was I rarely saw her. The old witch magically appeared at meal times or at my captor's command, but she was invisible otherwise. I could rip orgasm after orgasm from my body sitting on this huge rock, and no one would know.

Except me.

And the lizard.

Too embarrassing.

I don't care, said the turquoise animal as he gave the female beneath him the cloacal kiss to end all kisses.

And I knew it was true. The lizard wouldn't care. And, I found, examining my own mind, I didn't care either. They were my fingers, and it was my clit. If it bought strength to withstand my captor even another day, the plan was good.

As the sun took on its afternoon glow, an amazing peachy orange, I found myself looking forward to the dark cover of nighttime. My fingers would bring me orgasm after orgasm. I would come until I couldn't see straight.

Then. Then I would be more immune to my captor's charms.

Nestled in my tangerine-colored sheets, I lay in my bed, listening for the sound of his vehicle. I heard all sorts of things—frogs and bats and owls, I thought. But I didn't hear him.

I'd been crazed with anticipation since I'd hatched this plan, crazed with the idea of finally coming. But the thought of my captor electrified me like lightening sizzling across the grasslands. As I tentatively slid my fingers between my thighs, I wondered what full penetration would feel like.

The novelty of my shorn pubis enticed my hands, beckoned my finger. Desire rippled through me. I felt as famished for this as I'd ever felt for a meal.

With the touch of one index finger, the first orgasm of the evening came before I could truly begin.

With hunger burning deep inside of me, I had no choice but to use multiple fingers. I slid over the entire surface of the nerve-filled bump, gasping at the electricity of it.

Using two fingers, then three, then more, I caressed myself. I couldn't feel how many fingers were actually touching my clit, touching each other.

Then I slid one finger slightly inside, surprising myself with my own tight heat. I came with an amazing intensity that left me breathless.

Keeping one finger sheathed while pressed against my clitoris, I came again. It was all I could do to suppress a moan of pleasure.

Finally, I let the other fingers explore. And they wanted to. How many could fit inside me? What would a man feel like?

But my fingers weren't satisfied. They wanted more. I wanted more. They slid over my clit, into my vagina, then a little lower.

I'd never found my anus interesting before, but my captor made me think of things I'd never thought. The silky wetness from my vagina had slid around and down from my earlier efforts, and my fingertip slid easily around the unexplored area.

I wouldn't find this thrilling, I assured myself, but I tried it anyway. A lingering slide around the circle told me otherwise, and I gasped again in surprise.

Another glide around convinced me that my body held pleasures I hadn't yet imagined. Wave after wave of pleasure washed over me and finally brought me some peace.

Sleep came upon me that night, deep and relaxing. If wild beasts called into the dark skies, I didn't hear.

Squabbling and squealing baboons woke me the next morning, with the call of a flock of guinea fowl that had nested in the tree above my tent last night.

I had timed my masturbation experiment just right because my captor appeared just after Mariah had bathed me. She had also reshaved my pubic area with the dispassionate attitude of a farmer shearing a sheep.

When I thanked her, I received the usual expressionless response.

If I felt pleased to see him, I kept my face inexpressive. With the oil and rouge, he prepared me as before. I can admit that his gentle hands felt good on my body, but I felt pleased with the results of my experiment—I was not soaking by the time he had finished.

Which is not to say that I was dry, exactly.

After he oiled me, he said, "Now, we'll change the pace a bit. It's time for you to take a more active role. Before we begin, I want to warn you about escape. If you should dash out that door and across the path, you'll find only savannahs filled with buffalo, lions, and elephants. There are no people for many kilometers. Do you understand?"

"Yes." I tried to sound demure, but my heart raced. If he were talking about escape, perhaps freedom was more within my grasp than I'd thought.

He untied my ankles and wrists. Black ribbonlike snakes slithered to the floor. I tried to keep the hope I felt hidden.

He then sat on a chair maybe five feet from my bed and me. "Now," he said, "you will rub oil all over yourself, everywhere that I did."

I swallowed thinking of all the places he'd oiled. It was one thing to masturbate in the cover of darkness, by myself. But with him watching? I tentatively rubbed my arm.

"Oh, Samantha. You know that's not what I want. Why don't you close your eyes, for now, and oil those lovely breasts."

I did as he said, tilting my head back so that if I opened my eyes, I'd see only the dappled ceiling.

"That's better." With my eyes closed, his voice sounded husky, almost sexy. "Your nipples. Oil them, too. You have two hands. Use them both."

Despite myself, I pinched my nipples. "Yes," he said.

I knew him well enough to recognize desire when I heard it, and the appreciation in his voice loosened something inside of me. I ran my other hand over my well-oiled stomach, finding it hard to ignore the growing pleasure.

"Arch your back while you touch your nipples. And let that hand travel lower." His voice definitely sounded thick.

I did.

"Now touch yourself." I started to make a sound of protest, but he cut me off. "You know you want to."

I did.

"Are you getting close?"

I was. "Mmmhmm." I heard him almost purr with my response.

"Now look at me."

I shook my head. It was all too embarrassing. "I'm not giving you a choice. I want to see the fire in your eyes."

I looked at him and saw the fire in his eyes. "Do you want me, Samantha?"

Would an affirmative answer constitute begging? I shook my head again. The glint in his eye nearly made me wish I'd told the truth. He came toward me. "Don't stop," he said, "and don't stop looking at me."

I wanted to slide inside myself and end this. I wanted to look away from him, but I obeyed him instead. With my fingers sliding, now slowly, over my clit and with my eyes locked on his, he came even closer to me.

The whole thing struck me as surprisingly intimate. We seemed closer somehow than those times he'd touched me while I was tied.

Gently he pushed my knees apart. His hands were hot on my skin, and his chiseled features were flushed. He placed his hand over mine, and I couldn't help but thrust against him.

"Are you ready to beg?" he asked me.

I froze. "No."

"But you want me." It was a statement, not a question. Denying it was impossible, anyway. I closed my eyes and tried to escape him in any way I could.

"No, Samantha. I won't let you diminish this. But if you won't beg today, you will soon."

I feared he was right.

He left me alone, wanting him. I hated him.

When he strode into the tent, green waves billowing with the breeze he brought, my heart skipped a beat. That was the power he had over me. If he were ugly, maybe I'd have been able to ignore him. But he smiled a dangerous smile and his ice-blue eyes gleamed like knife blades.

I knew I was in trouble.

Wordless, he pulled me from the warmth of my bed, the scent of desire wafting around it. Brusquely he sat me on a chair. Like the other furnishings in my silk prison, the chair was ornately carved with forest creatures. Under my naked bottom it was hard and unforgiving. He began to tie me—chair legs and armrests served novel purposes.

Given the other things he'd done to me, tying me to a chair didn't seem so bad. Little did I know.

Yes, this was becoming so familiar, the same sweet, wild sensation of his hands on my bare flesh, the thunder of blood through my veins. I barely noticed the exhaust-free smell of the air anymore, or the screams of the leopards. All I noticed was him—the sound of his engine as he pulled up, his woodsy scent as he entered my prison, the fine lines around his steely eyes.

As if in a dream, I became aware that I was throbbing again, drenching the ebony beneath me. Lazily, my captor caught a handful of my hair and bent to inhale its lavender scent.

He brushed his cheeks against my face, and I stiffened. "Try to enjoy this," he commanded. "Relax."

I twisted my head, trying to draw my hair free from his grasp. It wasn't fighting exactly; I was just letting my preference be known. I didn't want him to touch me.

But he was in control. My captor tightened his grip on my hair—not cruelly, but leaving me no doubt that he was in charge, as always.

Slipping his free hand past my hair, he stroked the vulnerable length of my neck, the line of my jaw. A quick shiver traveled up my spine. His fingers felt warm and slightly rough against my skin. I could smell his musky desire.

"I will strip away your every defense and leave you helpless when it comes to your sexual needs. The sound of my voice will be all you need to desire my touch."

To my horror, I felt arousal tighten low in my belly. Its grip on me was hard, unrelenting. My nipples hardened, craving his tongue, his fingertips. My clit throbbed. Ignoring my need, I asked, "What exactly are you planning?"

"I'll answer this question, this one question. What I'm planning is . . ." His hot tongue flicked out and swirled around my earlobe. "A ruthless . . ." His teeth closed over the sensitive flesh in a gentle bite. "Seduction."

His hand dropped smoothly to the tip of my breast, and his teeth began to nibble my lips. The sensuous temptation burned, and my nipple tightened eagerly. Damn it.

"My body may say it's willing, but I'm still saying 'no.' That makes it rape." My breasts were aching for his touch.

"Mmmmm. You have a point." He lifted his hand to touch the center of my throat, and then he slowly ran his finger downward between my breasts along my tensed abdomen, right to the top of my naked pubis. He stopped there for a moment.

"I suppose then," he whispered, his gaze directed down at my naked skin, "that I'll just have to wait until you beg. Today, I wonder?"

"If you think I'm just going submit, you're wrong." I hoped he didn't hear the husky sound in my voice.

"I don't think even you know what you're going to do. But I'm going to do my best to convince you that this route provides the most . . ." He bent to capture my erect nipple in his mouth, and through his clenched teeth, he finished, "pleasure."

After a quick and brutal suck, he released me, leaving me gasping. Moving in front of me, he took my shoulders in his powerful hands and lifted me right off the chair, then he turned me around and gently, relentlessly, forced me to kneel in the seat, half bending me over the back. "Are you going to enjoy this, or are you going to fight me?"

"What the hell are you doing now?" I demanded. This man could invent any number of vulnerable positions.

To my outrage, he nipped my butt. "No more questions. No more talking . . . unless you're going to beg." I could hear the sardonic grin in his voice. "When you feel moved to moan, give into it, otherwise be quiet."

Taking my ass in his strong hands, he squeezed my cheeks, caressing them with strong, possessive strokes. "So muscled and strong," I heard him mumble to himself. "Magnificent."

I ignored him and said, "What is this really about? Ransom? Slavery? Vengeance?" I looked back over my shoulder at him and saw his face freeze. My blood ran cold.

"I told you not to speak, and you ignored it." The hair on the back of my neck stood on end at his tone. "You've earned another punishment."

Draped over the ebony chair, my captor tied my legs apart with his silky cords.

My captor then leaned closer to me, draping himself over me so he could reach the satiny tangerine sheet that had been wrapped around me. Tugging an edge, he freed a breast into the cool air. My nipple hardened, shamelessly eager for his fingers.

Then he shoved me forward, again gently and again relentlessly. My chin rested on the chair's soft back, and he tied my wrists together. The black snakes winked at me with wicked grins as they bound my wrists to the chair back. One snake, bolder than the other, flicked its tail high between my thighs then smiled at me.

As my captor oiled every centimeter of my exposed area, I felt my ability to think rationally slip away. I felt my labia softening, engorging. My clit was throbbing, searching for contact with anything, with him.

Then he dragged me against him until his erection pressed against me. I could feel the cloth of his pants absorbing my wetness. It seemed I had enough to fill a river.

When he spoke, his voice was thick and husky. "What would you know about slavery or vengeance? This is about pleasure. Mine," he rolled his hips, making me writhe, "and yours."

Despite myself, I felt the full roar of arousal. Shameful and reluctant, but strong. I couldn't deny its strength. Even through his clothes, he felt so . . . thick. I had the sudden intense image of his strong fingers sliding inside.

But icy fear poured through my veins. I didn't believe in his promise of freedom—that was simply a sick and cruel power play. Being slave to his whim was bad enough. How much humiliation would I have to endure?

I was no man's sex toy.

Suddenly, I'd had enough. What right did this man have to turn me into an animal, and what could he do to me that he hadn't already done? I was shaved. I was naked. I was in a tent in some foreign country that I had only barely imagined before now. I was tied and blindfolded, and I had no shoes. 'Beg for it,' he'd demanded. Well, if he wasn't going to rape me until I begged for it, I couldn't imagine any other punishments. I threw submissiveness out the door, which was not easy to do with my legs tied to chair legs and my wrists tied together to the chair back.

Again he leaned over me to cup my breast. Despite the delicious warmth, my nipple hardened further. He caught the stiff tip, pulled it and rolled it until I could no longer hold back a moan. He moved his face closer so that our noses nearly touched. "You see?" he murmured in my ear. "Pleasure."

I knew an opening when I saw one. Quick as a snake, I swung over and grabbed his lip in my teeth. I bit him hard. By the time I tasted blood he'd instinctively jerked back, bringing me with him. The chair, yanked from under me, splintered, leaving my naked legs unbound but my wrists tied together, free of the chair's back. I pivoted my body into a tight kick, landing a satisfying heel on his right shoulder. I heard a deep thud.

I hadn't walked the streets of New York without self-defense classes. Kickboxing, which I really enjoyed, had been the rage for the last few years. With perfect precision I reversed directions, planning to land another blow on his shoulder, but I couldn't catch him twice.

In a blink, he'd snatched my ankle and yanked. I landed with an "oof" on my butt. But even as he pounced on me, I launched another attack, swinging my tied wrists like a baseball bat.

I was hoping to hit his gorgeous face, or at least his nose, but I moved surprisingly slowly, as if in a dream. Like a scene out of *The Matrix* he dodged me, and I only grazed his cheek. It didn't seem to hurt him.

Before I could try again, he grabbed my wrists and pinned them over my head. "You don't want to do this. You can't win."

"Don't count your chickens." My voice came out as a growl, and I jerked my knee up toward his groin. The back of my brain caught his scent: the faint tang of male sweat, something woodsy. I ignored it and slammed quickly, as hard as I could. He imprisoned my thighs between his in a powerful grip. He kept me down, mashing my breasts against the hard wall of his chest. I tried not to admire his strength.

He was strong, and he was at least one hundred pounds heavier than I. My self-defense classes said I should scream or vomit or play dead. None would help in this situation.

With growing rage, I realized that the male body would prevail. Damn it. I had no choice but to submit and wait for my chance.

But . . . but maybe I had another choice, something no self-respecting self-defense class would advocate. The only thing I had to lose was my self-respect, and the way things had been going, I thought that was destined to fall by the wayside soon anyway.

I took a deep breath and forced myself to relax.

Feeling my body fall limp, my captor said in obvious satisfaction, "That's better."

Panting from my efforts, I appraised him as he sat on my thighs. His gaze was appreciative, and my traitorous nipples tightened in response. He noticed. "Much better."

I took a second deep breath and attempted to embrace my far-fetched plan. Locking eyes with him, I squirmed slightly, pressing the tops of my thighs against him. I saw disgruntled arousal in his eyes. Was my plan working?

"Do you finally want to play?" he growled and released my wrists to grab my breasts. He roughly massaged them, and I could feel the electric tingle run to my clit.

Yes, I wanted to play, but I hoped to change the rules.

Someone would beg, and it wouldn't be me.

I pushed my breasts toward him, shifting myself under his cock.

"You see?" my captor said. "You enjoy this as much as I do. Alone, tied, defenseless, and I'm the nasty villain. You can let yourself enjoy every second and heap the blame on me."

He wasn't on to me yet.

"But it can't be all pleasure." His words sent a zing of fear through my veins. "Hand-to-hand combat with you wasn't on the agenda. You've earned another punishment." I squirmed as his fingertips rolled over my breasts. I wasn't exaggerating the pleasure I felt.

"You're ready to beg, aren't you?" he asked. I didn't answer, and his smile seemed a little sad. "I must have dreamed you, you're so beautiful."

My captor slipped his hand down, between my thighs. A finger slipped easily over my clit in a slow, slick glide. My long groan was completely genuine, but I vowed that the word "please" would not come from my mouth.

"You're not real," he said, half to himself. Then he blinked. "God, you make me so hot."

I realized he was as tortured as I.

He said, "But punishment comes before pleasure."

My captor flipped me over quickly, and before I could object or entice him in some way, he'd bent me over the broken chair. Just as quickly, he tied me so that my nose was inches from the ground, my knees were on the floor, but every inch of my ass was exposed.

Then came the spanking.

At the first strike, I cried out, jerking against my bonds. Pain, surprisingly like pleasure, burst across my skin.

"Stop!" I gasped. I almost said "please."

His palm struck me again, too quick for readiness. Streaks of fire laced my vision, and my breath burned in my lungs, forcing out another involuntary cry. The rough wood of the broken chair pressed against my face. Again, he struck, and again. Agony blossomed in me with an unbearable and shocking pleasure.

I heard my own voice whimpering. With the last strike, I felt a splattering wetness as his hand met my flesh. It was my wetness. My head fell forward, and I wept with shame.

The stinging pain of the spanking camouflaged the pleasure. I only slowly became aware of his caress, his thumb gently gliding over my swollen clit. Through the haze of pain and pleasure I vaguely remembered my plan to capitulate. Could I do it? I arched my back, opening myself to him. By the pause in his caress, I had figured I surprised him.

I hoped to surprise him more.

But he surprised me, too. He stood, leaving me momentarily alone, and took something from the table.

It was a paddle.

Surrendering to the pain, one fact burned through my mind—I belonged to him.

5

"You've taught me something important, Samantha. Pain softens you, makes it easier for you. You're more malleable than you were this morning."

I hadn't intended this. I wanted to shake my head but didn't dare. I didn't dare move.

"Stand up."

I did quickly.

"Spread your legs slightly. You have to be able to withstand the blows."

I wanted to cry out, and through my tightly pressed lips, my sobs sounded very loud to me.

"Why are you crying when I haven't paddled you yet? Your ass is only a little sore from the spanking."

I felt the first crack of the paddle before I could answer.

Stinging pain exploded on the hot surface of my flesh. The second came more swiftly than I'd thought possible, and then there was the third and the fourth, and I cried aloud in spite of myself.

My captor stopped. Finally.

He kissed me gently over my neck, behind my ears. I wanted to collapse into him. I wanted him to cherish me, to adore me. Anything he wanted, I would give him.

"Let me tell you a secret about pain," he said. "You're tight as a drum. How could you not be? But the pain loosens you, makes you as soft as I want you to be." He buried his fingers between my thighs, deep inside. "Pain makes you as soft as you want to be, too."

Running his thumb over my clit, he ran his other hand along my jaw, tilting my eyes to meet his. He caresses were unrelenting. I tried to squirm away, to avoid giving him the compliment of my orgasm.

But I came, humiliatingly, right then. My walls pulsated, longing to be filled.

A wicked grin. An arched eyebrow. "See? A paddling is worth a thousand threats."

I said nothing. What could I say?

He lifted my chin again and spanked me again on my ass. My buttocks grew hotter and hotter with pain, and the cracks of the paddle were shattering. The sound itself was as bad as the pain.

When he stopped this time, I was breathless. My tears were almost frantic. The torrent of blows had humiliated me far worse than the pain had. But not worse than coming in his hands right after he spanked me.

This time, when my captor took me in his arms, I melted into him. Why couldn't he adore me?

My captor sat on the bed with a resolute expression, and he pulled me over his lap. I obeyed without question, fully expecting another rain of blows. I deserved them, and I wanted them. I was ready to embrace the pain.

Gently pressing his thumb against my other entrance, he said, "Do you know where your greatest vulnerability lies?"

He left little to my imagination, but I didn't tighten.

Instead his hand gently caressed my ass and thighs, his cool palm soothing my hot flesh. "Maybe you think the greatest danger is that I'll fuck you like a Viking, with no regard to pain or no regard for dignity. Maybe you think cruelty is the greatest danger."

His thumb circled that entrance with growing pressure, exuding heat and a promise to fulfill. I didn't move a muscle, listening to his every word.

My captor continued. "But it isn't. Brutality isn't at all where the greatest danger lies."

His other fingers danced maddeningly around my clit. Then he touched me, light as a moth touches a flame before it explodes into death. He increased the pressure of his strokes both front and back until I was sure he could feel heat radiating from inside me, despite my fear.

I opened my thighs.

I was his. Anything he asked, I would give. I wanted his fingers to plunge deep inside of me. I wanted to come until I roared like the leopards on the savannah. I thrust my ass toward him, asking him, begging him without words.

But he pulled back, and I wanted to cry at the loss. I squirmed toward him, craving fulfillment.

"No," he said in his whisky voice. "You can't have this. Your greatest vulnerability lies in the fact that now that I have you, I might never let you go. Not even when you beg."

Not if.

Ozone crackled in the air around us, and the old witch appeared in the doorway, haloed in fluttering silk.

"Mariah, leave us," my captor said, raising his voice above the growing wind.

Then, in a voice that sounded like water pounding through the bouldered riverbed, the old woman spoke. "You've both become captors on this day," she said.

I was glad for the warmth of my captor's arms around me.

Lightning arced across the sky and struck just outside the tent with a deafening crack. Baba Yaga was gone.

"I thought you said she couldn't speak," my captor said to me.

"What?" I said. "You told me she couldn't hear."

Then my captor dumped me on the mattress, alone, and left.

Bright sunlight sparkled through the green silk, showing me the gnarled finger shadows of the tree above the tent.

I'd had enough.

Mariah would be back in moments, if she followed her regular pattern. But I was too angry to wait for her soothing ministrations. When he left, I tried to rip myself free, wrenching both wrists and shoulders in the process. I didn't care. I needed to get home—now. Whatever it took.

When I broke through the bonds, no one was more surprised than I. I'd like to think it was my determination, but really, we'd probably loosened the ties in the melee. The black snake ties slithered away, giving me a baleful look as they melted into the shadows.

I grabbed a peach-colored sheet and stomped barefoot out of the tent. I don't know what I thought I would do—scream at the sky maybe or smash some rocks with my bare hands.

I didn't expect to find car keys sitting on the bench outside my tent, and seeing them there should have cooled me, but it didn't. I grabbed them and tramped to the beaten-down grassy area that served as the driveway. I was still too angry to think clearly. Ignoring thorns impaling my feet, I huffed up the hill toward a Landcruiser.

Muttering under my breath, I jerked the car door open, hauled my sheet-wrapped self inside, and fumbled with the keys—only to find myself looking at the glove compartment. Wherever I was, they drove on the left side of the road.

That marginally cooled me. I got out, careful to close the

door quietly. I walked to the other side. The key went in smoothly, and the engine purred with a soft confidence. I blinked, realizing I'd have to shift gears with my left hand, but my brain quickly adapted to the concept. I drove.

When I didn't stall the truck as I sped down the dirt path, pride splashed through me. Fuck this crazy asshole. I was getting out of here.

The pathway ended at a wider dirt track. Thorny scrub trees arched over the path. I had two choices: east or west. The trees were equally thick in both directions. *Fifty-fifty*, I thought to myself and turned east.

The truck handled nicely, but I could only go about thirty miles per hour without fishtailing in the sandy track. I went twenty-nine.

The heat from the engine seeped through the firewall, roasting my foot. I had no shoes. That made me realize I had no shirt, no pants, and no underwear. I had no money. Had my captor left any water in his car? Glancing around, I didn't see any, but I couldn't see in the back seat. Had he brought food? A sharp corkscrew of fear twisted through my stomach. What had I done?

While I had a good vehicle, if I stopped anywhere besides an embassy, I could be in trouble. Big trouble. What would happen if I pulled up nearly naked to a gas station? What would happen if a naked woman pulled up to a gas station in Brooklyn? Nothing good.

Likewise, if I ran out of gas before I found anything remotely civilized, what would I do? Naked, I could hardly walk to safety. Without food and water, walking would be particularly dangerous.

Carefully bumping the truck over a huge tree root, I tried my best to convince myself that I wasn't embarking on the stupidest gamble of my life.

* * *

I cursed and cursed, and I wanted to shake my proverbial fist into the sky. East had been the wrong direction. Very wrong. The track had petered out into nothing.

I couldn't make myself turn back—it would be like returning to the lion's mouth—so I kept forging ahead, hoping that the track would magically appear. Instead, branches slapped my windshield as I drove in an ever-darkening direction. I jumped with each smack. Thorns scraped the truck's side like fingernails on a chalkboard.

Wiping tears from my cheek, I cursed again. I wanted to go home.

Then I spied a clearing under a stand of acacia trees. I headed toward it. I knew it was the road. I was on my way!

But halfway through the clearing I heard a loud hissing, and my truck lurched to one side. I hadn't driven into a gully. Dear God. I had a flat.

I stopped and gingerly tiptoed around the truck, careful of my bare feet. Stepping over myriad acacia branches, I saw the problem. Acacia trees apparently armed themselves with medieval cavalry snares. On their branches, two thorns always pointed toward the sky, and those wicked thorns had penetrated my tires. I couldn't believe it.

I had three flats.

When I saw the first flat, I was angry; the second worried me, and the third had me terrified.

But I kept my head. I found two spares, one on the hood and one on the back door. I searched the back of the truck hoping to find one of those mini spares so common at home, but the Landcruiser had none. I decided to change the two tires and drive on one rim. I knew I wouldn't get too far on this terrain with three flats. I wasn't sure how far I'd get with one flat, but what choice did I have?

Changing the tires while wearing no shoes wouldn't be easy,

but it wouldn't be impossible either. I found a thick canvas tarp with the tools, and I laid it on the ground where I would stand.

I had fitted the lug wrench around the first nut when the lions arrived.

As I began to jerk the wrench, a warthog shot past. The wind it stirred wrapped around my bare leg. Then a lioness sped past taking my breath with her, then another, then another.

Frozen, I watched the first lioness send the warthog flying with a swipe of a paw. The second lioness pounced. All three descended on the screaming, bloody meal.

Sense finally kicked in and I dashed into the truck, heart pounding. I could have touched the fur of the first lioness as she'd run past me. It was closer than I ever wanted to be to a wild lion—to any lion.

Throwing myself into the truck's interior, I slammed the doors closed and rolled up the windows.

The lionesses reduced the warthog to cracked bones and tufts of hair within minutes, and all three laid down for a nap.

I waited. And then I waited some more.

As dusk began to fall, I began to feel despair. I'd found only one bottle of water in the truck. No food. No shoes. No money. I could easily die out here—eaten by lions or starved to death—and no one would find me for years. Fat tears dripped down my cheeks, and I wiped them with my flimsy sheet.

But feeling sorry for myself would solve nothing. Perhaps the lions would be gone by morning. Perhaps I could see the path in the daylight and drive the truck back to the main track. Failing that, maybe I could walk back to the main road. Although that seemed like a scary idea: walking nearly naked and barefoot through some lion-infested savannah.

At any rate, I would reassess the situation when the sun rose.

I focused on calming myself. A small brown owl sat on a branch just outside my window. Its eerie chirp filled the air. Bats dived after bugs, making high-pitched piping calls. "What should I do," I asked the night, but no one had an answer for me. I missed the turquoise lizard with his orange throat.

I breathed deeply, relaxed my eyelids, and nestled back as comfortably as I could. I would sleep.

Suddenly, one of the lionesses roared, and I jumped out of my seat. The lioness sounded like she lay at my feet. Sitting five yards from a roaring lion felt a lot more intimidating than watching one from across the river.

The noise had begun with a few moans, forsaken and desolate sounding things. My skin crawled. Then came eight or ten full-throated, thunderous, deafening roars, and the hair on the back of my neck prickled. The howling lioness finished with a few grunts.

I wished that a river still separated us.

What if the lioness wanted to eat me? I wondered if a lioness could or would pull my screaming body out of the truck for dinner. Could they smash the window? Didn't bears do that? I locked the doors.

As if that'll help, the small, rational corner of my mind chided. I thought about honking the horn, but what if that just brought me to their attention?

I'd found a fire extinguisher in the back. I picked it up and pulled out the pin. Could I blind the lion with the contents? I'd try if I had to—I wasn't going to get eaten without a fight. My fingers on the trigger, I perched on the end of my seat and peered fruitlessly into the darkness.

Minutes later—maybe even hours—my mind began to wander. What would have happened if I'd met my captor someplace normal, or even a bit glamorous? Although I dreaded formal affairs, my parents threw enough black-tie parties so that I felt like I'd been weaned on them. What if I'd met him there? Surely I would have noticed him. He'd look great in a tuxedo.

Easing back into the car seat, I could almost smell the canapés and hear the tinkling of background piano music. Our eyes would meet across the room. He would admire my curves, highlighted by a red-sequined dress instead of the drab black pantsuit I usually wore. I'd drop my eyes and pretend to find old Senator Stodgy's conversation interesting. When my captor—who still remained nameless—approached with a glass of champagne, I would accept, meeting his glance, briefly. Immediately, we'd see the mutual attraction.

Okay, I have an active imagination, but I was stuck naked in a truck surrounded by lions. It was the only escape I had. I went back to my daydream.

But after I noticed him—no, after we noticed each other—what then?

Well, it would depend on who his family was. Were they friends or foes? If he came from a family of foes, I might have flirted with him to get him to at least consider the idea that his family was wrong and mine was great. If he came from a family of friends, I might have flirted, too—but not too much, because I'd have all the foes to conquer. In neither case would I have ended up in bed with him.

What had I been missing with my political life?

The moon had risen, thick and yellow just above the horizon. Dark, grey clouds scuttled quickly across the sky. I envied their easy departure.

Right next to my window a lioness stood in her roaring stance, neck held elongated, a roar pouring from her mouth, loud and terrible.

From my tent, I'd seen lions across the river call like this, mostly in the evening. This animal was a step away from me. I could see the black lines—like kohl on an ancient Egyptian priestess—around her eyes. I could see individual hairs on her face.

Then, through the moonlight, the lioness stared at me. She saw me. Me. I froze, and she looked away after a minute. Had she locked eyes with me, or was it my imagination?

I licked my lips, and my hands began to sweat. Could I go mad overnight?

Was madness already upon me? I didn't believe my eyes. Salvation. Two shining beams snaking in tandem toward my truck. What those lights did made my heart flip with hope—they herded the animals back about ten yards.

It wasn't much, but it was something. Why hadn't I thought of that?

My captor drove his truck so that his passenger side lined up with mine. He opened the door and waved for me to get in. I hesitated, imagining the slathering beasts waiting for me in the bush. Then he picked his rifle off the gunrack. Somehow I knew that he was threatening the lions, not me. Never had I been so happy to see a firearm.

I didn't say anything to him when I got in. I just looked at him. My face must have been as pallid as the moon because it was only then that my captor spoke. "Oh Samantha, let's get you away from here."

He drove quickly, finding the main track quicker than I would have thought possible.

Under his masterful guidance, the truck smoothly crossed the unmarked path. Nightjars flew and scattered at our approach.

After he shifted the vehicle into fourth gear, he put his arm across my shoulder and caressed it. I didn't pull away—I snuggled in closer. I was still trembling when we reached the camp.

It was the lions.

Really.

6

My emerald tent was gone. My captor must have replaced it. The tent now looked like one from M*A*S*H, only it had a thick, thatched roof held over it by wooden poles. Inside stood a table, a chest, and a bed.

Seeing no shackles and no razors, I breathed slightly easier.

My captor came into the room carrying two glasses of what looked like scotch. He was gorgeous, and definitely he would have looked great in a tux. His chiseled features and rangy form—those I liked.

But the fire in his eyes really turned me on. That softening he'd noticed earlier, it was happening now. I knew what wanting felt like, and I wanted him now.

My captor didn't look angry—he looked consumed.

"Are you feeling better?" he asked quietly. It was the first nearly normal thing he'd said.

I managed a feeble grin. "I had to pee like nobody's business . . . that was almost the worst." He nodded and took a sip of his scotch. Somehow it had turned to rum. Why had he switched it?

Then my captor stepped in very close to me, handing me the drink. Amaretto now? I didn't step away. The smell of his skin registered in the heat of the night. It drove all confusion away.

"I was terrified when I saw you drive away," he admitted in a soft voice. "Even now, I'm too damn shaken to find the right words." His slow-moving hand pushed the hair from my eyes, and he tilted my chin up. "I'm so very sorry."

I didn't know what to think—the change in our relationship seemed too dramatic to make sense at the moment. Nothing made sense. For what, exactly, was he apologizing? How had he found me? And why had he kidnapped me in the first place?

But I didn't have time to reply. He kissed me first. I realized that he'd never kissed me before this—not on my mouth, at least. Slow and deliberate, he tasted better than I'd imagined, and I realized that I'd been imagining his kiss for some time now. Velvet on velvet. His tongue teasing mine.

Tension and passion filled it. Wildness and hunger. I answered him with desire of my own. His strength felt like the world to me.

He felt like forever.

My captor dropped his hand from my shoulders to the small of my back, then lower, cupping my ass, pulling me against him. His cock pressed eagerly against my pubis. My shivers of desire matched his.

He was no longer my captor. Somehow I was now his.

Meeting him with freedom was intoxicating. I could not resist. I pressed myself closer to him, running my hands through the long, dark hair at the nape of his neck, tugging it. His hair ran like silk through my fingers. I couldn't believe he let me touch him like this.

I could believe I wanted to.

This freedom set me on fire, after all that time having my hands literally tied. My fingers and palms savored his broad shoulders muscled under his shirt. My fingertips delighted in

MY CAPTOR / 57

the soft skin behind his ears. The muscles in his arms flexed under my lips.

And then I kissed him. My lips couldn't get enough of his. I sucked his lips into my mouth, proud of my power over him.

My body responded to his the way it always did. It lit with pleasure. I thought of the spanking and the shaving, and I felt a flash of contempt for myself.

I hated him for a moment for making me loathe myself. I began to pull back.

But he would have none of that. Thankfully. He pulled me toward him. Pushing my sheet away, he began grazing his teeth across my skin. The sensation of his teeth on the side of my neck was almost more than I could stand. My pride and doubts retreated to some far recess in my mind and stayed there.

My peach-colored sheet fell to the ground with his touch, puddling at our feet. I was his in that moment. I surrendered myself to him completely.

He didn't need ropes to make me his. My captor didn't need shackles. Standing with my legs apart, I offered my breasts to him. But when he grabbed a nipple in his teeth, my world teetered.

I knew it wouldn't work. My desire was too strong. If I stood here, I'd collapse.

The games were in the past, but my pride had been hurt. Mangled. I could still hear his sexy voice telling me that I would beg for him. I suddenly knew a way to put the games in the past forever. I took his face in my hands and brought his lips to mine.

I knew what I had to do.

"Let's go to bed," I suggested in my huskiest voice.

For a moment the world shifted, became strange and confusing. As if in a dream, I led him to the bed with more grace and confidence than I had ever before experienced.

Without a word, he ran his palms over my breasts, down my

waist. The look in his eye as he studied me, the intensity of his gaze . . . I felt worshipped. With that look, he gave me more power than I'd ever had.

I knew then that he was absolutely mine.

In slow motion, he reached to kiss me. My heart pounded as he neared.

His lips touched my cheek and then my lips. The world shimmered again. Strange magic. This is what the first kiss should have felt like, I thought to myself.

His clothes melted away. Had he been wearing any?

I gently pushed him onto his back, my mouth never leaving his. I took his wrists and held them above his head. It was only a token symbol of submission—he outweighed me, but I made my point. He was at my mercy.

Filled with an odd lethargy and that overwhelming power, I kept his hands pinned above his head and let him caress my breasts with his face and lips. "I don't know your name," I said.

"Phillip."

"Phillip," I repeated as I kissed him again, "my captor."

"But you're my captor now."

"How?"

"You've got my heart," he answered.

Freeing his wrists, I wrapped my palm around his cock and caressed it. It throbbed with my touch. "I've captured your cock," I corrected.

He paused for a moment, and I couldn't guess at his thoughts. Finally he replied, "I can't deny that I want you, but you've won my admiration."

I caught the tip of his finger between my teeth and bit gently. "Really."

"Your bravery and courage is something I've only read in books."

When I lightened my grip, he slid his fingers between my

legs, drawing spirals around my clit. "You leave me breathless," he said.

But I'd thought I was the breathless one.

The feeling of unreality passed as he rubbed his cheek against my shorn area. I throbbed with need for him. A single pass of his tongue over my clit teased and promised.

Like his words.

Then his tongue touched me again, pushing delicately. Deliciously. He found my clit and circled it with hot flicks. The lack of friction astonished me. His teeth closed in for a gentle nibble, and then I realized that I could no longer describe his actions. I was breathless, as he'd promised.

But I wanted to trust him. I really wanted emotional satisfaction to come with the physical fulfillment.

"Prove it," I said.

"That I want you?" Phillip asked, only his eyes visible as he looked at me from between my legs. "I thought I was." He sucked me hard to make his point.

I rolled over in consternation, tangling him in the process. "Hot seems to be my permanent state when I'm around you."

Apparently undeterred by my position, both literal and figurative, he began to massage my ass, teasingly brushing against more sensitive areas. I moaned with pleasure, encouraging him to touch whatever he pleased, however he pleased to do it.

Surrendering to him was easy. Now.

But could he surrender to me? As his thumb trailed the sensitive area between one entrance and another, I shifted to give him better access. I knew I could ask. "Would you give to me what you asked me to give to you?" I could hardly get the words out for the pleasure his touch lit up in me.

"What?"

"Beg for me." I couldn't see him, with my face buried in his pillow, but the pause in his caress made me crave him even more. It filled me with fear. If he refused, I might cry.

Or worse, I might fuck him anyway.

I rolled over again, so I could see him, and I could see consternation on his face. I sat up and kissed him, and he returned the kiss ferociously. His strong fingers insistently plucked and played with my nipples, and I could think of only one thing. Regardless of his answer, I wanted to feel his cock deep inside of me.

"Please, Phillip," I said. But whether I was begging him to beg me, or I was begging him to satisfy me, even I didn't know. "Please."

He quickly straddled me. "Please," he whispered into my ear. "I beg you. Please let me love you."

My body had only one answer.

I pushed against him with my hips. I wanted him inside me and I wanted him now.

"Please!" he all but roared. Quieter now, he said, "Please. I beg you." I could feel him so close to slipping inside, so close to losing that self-control.

"Yes," I said softly, and then more loudly, "Yes!"

We were both too far gone, and he thrust himself inside me with one fluid movement. As he shoved past the thin membrane that had lasted all of these years, I gasped—almost, but not quite, in pain.

Pleasure built with every thrust, and the power of him reminded me of the natural grace of a wild animal. Pleasure built and blossomed. I wrapped my legs tightly around him, pulling him inside of me. Our bodies connected, as did our mouths and hands. Together, our breathing became shallow, quick. I had never felt so wild and wanton. I'd never known I could. Wave after wave washed over me, shook me, until I cried out his name. "Oh, Phillip," I said as I wrapped myself around him as completely as I could.

His answer shook through him for what seemed an eternity.

I lay on top of him, warm, wet and comfortable. I felt like the savannah plains must feel when the rains start to fall after the end of the dry season. He'd filled all of my needs and left me feeling strangely content.

I looked over at him, at his possessive expression. But I didn't know what to say. He said nothing, either, but a secret joy filled my heart. Did he feel the same way? I peeked another glance at him. His drowsy smile made my heart fill with happiness.

I kissed his cheek and snuggled in. As my mind drifted into sleep, I realized that his eyes were the color of cobalt in this light. The delicious color suited him. My hazy thoughts realized that if we had children, their eye color would be remarkable. I fell asleep before I could chastise myself for such a presumptuous thought.

I woke in the middle of the night, awash in moonlight. Phillip was still asleep, unperturbed by the night's brightness. Looking at his eyelashes lying on his cheekbone, I found it hard to reconcile his face with the brutal man who'd captured me and the tender man who'd rescued me from the lions.

I pressed my breasts against his side, appreciating the well-defined muscles of his chest and abs. I couldn't help myself. Still smiling, I began to stroke that lovely curve of his bicep. Gently, gently. He wasn't awake yet. I moved to caress his cock. Woken in the sweetest way, he pressed against my thigh.

Unable to resist, I straddled him again. Our bodies spoke the natural language shared by all wild creatures.

7

I didn't open my eyes at first, relishing the previous day. The lions. And Phillip. In my mind, I rolled his name over my tongue. I liked it. It meant "lover of horses" and, being a horse-lover myself, I liked it. I thought about the earnest look in his eye, about how satisfied I'd felt drifting off to sleep . . . both times.

I couldn't believe he was mine. He'd begged for me as I'd begged for him.

In the real world I would never have asked for so much. I didn't have the confidence. I'd been too cautious in my love life. His desire gave me authority I'd only dreamed of having.

I thought back to all of the handsome men who'd asked me out. I'd rejected each of them, using my family as an excuse. The truth was I just hadn't wanted to give any man that sort of command over me.

Fool that I was, I hadn't realized that sexual power ran both ways.

I rolled over to nestle against him. He smelled so good. But the bed was empty. It was then I noticed the absence of faunal sound. No baboons. No guinea fowl. No songbirds. No animals at all.

Instead I heard the honking of horns, a garbage truck, someone shouting in English—the frantic sounds of Manhattan.

My eyes flew open and I sat up. I was in the Morgan Hotel. Alone.

I sat up and rubbed my eyes. Bits and pieces of the dream clung in my memories, the flavor if not the contents. Most of the dream fell away like tattered ribbons in the wind.

Phillip, my mind cried. He'd just been a dream! How could he just be a dream?

I heard a lion's roar and looked around quickly in mad and crazy hope. Then my eyes landed on the television, tuned to the Discovery Channel. A commercial advertised an upcoming special—highlights from Tanzania's savannahs.

I wanted to cry. Phillip wasn't a dream. How could Phillip have been a dream?

I looked in the bathroom, all shining chrome, white porcelain, and fat towels. Empty.

Scanning the room, I saw rich bedding, sage green. An art deco light fixture, elegant blinds. But I was the only one here. The suitcase I'd packed what seemed like a lifetime ago sat forlornly on the valet next to the television.

Fighting a desperate sadness and a growing headache, I lay back on the bed. I wrapped the comforter tightly around me but found no comfort. Its muted green was no match for the tangerine of my dream memory. I thought about taking a hot shower in the luxurious bathroom. The water would be steamy hot and the towels would be like clouds.

But I didn't want to bathe by myself.

Oh, get over it, the rational part of my brain said. *Would you really be pining for a guy who kidnapped you and tied you up and spanked you?*

And yet . . . and yet, the spanking at least was something I might have been able to forgive. His strength seemed real enough, and worthy of missing.

I tried not to cry as I headed to the shower, but I cried anyway. I must have truly needed this vacation.

Or a man in my life.

As I took a shower in the absurdly opulent bathroom, I thought about my usual dread of these formal affairs. Why did I hate them? I shaved my lathered legs, and an answer occurred to me.

I hated repressing myself continually. I used my family as an excuse. "Dad would be so disappointed," that sort of thing. But the truth was, trusting someone enough to sleep with him was a scary proposition. I hated to give him that power over me. I really hated it.

As I scraped the lather, I wondered if maybe I'd been thinking of relationships in the wrong way. By approaching affairs in terms of politics and power, I could have been missing the point. My animal instincts might serve me better than I'd given them credit for.

My legs were now satiny smooth, and I went to set the razor on the edge of the tub. But then I thought better of it. I picked up the bath gel and lathered between my thighs, thinking of the wicked grin of my dream man.

I wanted to try something new. I wanted to be smooth everywhere.

8

"Samantha, you look beautiful," my mother said to me. "I'd forgotten you look so good in red, and I love the sequins! So festive. You usually wear black to these things." She made a wry face and added, "Ugly, baggy black."

"I'm glad you approve, Mom," I said, giving her a kiss. "Happy birthday!"

"I'm serious. You're absolutely glowing. That vacation must have agreed with you. And whoever put your hair up did a marvelous job."

"I did it. I'm glad you like it."

"It makes you look so elegant, and it shows off your long neck. I'm glad you inherited mine and not your father's." We laughed together. He looked like a bull, a tall bull.

"What did Dad give you for your birthday?"

She made a clicking noise of appreciation. "A rosebush. It's supposed to be a wild type, ancestor to all modern roses. It's supposed to smell heavenly, pale pink blossoms. I can't wait to plant it and see what it looks like when it blooms." Some women loved Tiffany's, but Mom loved roses.

"Do you know where you'll put it?"

"I've just the—look, there's Senator Stodgy. He's coming over here." A harried look crossed Mom's face. "You talk to him, Samantha. I don't want to, and it's my birthday."

"Okay," I said as she rushed away. It *was* her birthday.

The old senator ambled over, an amiable expression on his face. "My goodness, Miss Samantha," he said. "You look more beautiful each day. You remind me of your momma in her heyday."

"You mean yesterday?" I smiled and touched his arm. "Thank you."

"You have that special shine tonight. You must have a fellow on your mind."

"No. Not really." I laughed a little. The truth was too bizarre to explain to anyone, especially this ancient conservative. "But you look good, too, Senator." And he did, for someone nearing his eightieth birthday. "How do you do it?"

"I love my job, Samantha," he said with a grin, raising his white, hairy eyebrows. "That's the trick."

"You're certainly good at it." I meant it. His was one of the few states where more than 90 percent of the people had health-care coverage. But then he started what my mother would call blathering, a friendly but meaningless stream of words that required little from the listener but a polite nod and an occasional, "Mhmm." I let my mind wander, scanning the crowd for anything interesting.

Suddenly my heart stopped. Across the room I saw a gorgeous man prowling through the throngs. He looked like a young Pierce Brosnan—jet hair, classic lines, lovely crinkles around his eyes.

I blinked with a sense of déjà vu. Hadn't I envisioned just this scene when lions trapped me in my dreams? "Senator," I interrupted his soliloquy. "Who is that?"

"The lanky, dark-haired fellow?" The senator was right. The man was lanky.

"Yes. Don't stare."

"That's Senator Benfield's nephew. His name is . . ." The senator mused, looking at the ceiling for an answer. "What's his name?"

"Don't tell me it's Phillip."

"No, that's not it. It's . . . James. James Benfield. Apparently he's been long lost. His momma was Spanish or Saudi or something. Prodigal son coming home and all that. Look, he's heading this way." I suddenly didn't know whether I wanted to run away or run to him. James approached before I could make up my mind.

"Well, hello there, young Benfield," said Senator Stodgy. "This young lady was just asking about you."

I cringed to myself.

"She was, was she?" I could hear the smile in James's voice. "Would you like a glass?" he asked, handing me one of the two champagne flutes he carried.

I took a deep sip, grateful for something to do with my hands. And mouth.

James offered the other to the old senator, but he waved it off with a touch to his stomach. "Thanks, no. My drinking days are over, son." The old man then grinned and said, "You're a lucky lad, to have such a beautiful woman asking after you."

"Yes, I am," James agreed, drinking from the refused glass.

"Let me introduce you properly. James, this is Miss Samantha Thornton."

I smiled weakly at him, relying on countless years of good manners to get me through this. My heart hammered while my brain tried to make sense of his appearance.

"Hello, Miss Thornton." His accent was smooth and polished, not at all the strange clipped thing of my dreams.

"Please, call me Samantha."

"Samantha," he replied, tilting his glass to me.

"Samantha, this is Mr. James Benfield."

We shook hands then, and I found myself asking, "I'm sorry, but have we met before?"

His eyes locked on mine. Shocking. They were as blue as my captor's, but the gleam seemed less predatory. Seeing that, I breathed a little easier.

Senator Stodgy clearly wasn't interested, or was polite enough to give us some privacy. "James, you look after lovely Samantha, will you? I want to find my wife before she makes too many campaign promises on my behalf. She thinks big, that woman," he muttered as he walked away.

Standing alone with him, I could barely meet his eyes. My mind was racing. How could I have dreamed him so vividly?

"Samantha," he said in that husky voice.

I looked at him, feeling so nervous that my heart threatened to pound out of my chest. "You look as good in a tux as I imagined," I said. Where had that come from? I'd never been so forward with a stranger in my life.

He looked pleased at the compliment but answered smoothly, "You didn't have to imagine it. The last time I wore this tux, we met—well, sort of met."

"We were together? And you were wearing a tux?" The last time I remembered seeing him, he wasn't wearing anything.

"We didn't meet exactly, but I certainly noticed you."

"You did?" I asked, at a complete loss. Had I actually met this man?

"At the Kennedy Center in March?"

"Oh, yes. D.C. I was there. The Russian ballet, right?" I'd had to rush out for some emergency of Dad's.

"You left too quickly, before I could get someone to introduce us."

"Yes," I agreed, still puzzled. "Someone had leaked Dad's

budget to *The Washington Post.* I was supposed to convince the reporter to sit on it for a day." I paused, looking at his strangely familiar face. "But I don't remember you."

He smiled, looking adorably abashed, and said, "We saw each other across the room. Before I could get over to you, you left. Like Cinderella."

And then I remembered. I *had* seen him. Across the crowd, his angular face and vivid eyes had momentarily caught my eye. I hadn't thought about him since I rushed out that evening. I hadn't thought about anything but work.

At least not consciously, I amended to myself.

"I never imagined you in such a dress," James said with the crooked grin familiar from my dreams. But the actual smile was kinder than that of my captor.

On firmer ground, I realized what must have happened. Incorporating the television special on lions and James Benfield's face, my subconscious must have been working overtime in the tight box I'd built for it.

"What did you imagine me in?" I finally replied. If he said a peach sheet, I was going to take the next cab to Bellevue.

He laughed and then answered, "I imagined you in my arms."

Normally I would have cringed at such a bold line and promptly brought the Ice Queen out to deal with him. Tonight, though, the world seemed rich with potential. I brazenly answered, "You have a smooth tongue, Mr. Benfield." I'd love to find out how smooth.

"Would you like to dance?" he answered.

"Yes. I think I would."

He graciously nodded and led me toward the polished wood floor. The band played a quick waltz, and as we began to twirl around the floor, I met his direct gaze. The intensity of *that* look seemed so familiar. I said, "I had the strangest dream last night, and I'm certain you were in it."

James stopped in his tracks, causing me to bump ungracefully into him. "Sorry," he said, resuming the steps.

I looked at him curiously. "What is it?"

He shook his head, "It's nothing."

"What?" I insisted.

"I dreamed about you last night, too." He couldn't meet my eyes, and my pulse raced.

"What was your dream about?" I asked, striving to keep my voice light. What if they'd been the same dream?

"You first," he said.

I thought about the razor and the ropes and felt the blood rush into my face. They couldn't possibly have been the same. "No way. Besides, I asked first."

James looked at me speculatively for a moment, perhaps intuiting at least the sexual nature of the dream. "Maybe we should save that for the second date."

A second date? I rarely allowed first dates. This man was serious. "I like the sound of that."

"Exchanging secrets or having a second date?"

I then envied the woman I'd been in my dream—so bold and confident. She'd have a cocky answer to this suggestive question.

But she was I, wasn't she?

"Both," I said.

The waltz slowed, and he pulled me closer, just a bit. "What should we do on our first date, then?"

"Is that what this is?"

"If you'll permit it."

The waltz thrummed its three-beat melody, and I let the music carry us while I thought.

"Then let's dress in our finest, drink a little champagne, and waltz the night away while staring into each other's eyes." I became increasingly aware of his mouth, the curve of his lips. He was so close, so close.

"And could I kiss you on our first date?" he murmured.

I wanted him to. I knew exactly how it would feel, and I craved it. "Did you dream about it last night? This kiss?" I asked, softly.

"Yes." His voice had grown husky.

"So did I."

In the middle of the dance floor, we stopped.

He kissed me then, and I gave my mouth completely to him. More brazenly than even my dreaming self had imagined, I luxuriated in the silky caress of his lips and tongue. His kiss tasted like something from paradise—glorious and powerful.

James Benfield drew me into his arms, ignoring the dancers moving politely away from us. "It's the same, isn't it?"

"Yes," I agreed, "it is."

"Or better."

"Mmm," I hummed, letting the music wash over us, calming my rapidly beating heart. "This scares me."

James looked me in the eye, eyebrow cocked. He didn't look scared at all. "Why?" he asked.

"I don't know exactly what you did in your dreams last night, but the second date might have us in for a wild ride."

James grinned then, and the intensity of his wickedness was exactly the same as the man in my dreams at his worst. I could almost smell the savannah dust. "I think you know exactly what I dreamed last night," he said.

I was afraid that I did.

Just then Baba Yaga capered past us, carrying a flute of sparkling champagne and cackling a happy tune. She winked a raisin eye at us, and floated away on the spring breeze.

"I can't wait for that second date," I said to him.

Winged Dreams

1

More brazenly than her waking self imagined possible, Iole gave her mouth to him, luxuriating in the velvet caress of his lips and tongue. His kiss tasted like something from heaven—sweet and powerful.

But fear rode in on the waves of surrender.

Sensations she hadn't known existed flashed through her with a burning intensity that left her breathless. The glide of his lips over hers made her instantly aware of her breasts, her thighs.

Her thoughts roiled, charged like a summer storm. Power raced through her fingertips. Might coursed through her veins, immense and building.

Like lightning in the summer night sky, she could sense emotions hidden by darkness. Something—someone—lurked behind the shadows of this tempest. Never had she known that nipples could long for something, that the space between her thighs could feel so empty. He, whoever he was, caused this.

The electric shimmering gave way to something more permanent, more pervasive. Yes, her breasts wanted his touch, his tongue and lips, but the molten feeling between her thighs was becoming insistent. The storm was building, and she couldn't ignore it.

Iole could only yield. She could only give herself over to a pleasure she'd never understood.

But even as she ceded to his touch, even as she expanded with it, Iole sensed an incredible presence. Someone wanted her attention. Someone as mighty as an autumn storm over Mount Olympus.

A god, then. Which god? She couldn't tell.

She opened her eyes, searching, wanting to see her lover's face. What did magic look like?

But in the disjointed manner of dreams, he melted away. A pair of doves replaced him. They soared across an oddly colored sky. Green clouds, a purple sky. Then her perspective shimmered, and for a breathtaking moment she became one of the doves.

The warm air under her wings gave her the sky's freedom. Leagues of forest and farmland passed under wing. The Aegean lay open before her. With a powerful stroke she flew toward the open horizon . . .

The dream melted to another.

No more wings. Now she lay on a rich mattress of feathers, subject to his authoritative touch. Who was he? As his mouth traveled from her hip inexorably toward her breast, she shuddered. As if lit from within, golden highlights shone wildly in his coppery hair.

With preternatural clarity Iole knew the line along her midriff that his lips would follow, that his tongue would lick. He traced the path, claiming every bit as his. Every bit of her longed for his heat.

His lips passed her navel, and Iole shivered in delight. The area between her thighs burned like a sun. She belonged to him.

She belonged. To him. Like an aphrodisiac, the thought enflamed her, from her heart to her fingers.

But that wasn't right. She belonged to no one, not like this. A chaste maiden, she belonged to her father, to marry as he saw fit.

Iole struggled to sit, to run. But her dream lover stopped her, sliding his long, hard body against hers.

His touch stopped Iole midflight—his body fit perfectly. He belonged there. And her dream lover took advantage, slipping his hands over her breasts as lightly as a spring breeze over the Aegean. The broad power of his finely formed fingers let her revel in his strength. She'd be safe in his arms. No one could hurt her here. His strength gave her the freedom to let go, to savor the new sensations he offered.

His fingertips danced over her nipple, hardening it. Mouth watering, she swam in the delight. He pinched, sending waves of shock through her. Who'd known that pinching would be pleasurable? Iole rolled her head back, wanting him to caress more of her, to caress her harder.

But still she trembled, and not simply with desire. No man had ever touched her so. This was wrong. As his fingertips slid over her nipple, fear slid down her spine.

Still, breathless and weak with desire, she allowed him to ease her back onto the bed, trap her balmy body. He licked her stomach then, and the moan that escaped her dreaming self surprised the still-rational part of her mind. She sounded like a different girl, a different woman.

When he cupped her breast in his hand, thumb still toying with her nipple, her head began to spin, deliciously. She writhed, arching her back toward him. Was she too forward?

She should wake herself. She should run.

But his hot tongue flicked over the curve of her hip. She knew she wanted more.

And he gave more.

When he captured a hard nipple and languidly licked it, she could only whimper.

Iole watched light from some unknown source play over the coppery highlights in his hair as he bent over her. She wanted him in ways she couldn't have said, even awake. He'd fill an emptiness in her she didn't know existed until now. He'd feed this growing, expanding hunger.

Each kiss worked its way to her head like strong Athenian wine. Each kiss weakened her resolve, her need to escape.

"That's right," he said, when he took her earlobe between his teeth. And when he kissed that ticklish spot behind her ear, her defenses weakened further. "It's only a dream," he said, his voice deep and melodic. Hypnotic. "Fly with me."

Her dream-self acquiesced. He was right. What harm could come from a dream?

She wound her arms around his neck, drawing him closer, inhaling his tangy scent. Iole could not resist his call. When his mouth enveloped hers, she parted her lips, welcoming his tongue inside. She embraced his wet heat, his soft strength, with a feeling of safety and well-being. She belonged in his arms.

That gods gave gifts, she knew—and she wanted this one. Iole took his hand in hers, and after a moment's hesitation, slid it between her legs. She'd never done such a thing! Exhilarated with her daring, she widened her thighs, pressed his hand hard against the swollen nub that cried for his attention, for relief.

And the exquisite pleasure that came! White sparks exploded. The eruption of Thera's volcano couldn't surpass the power of this feeling.

As she molded to his touch, she dreamed that he cried in desire.

But it was only a dream.

* * *

Drenched in sunlight, Iole woke. Her attendant still slept soundly, oblivious to morning's arrival. As Iole stood, she became aware of the strange slickness between her thighs. Had she dreamed about . . . a kiss? As she tried to remember, snippets of the dream fell away, leaving her with the sensation that something important fluttered just out of reach.

Something very important.

2

In the stable he and his father had built, Lord Echion stood, inspecting the aisle with a critical eye. Halters and leads hung neatly on the stall doors. The cobbled floor had been swept, and the fresh scent of barley hung in the air. Out the large door he could see brood mares on the green hillside grazing with their new foals, all knobby knees and big ears.

The perfection of it all wrenched his heart. He wanted to keep this rightness. He wanted to grow it.

Echion walked to the first stall and peered in. His lead horse, a lanky bay stallion, pricked his ears sleepily at his approach. Echion entered the stall, and Ampyx shoved his muzzle in Echion's hand and licked, obviously hoping for some treat. Laughing, Echion offered a honeyed fig, and Ampyx quickly ate it. Looking at this serene pet, Echion knew few would guess that he ran more swiftly than any other stallion in the land.

Echion ran his hand down the stallion's front leg, appreciating the tautness of tendon and the solid hoof. No cracks. No nicks. His muscled chest and thick hindquarters spoke of power to those who could read horseflesh. Ampyx had winning in him.

He'd done all he could, Echion told himself, for tomorrow's race. The horses were fit and trained. He'd oiled the tack himself, bringing each leather strap to a polished shine. Although his father had inspected the chariot, Echion made a mental note to recheck the reinforced axle and wheels.

As Echion secured Ampyx's stall door, a scent caught his attention. Male sweat. Nervous sweat. He froze, listened.

The assailant flew from his left side, wooden staff swinging to crack his skull. But Echion spun and caught the weapon in his hands, powerful from a lifetime of training and handling horses. He pressed the staff against his attacker's chest, forcing him to step back until the man was pressed against the oak wall.

As Echion grabbed for the man's throat, the attacker jerked up the staff, knocking Echion's chin and jaw. Ignoring the hard click of his teeth, Echion landed a solid punch in the man's solar plexus.

With a heavy grunt the man stumbled but didn't fall. He aimed a knee at Echion's groin, but Echion caught his thigh and pulled up with all his strength. The attacker landed flat on his back, head thumping the stone cobbles with a loud "thwack."

Echion spat a mouthful of blood. The man was no longer conscious, but as Echion secured his wrists and ankles with lead ropes, he saw his assailant was most definitely alive.

"What have we here, son?" Lord Kadnus asked walking down the aisle.

"Father," Echion answered, panting and wiping sweat from his forehead. "I didn't hear you sneak in."

"Well, you wouldn't, seeing as you were busy pummeling someone."

Echion laughed wryly and said, "He started it."

Kadnus looked down at the trussed would-be assailant. "What did he want?"

"I didn't get a chance to inquire. Want to help me ask?"

Kadnus grunted his assent and grabbed the man's feet.

Echion had his wrists, and as one, the two men lugged the victim to the water trough and tossed him in.

"Well, you whelp," Kadnus said to the sputtering man. The narrow trough folded his torso and forced his legs and arms to hang out awkwardly. "What do you want with us?"

"Like you don't know," he snarled.

Without batting an eye, Echion punched the man's nose.

Seemingly oblivious to the streaming blood, the dripping man continued to glare from the trough. "Kill me if it pleases you. They'll just send more men."

"Who, you bastard?" Echion demanded.

"You owe money, fool, and you owe it now."

Clenched fist, Kadnus plowed him this time, in the eye. Age hadn't diminished his strength in any way that Echion could see. "Watch your tongue when you speak to my son, Whelp."

"Whether or not I watch it, you owe and you'll pay."

"The race is tomorrow. Your employer knows we'll win, and we'll pay then," Echion said.

"Yes," the man said, wiping blood from under his nose and water from his eyes. "My employer wants to ensure that you're properly motivated to win. The next time you miss a payment, it won't be your pretty head I crack. It'll be the stallion's forelegs."

Echion pulled a knife from his belt and held the wicked blade beneath the man's nose. "If you hurt that horse . . ."—He moved the knife toward the man's middle, stopped above his testicles, and quick as a blink, cut the binds at his wrists—"I'll cut off your manhood." He freed the man's ankles and left him wallowing in the trough as he sheathed the blade and put it away.

"Get out of here," Kadnus said, kicking the trough over abruptly.

The man pulled himself from the mud and stood carefully.

"Leave!" Echion demanded. "Before I hurt you!"

Father and son watched the lackey for the moneylender scurry away, but Echion felt little satisfaction in his departure. He sighed and looked at his father.

"How does Ampyx look, son?" asked his father.

"Perfect. Glad you arrived when you did."

"I was looking at the mares. Phemie will foal soon—maybe tonight."

"Do you want me to look at her?"

"Perhaps later. I'm having one of the lads bring her in." Kadnus looked his son over and asked, "He was a brute of a man. Are you hale for tomorrow's race?"

Echion felt as fit as Ampyx. He'd been running horses all season in races big and small across the countryside. Echion had won many of them, most of them. Despite the brawl, he felt ready, like he could run the race himself.

"I'm fine, father," he replied. Echion noticed a faraway look in his father's face. "But it seems like you're brooding yourself. Did you know this mongrel was coming?"

"No! No, nothing like that." Lord Kadnus scratched his head, apparently looking for the right words. "I've done something you won't like."

Alarmed, Echion asked, "What is it? Did you borrow more money? We don't need it. I—"

"No, not money. It's just—"

"What?"

"I've asked Lord Aeson to consider you as a potential suitor for his daughter."

"What?!"

"Echion," the older man said, putting his hand on his son's shoulder. "I know you like the fillies, but you're not getting younger. It's time to settle down."

He'd be damned if he were settling down. Echion was meeting the fair Hyades tonight, and perhaps he'd meet sloe-eyed Calliope at tomorrow's celebration. "I don't want to marry."

"It's not just about marriage. Think, son," Kadnus urged. "If you marry money, we'll never be under this kind of pressure again. Moneylenders will never jump you. I know Lord Aeson can't help with tomorrow's race, but if you marry into that family, no one will be able to take this farm from us. You'll never have to worry about losing the mares and the barns and the foals."

"True . . ." Echion said, looking through the barn door. Two sorrel babies capered together.

"And it isn't just the money," Kadnus continued. "Lord Aeson has the emperor's ear, doesn't he?"

"Yes . . ."

"Who better to buy horses from, if you're the emperor, than Lord Aeson's son-in-law?"

"Mmmm," Echion said.

Kadnus took the noise as dissent and took up yet another argument. "And when you win this race, no one will doubt who has the best horses. Aeson's daughter will be fawning over you, and the emperor will see for himself these beautiful horses that will be so easy for him to buy."

Biting back a smile, Echion finally gave his father the answer he wanted. "Father, you're a genius!"

"You're mocking me."

"But I love you, nonetheless."

"It's a good idea, Echion."

"It's a great idea," Echion agreed, letting his appreciation for the idea show on his face. "And what of the girl?"

"I know little. She is older—early twenties, I think—and I hear she is pretty enough."

Echion imagined a fair maid with a quick smile and an easygoing manner, enjoying herself at his side at the many parties they'd attend. He relaxed at the vision. Her family had money and connections. She'd love horses, and together they'd become rich beyond their wildest dreams. Their sons would carry on his line.

Hyades and Calliope and Syna wouldn't bother his imaginary bride. Not too much, anyway.

His heart pounded at the vision. He'd win the race. They'd pay off the cursed moneylenders. He'd gain the heart of the girl holding the key to his golden future.

His dream was certainly worth a visit to the oracle and the temple. A horse nickered in the background, and Echion knew he'd do whatever the gods asked to see this realized.

He'd plead with Zeus himself.

"Halooo," Lord Arcas cried to his men as he reined in his mare. His call echoed strangely in the open air, as if muffled by an invisible mist.

No jangling bridles. No hoof thuds. In response to his call he heard only the rustle of unearthly wings. A mist grew, almost imperceptibly, and his mare shifted uneasily beneath him. The heat from her body reassured him. Some measure of reality still existed.

And then: "Arcas." The voice, if that's what it was, sounded ethereal, as if songbirds invented it from bells and lullabies.

Fear wrapped a cold hand around his heart. Five trained soldiers were accompanying him from his country home to Athens in order to secure the hand of his childhood sweetheart in marriage.

Five well-armed men and their horses had simply disappeared.

"Hello?" he replied, quietly.

"Arcas." The voice now seemed more substantial. A flock of doves appeared from the thickening mist. Then they clustered tightly together so that they seemed to coalesce into something else entirely.

He blinked, and a woman of surreal beauty took their place. The maiden whose hand and heart he journeyed to win was exceptionally comely, but the woman who'd just appeared before him was beautiful.

As Arcas inhaled, he caught her scent. Soft lovers, touching, exploring. Ignoring his pounding heart, Arcas reached behind his saddle for his sword. "Where are my men?"

The question was directed toward himself, but the apparition replied, "They will rejoin you shortly. I will not harm you."

"Gods and goddesses do not interfere in mortal affairs for the benefit of the mortals," he replied. "Just ask my mother."

Her eyes gentle, she replied, "I am sorry for your loss." Her bowtie lips curved invitingly. He could forget himself in such lips.

"What do you know of my loss?" Arcas heard despair in his own voice.

"Lady Penelope's appreciation for beauty caught my attention years ago. Each time she took moments from her hectic life to savor my gifts, she brought me pleasure. When she shared her love of beauty with you, she prayed—to me. I, too, miss her."

Arcas stared at her, finding no appropriate words.

"Your mother would have approved of your choice for a wife. I will help you win your bride," the apparition said.

She looked Arcas over in an appraising manner, lingering on his chest, which had been unaffected by Hera's hand. "Lady Penelope herself brought great beauty into this world."

The goddess's power rippled through him. For the first time in more than a year, Arcas felt like a man. He nearly forgot his bristles, his warts. For the first time since that terrible day, Arcas grew hard.

"I am no longer pleasing to the eye, as you can see."

"To those with the right eye, beauty shines forth."

Arcas felt his heart pound anew. Perhaps his maiden had the right eye.

The goddess paused, giving Arcas a moment to appreciate the luxurious wealth of her luminescent hair, which was exactly the color of a dove's wing. What would it smell like? What would it feel like if he brought it to his cheek, to the cheek free of warts?

"Aphrodite," Arcas said finally into the silence, identifying her. "The goddess of beauty."

"Yes," she breathed.

"You honor one as ugly as I."

"You are on your heart's quest. I will give you aid."

"I've no need." Pride. Stupid pride.

"I disagree. You are awash in self-pity. Your mother would have wished to give you something to help you on your journey."

Lord Arcas looked at the goddess, at a loss for words. What did she know? Had she gone from having everything—loving parents, a secure future, the favor of fair maidens—to having nothing? No, sitting atop Mount Olympus, she hadn't.

But Arcas had. His mother was now dead, smashed to bits at a cliff's bottom thanks to Hera's hand. Hera intimated that Lord Knaxos had not sired him. His paternity was now questionable. And maidens now shunned his company as if he bore leprosy or the pox.

Aphrodite's gaze seemed full of understanding. "Do not fret so, Lord Arcas. Hera's wrath brings madness. Remember, her touch made Heracles murder his beloved children and wife." She paused a moment as if considering, then said, "If she's filled you only with despair, perhaps you've hope of escaping your sorrow."

The shimmering goddess leaned forward and kissed him full upon his lips. Cool shady brooks. Sparrow song and the drone of bees. The scent of blooming fig flowers.

Her kiss bore no taint of Eros, but when she ceased, Lord Arcas found he throbbed with desire.

"Perhaps," Aphrodite continued, "you will find that my touch can dispel her poison."

And it was true, at least to some degree. If his brooding thoughts still haunted him, the muscles on his forehead, which had been pulled into a perpetual frown, relaxed. His shoulders too uncoiled. Arcas wanted to laugh, or perhaps simply to smile.

"Can you do this for my father, too?" Arcas asked.

Aphrodite smiled. "No, handsome one, I cannot. King Knaxos's grief is natural, and only Chronos can salve that wound."

"With time, then."

"Yes," she said. "Which brings me to my gift."

"My lady, your kiss is gift enough." And he believed it. At this moment all felt right in the world. His men had seen him at his hunched, half blinded, and warty worst and remained loyal. His father had cultivated a prosperous and happy land that he would inherit. His father loved him, as his mother had.

Regardless of who had sired him.

"But I need bid you welcome to the family, my cousin. I bear a gift." With a graceful turn of her hand, Aphrodite proffered an amulet wrought in gold. It dangled from a black leather cord. "Wear this when you have need."

"What sort of need?"

But Aphrodite evaporated with the sound of fluttering. Arcas heard words echoing in his mind: "Beware of Hera."

Like he needed that warning.

Holding the amulet alone in the glen, Arcas wondered if he'd lost his mind. To his horse he said, "Did you see that?"

The horse snorted, tossing her strawberry mane.

Then the implication of Aphrodite's words sunk into his thick, addled skull. "Cousin," she'd called him.

Zeus truly was his sire.

———————

"I'm giving you an ultimatum, daughter. You must select a husband. Or I will do so for you."

Iole sat across from her father, separated by a massive oak table that must have cost a fortune. Oak trees were becoming scarce around Athens. If men kept chopping them, what would her sons use for lumber, and what woods would her daughters explore with their grandfather?

Through her worry, Iole suddenly realized that her father was talking—almost shouting—at her. Lord Aeson's linen chiton was rumpled, and his bulging eyes were red rimmed with frustration . . . at her.

"You must select a husband!"

"Husband?" Iole blinked.

Lord Aeson answered with exasperation, "Your sisters—even your younger sisters—have been betrothed for years."

"But—"

"Choose!"

"But—"

"I don't want to hear it. Lord Echion or Lord Arcas. Pick. Now." Lord Aeson glared at her.

She crossed her arms over her breasts and glared right back at her father. "How am I to select one? Alphabetically?"

"You know their families as well as I! You grew up playing with Arcas." He drew a deep breath, and tight lipped, Aeson looked away from her for a moment. Then he burst, "Don't play daft with me!"

In the face of his fury, Iole kept her voice steady. "I have not seen Arcas in ten years, as you well know. And I know nothing of Echion."

"I am weary of argument, daughter! So few maidens get a say in their betrothals, and I am beginning to understand why." He shook his head and muttered under his breath. "I have spoiled you too much."

Satisfying her father had been the goal of her childhood. She'd learned philosophy and mathematics to please him. They'd spent hours rambling through dwindling forests, discussing ways to make their city-state more powerful, more just. That she should cause him such dissatisfaction in her womanhood upset her.

So did his words.

"Father, I'm sorry. I don't mean to be ungrateful." She put her palm over his hand and looked at him hopefully. "I love you."

"And I love you." She saw the stubborn set to his jaw before she heard the words. "But your charms will not work. Not this time."

"Let me meet them at least," she pleaded. "Please? I don't want to pick the wrong one."

Her father answered in a tight voice. "They are both young. They are both rich. They both come from politically useful families. There is no wrong choice."

"Remind me of their families," she pleaded, hoping to calm him. "Why did you select these two?"

"Iole . . ." he said, with a clear lack of patience.

"Father, you taught me to think and question! I am doing so now. I must spend the rest of my life with one of these men. I think it is wise to seek information before I bind myself in marriage!"

"Our families must spend that time united as well, Iole. Daughters should trust their fathers."

"You know I trust you!"

"Then believe me when I say that I have made inquiries into both, and both are good matches. What other maid gets such assurances?"

"If it is an important decision for both our family and for me, then it is doubly important for me to weigh in on the issue. I may see something that you missed."

"Like how beddable the boy is!"

"Father!" Iole gasped. Heat raced to her face.

This time Lord Aeson looked abashed. "Iole, I'm sorry. What you say is true: I've taught you to seek the logical path. I've never known you to let beauty sway you from the path of reason."

Iole did not mention the trees she wanted to save, only for their beauty.

"And," Lord Aeson continued, "you may indeed see something in these youths that I did not."

"Youths?"

"To me, yes," he answered with a self-deprecating smile. "They are both in their thirties."

"What else?" she prodded.

"Lord Arcas and his family outfit the army with arms—the best swords."

Iole tried to reconcile this image with the thoughtful, almost shy boy she'd known as a child. Her twelve-year-old self had believed she was in love with him for his smile. Unlike the other boys, mainly her brothers, he hadn't impaled frogs and worms on sticks. His reluctance made her seek his smile, do whatever she could to earn it.

"And of Echion?"

"He and his father breed the best horses in the region. Persian bloodlines. They want to expand their market to the armies."

Persian horses. Gorgeous creatures with long, arched necks and intelligent eyes.

"I see armies were on your mind when you made these choices," Iole said.

"I knew that wouldn't get past you."

"So, may I meet them?"

"Zeus's thunderbolts," he said, rolling his eyes, but she knew she'd won some quarter. "You have a month to decide. Go with your sister to the races. Both men will be there."

"So, father is finally ready to marry you off?" Calandra asked as the horsemen prepared for the final race.

"I suppose he is."

"You should be happy!" Calandra had been betrothed for years to an Egyptian lordling, and unpromised Iole was two years older.

"I am. I just hope . . ." Iole's voice trailed off.

"You just hope, like all brides, that he's young and handsome and rich."

"Of course," Iole replied. "But I want him to do important things. And I want to help him." She looked at her sister and added, "And I want him to be kind."

"How sweet!" Calandra fluttered her lashes and crossed her hands over her heart. "You want to save the world together with your true love."

Iole bumped her shoulder against Calandra's and laughed. Something caught Iole's eye, and she inhaled sharply.

"What is it?"

"Calandra, can you see who's in Arcas's box?"

Calandra peered around her attendants. After a moment she answered, "It looks like . . . two men. And their slaves."

"Does the close one look lumpy to you, or are my eyes playing tricks?"

"No, he looks misshapen. What's *wrong* with him?" Calandra looked again and let out her breath appreciatively. "But the other . . . He looks more like how I remember Arcas."

Iole saw the breadth of his chest as he turned. "Arcas wasn't lumpy, was he?"

"Definitely not."

"That was ten years ago," Iole said doubtfully. "We haven't seen them since they moved halfway to Sparta."

"Well, I hope Lord Arcas hasn't turned into Lord Lump! Wait. We can answer this question." Calandra whispered something to her youngest attendant, and the girl slipped away with a happy smile on her face. "She'll find out. She loves to snoop."

Around them, the crowd began to chatter excitedly as the chariot teams trotted around the track, letting viewers see them one last time before the race. Seven teams were racing, but the crowd talked only of two men: Castor and Echion.

Calandra's girl scampered back, breathless. "For you, my lady." The girl handed Iole a bouquet of wild flowers. "Lord Arcas said they're for you."

"To the point, girl! Was he the handsome one or not?" Calandra demanded.

The girl shuddered and looked at Iole. "Lady, Lord Arcas is not well proportioned, and it is he who sent the strange flowers."

Iole looked at the bundle of purples and blues. They were tied with an indigo ribbon. Iole asked, "How are they strange?"

"He said they're from the great oak forest north of Athens."

Iole blinked. She'd just been thinking of these woods—the

forest she and her father walked through on the hot summer days of her youth, the forest dwindling as the number of ships in the army grew.

"Iole?" Calandra asked with concern. "What is it?"

"I remember Arcas being quite handsome. Don't you, Calandra?"

"Mhmm. He was cute, in a serious way. Tall. Great eyes. I wonder what happened to him?"

"What does he look like?" Iole asked the slave girl.

"He only has one eye. And his back is hunched, my lady, like this." The girl curved her spine awkwardly, making a mockery of her youthful beauty.

"He wasn't disfigured all those years ago, was he?" Calandra asked.

"No." Iole swallowed. She looked down at the flowers, and her world shimmered. For a moment she could hear wings beating in the night air.

"What is it?" Calandra asked with quiet concern.

Iole shook her head, trying to clear her mind.

"And he has warts all over his face," the slave girl continued.

Perhaps mistaking Iole's expression, Calandra put her hand on Iole's knee. "Don't worry, sister. You will marry Lord Echion instead. Look! Here he comes now!"

Charioteers waved to the crowd. Unlike Arcas, Echion looked as strong as the stallions he drove. Iole breathed a deep sigh of relief. Deciding between these two would be easier than she thought.

And her father would be happy—joyous—for a quick decision. Lord Aeson couldn't have known that Arcas had changed so. Not even Calandra with her gossiping ladies had known.

As the charioteers drove their horses into the starting gates, the crowd hushed. From their pavilion, Iole could see equine nostrils pulsating behind the gates. She watched the dancing of anxious hooves, and her heart fluttered in anticipation. Along with the crowd, Iole fell breathlessly silent. A high-pitched challenge from a stallion broke the hush, and someone in the crowd laughed nervously.

The sheen of a chestnut horse's coat—copper and bronze over solid muscle—reminded her of someone's skin. Who was it? The fleeting memory sent an unfamiliar sense of excitement through her. Iole slid closer to the edge of her seat.

Just then, the gates flew open.

Horses, men, and chariots raced toward her—glossy necks, outstretched legs, leather straps, wheels, and whips. At first, she couldn't tell what part belonged to whom.

Then she focused. Thick forearms held taut reins. Chiseled calves balanced on chariot edges. Iole's heart thudded at the raw, surging power.

By the first turn, three teams had fallen back, obvious non-contenders.

Through the excitement, the weight of someone's gaze caught her attention. Lord Arcas watched her. Across the crowd, his gaze seemed loaded with meaning, like he willed her toward action. Or maybe like he could see into her soul.

Disconcerted, she gave a little smile. She pointedly dragged her attention back to her other potential fiancé—no, to her fiancé. Lord Echion was hers for the choosing.

The remaining teams approached a curve. Iole watched a horseman on the outside track authoritatively shift his weight to his inside leg. The muscles in his upper arm rippled as he cracked his whip, and he daringly cut across the racing mass. The charioteer's grace and audacious courage left Iole breathless.

As his team approached the favored inside track, she saw his bravery had paid off. He'd found exactly the right spot! Suddenly, the team behind him overran his chariot's edge. Iole watched in horror as the two groups avalanched.

She looked away from the carnage—only to find Lord Arcas

staring still. Without bidding, bits of last night's dream flitted back into place. She'd been a bird! Soaring in the strangely purple sky.

Only Castor and Echion remained on the track. Their pounding hooves thundered over the ground, and the reverberation echoed up Iole's spine, making her heart pound in rhythm.

Castor's sweat-drenched team held the lead. Swallowing, Iole saw that Echion needed to pass before the next turn. His bay horses looked willing and eager. Even at this distance, she could plainly see that Echion ached to win.

Toward the turn, both teams ran flat out, nose to nose.

The chariots themselves were only a handsbreadth apart around the curve. She watched Echion's arm flex as he raised his whip, and she—along with the entire crowd—stood to yell him on.

But her cheer turned to a gasp as Castor rammed his elbow into his competitor's solar plexus. The light leather armor must have provided little protection; she could see Echion struggle to remain upright. His whip fell uselessly into the roiling dust.

A straight run stood between the horses and the finish line. Echion's horses faltered with lack of guidance while Castor's, covered in foamy sweat, kept the lead. She watched, not daring to breath, as Echion straightened himself and gathered the many reins. He pulled them tight, steadying the balance of the racing animals, and he gave an almighty roar. The overwhelming cheer of the crowd told Iole that even the stadium spectators could hear it.

So could Echion's horses. They answered with power, surging past Castor's team.

From the corner of her eye, she could see Arcas watching her cheer for Echion. Self-consciously, she tried to control herself.

Echion had won. The gods had blessed him, and Echion had won.

Calandra hugged her sister. Then she saw Iole gasping for breath. Calandra laughed. "Good thing your new husband likes the races as much as you do."

"What do you mean?" Iole asked.

"Look at you! I think it bodes well for Lord Echion. Your eyes are wide and wild. Your lips are blood red. And this . . ." Calandra gently caressed Iole's throat. "I can see your heart throbbing like a captured bird's."

"Oh," she answered, weakly. At her sister's words, the texture of last night's dream glimmered again in her memory. An erotic heat flushed through her veins. In confusion, Iole looked to the sky.

She could almost imagine taking wing.

Standing outside the pavilion waiting for the crowd to disperse, Calandra chattered happily, but Iole listened with only half an ear. Memories of her dream danced just out of reach. It'd been . . . erotic? Iole blushed. But perhaps talk of marriage normally led ladies to such dreams.

"Iole, look!" Calandra exclaimed.

Accompanied by several guards, the now-famous Lord Echion left the stadium. The men bantered casually, and the horseman exuded power. The man's jaw muscle was so defined that Iole knew she could trace it with her fingertip. People fought to get close to him, heaping his arms with flower bouquets and other small presents. He greeted everyone with an endearingly lopsided grin.

"He looks like Apollo!" Calandra said in a husky voice. "I hope my Egyptian is half as gorgeous. And so skilled!"

"Mhmm," Iole concurred. She surprised herself by wondering what bedding such a man would be like. Her half-remembered dream suddenly came into focus, and she inhaled sharply. She could remember the texture of her dream lover's skin, the taste of his sweat. And how she had touched him.

Sizing the horseman up, Iole decided that Echion's skin was definitely lighter, less golden.

She also decided that it didn't make him less gorgeous.

"Lord Echion," Calandra said in a half whisper, "your new betrothed!"

Iole hushed Calandra with a look, but she had to admit the idea excited her. With horses, his hands had seemed so masterful.

What would he be like with her?

Lord Echion caught her gaze across the sea of people. With a quick wink, he bowed to Iole and Calandra. When the crowd turned to see who had his attention, he threw her one of his many bouquets. She caught the bloodred blooms deftly. Their polished beauty overwhelmed the muted wildflowers she already held.

With great strides Echion walked over to the girls, giving them an elegant bow. "Ladies," he said.

"Hello, Lord Echion," Lady Calandra said as coolly as if she spoke with Olympian-looking men regularly.

"Lord Echion," Iole said in a more subdued tone.

"We enjoyed the race tremendously, especially my sister," said Calandra, sending Iole an impudent wink.

"You take pleasure in horses, then?" he asked. Was that hope Iole heard in his tone?

"We do," Iole answered, knowing it to be an understatement. She and Calandra loved horses. Their muzzles felt like the finest cloth, and they smelled like freedom. Even to women, horses lent great power and speed. "My father says you have Persian broodmares. Bred by Darius I himself."

"Ah! You know horseflesh. Would you like to tour our stable?"

Unlike Iole, Calandra had no need to restrain herself. Calandra clapped her hands together in delight. "That'd be wonderful! We'd love to see the barn."

"Yes," Iole answered. "That would be lovely."

"And might we ride?" Calandra asked. "Perhaps on the beach?"

That earned a quick crooked grin from Echion. "That could certainly be arranged." As his slave waved at him from across the plaza, Echion said, "My apologies, ladies. I must run. Shall I visit your place this evening to set the plans?"

"Yes," answered Calandra. "We look forward to it."

As Echion departed, Iole's gaze caught an amber eye—great beauty swimming in a hideous sea. He walked toward them. "Lord Lump," Calandra hissed.

"Your manners, sister," Iole said quietly to her, although she had to agree that the horror shambling toward them little resembled the lithe boy who'd played with Iole, Calandra, and their brothers all those years ago.

"Lord Arcas," Iole greeted, firmly. "Thank you for the lovely flowers."

"Lady Calandra." He nodded in greeting. "Lady Iole, you are quite welcome." He paused awkwardly, perhaps at a loss for words.

Calandra's maid had spoken truly. Iole tried not to stare at the warts erupting across his cheekbone as she said, "They come from the woods, I am told."

"From the Northern Forest, one of my favorite places," he agreed. "Do you remember games of hide-and-seek there? Lady Calandra's ready laugh always gave her away, and no one could ferret you out, Lady Iole." His voice was as deep and rich as fertile fields.

"We had fun then, didn't we?" Iole replied. "Again I thank you. The flowers are beautiful, as are the memories."

"Not as beautiful as you, but alas, far more beautiful than I."

Looking at Arcas's hunched back, Iole could only agree, silently. What had happened to him? A bear? A Spartan?

"Despite that," Arcas continued, "I am visiting your land in order to convince you to return with me—as my bride."

"I, uh—" Her gaze caught his empty eye socket, a flap of red skin hanging loosely over it. Iole stood, nearly speechless. "My—"

Calandra rescued her, grabbing her shoulder and pushing her down the path. "We must return home, Lord Arcas," she said over her shoulder. "Perhaps you can visit tomorrow evening."

Iole watched what looked like pain cross his face, but he only bowed to them and said, "As you wish."

4

Lord Arcas cursed Hera. If he could, he'd strangle her—just to hear her choke and gasp, just to hear her suffer as her victims suffered.

Arcas replayed the instant after the race in his mind, the instant fraught with cruel hope. Iole's classic beauty, her full lips, her steady gaze—she'd grown into a magnificent woman. He'd known she would.

After the race, she'd turned that beauty toward him, addressing him as if he were normal, as if he had no hairy warts. As if he were a man in full.

In that heartbeat, hope, burning hot like molten gold, flooded his veins. Maybe she knew. The geas was upon him— he couldn't speak it, but perhaps she knew! In that moment he'd thought Iole had seen behind the facade, behind the eye socket and warts and hunched back. For the briefest moment, Arcas believed she'd seen his true self.

But he'd pushed it. He had. He had mentioned marriage. And before Iole politely schooled her expression, he'd read horror and disgust, as clearly as words on a scroll.

And it was all Hera's fault.

He'd been blaming her for ages, but it had gotten him nowhere. Aphrodite made that clear. The mourning period was over. He would no longer remain hostage to her whims.

He needed to discover what his heritage was worth.

"By Zeus," Echion said to his father as they left the money-lender's stall. "Our sacrifice at Apollo's temple certainly paid off, didn't it."

"Yes, son," Lord Kadnus replied, "I was loathe to offer up that mare, but we have our freedom. Our pockets are empty, but that crushing debt will hound us no longer."

"And that race! We won it!"

"That spineless bastard Castor," Kadnus shook his head. "Apollo must have interceded on your part."

"When Castor punched me, I thought I'd be eating dust."

"The question is, will Apollo follow up on the second part of our request?"

"Mmmh," Echion replied, enigmatically. When he'd seen Lady Iole standing outside the coliseum with her sister after the race, the phrase that danced through his mind was "matched pair," two perfect fillies. Both had flawless skin and almond-shaped eyes. Both had hair the color of amber. Lady Calandra's was a shade darker, like dark honey.

"What do you mean, 'mmmh'?" scoffed Kadnus. "Those girls are more beautiful than any of your hussies. Lady Iole's smile is as pleasing as any marble-columned goddess's."

"It's true," Echion answered. She looked as cool as a marble statue, too. Still Echion said nothing more; he didn't want to give his father any clue to the depth of his emotions. In truth, the sisters took his breath away.

"Beauty must run true through their bloodlines," Kadnus continued to cajole, unaware that his argument fell on the ears of the converted.

"She's pretty enough," Echion answered, cringing at his answer. His words made him feel like he betrayed her. Even without her family money and political connections, Iole was herself a treasure. As beautiful as Hyades or Syna or any of his other women, Iole expressed interest in his horses. With intelligence! And when Iole caught his flowers so gracefully, pride pounded through his heart. What more could a man ask for in a wife?

"Did Ampyx kick you in the head when I wasn't looking, man?"

"She likes horses," Echion added, as if that was the only thing he could possibly appreciate in her.

"She loves horses!" Kadnus said, twisting the nugget of information into its most positive form. "There's never been a woman that Ampyx couldn't charm. Take her riding!"

Echion walked next to Lord Kadnus in silence for a moment. He couldn't explain it to his father. His brief encounter with Iole had changed him somehow. He'd been thinking of a wife as an impediment, someone who'd make him stay home and keep him from carousing.

But Iole would be an anchor. A lifeline. She wasn't one of his hussies. She wasn't a means to an end. No, Lady Iole embodied the entirety of his golden future. Marrying into her family—marrying her—would bring him everything he dreamed of.

The dream was too huge to describe to his father, too important. Kadnus looked at Iole and saw an easy way to spend an evening, an end to their ever-present financial need, and a path to the emperor's ear. Kadnus wouldn't understand the way Echion's heart had changed.

"You're right, father. I'll take her riding." Echion looked at the sun in the sky. "Let's hurry. We have just enough time to follow the second set of the oracle's instructions."

He'd do anything to secure his future, to secure Iole's heart.

※　※　※

The lips of her dream lover burned a path along her thigh, her hip. Kisses circled her belly button. She groaned as his teeth gently grazed her collarbone.

These sensations, they were as delicious as she remembered.

His tongue found a quivering tendon, and he began to trace a hot, wet trail downward. Iole caught her breath as his hands explored the length of her thigh. Inexorably, his tongue approached the soft vee between her thighs and—

It was too much. "No!" she exclaimed in her dream. "Do not touch me!" She twisted away from him.

Stroke. Lick.

Iole felt her core softening, engorging, knew her nub was swelling, protruding from its hood of flesh. Her lover's arms tightened around her, a strong hand covered a tender breast.

She pushed his hand away. "Leave me be!"

She fell back into a dreamless sleep.

And then . . . Iole walked on an unfamiliar path, feet nearly floating above the rich earth.

"Iole . . ." She heard him call as the path passed magically under her feet. Leaves from shrubs and grasses, ethereal greens and blues, caressed her toes as she billowed above them.

And then he called her name again in a voice that seemed to come from all directions. "Iole . . ."

Strange magic drifted her over the narrow lane, and Iole looked around carefully. Flowers bloomed in a riot of colors from the shrubs, their scent sweet and pungent.

A flash of feathers danced in front of her, long and graceful. Iridescent blues and metallic greens melted into the trees. The birdsong from the foliage made her think of the laughter of children.

"Show yourself," she called. After a moment's consideration, she added, "And name yourself."

No answer.

Stubbornly, she stopped. Her feet gently touched the

ground, and reality tightened its grip on her mind. She would not be his pawn.

"Iole . . ." She heard laughter in his voice, but it sounded slightly sad.

Still she stood, jaw set.

A white dove fluttered near her face and landed an arm's length away. Unearthly, its feathers glowed against the verdant background. Fireflies—strange violets and ambers—lit up the trees, even though the sun's rays peeked through the branches.

Another dove landed nearby, glowing white. The birds approached one another with a gentle "coo," and they began to preen each other. Trills of happiness fell from their throats.

Like a portent, the pair flew up the path, wing to wing.

"They're just pigeons!" Iole called into the strange twilight, unimpressed.

"Aphrodite's symbols of love and peace," she heard in the voice that rang from each bluegreen leaf.

"Delicious in a marinade of rose hips."

"Iole . . ." Chagrin tinged his voice.

The dream shifted.

He stroked her breasts lightly, tantalizingly. "Your breasts are as beautiful as I remembered," she heard.

"Who are you?" she asked.

"Tell the truth, Iole."

"I am truthful."

"Do you really care at this moment who I am?"

Hearing the raw desire in his voice, Iole's mouth went dry. Still, she remained calm, steady. "I did not ask for your advances. If I knew who you were, I could perhaps stop you. You are not a gentleman."

The very air around her crackled. Anger? Humor? She didn't know.

"But I can be gentle," he finally answered. And as if to prove his point, he dipped his head. She knew at once what he was going to do, but stopping him was impossible. She tried to wake herself, to shift the dream, but the dream remained as firm as reality.

His mouth covered her nipple with electrifying heat, and her body traitorously pushed toward him.

"This is a gift, Lady Iole. Accept it graciously." He licked her bare nipple, and slow heat burned through her. "Fly with me!"

"I do not want your touch. Please," she gasped as his tongue danced hot and slick over one nipple then the other. "Leave me be."

"And you called yourself 'truthful,'" he said, roughly cupping both breasts in his hands. He pressed both thumbs against her nipples, still wet from his mouth, and Iole moaned in pleasure.

"You want this," he said. "Confess."

"My body wants it . . ." she said, as his kisses made her melt into him.

"And soon your mind will follow."

Iole feared he understood her too well. She feared he would win her over, despite herself. She knew she should try to pull free but didn't have the strength to try. He sucked away her will to resist with each tug of his wicked mouth.

The desire coursing through her veins, the need in her very core—those sensations pushed all good intentions aside.

Nothing else mattered, not his identity, not her fear, not her innocence.

Nothing mattered but her need to feel him touching her.

Iole threw back her head, riding the storm of pleasure, pressing her face against the hard bulge of his biceps. Her heart beating loudly, horse hooves pounding over turf.

Barely aware of her actions, she bit into his muscle. He tasted real—delicious, but not godlike, not dreamlike.

Her dream lover tasted like desire and male sweat.

He growled, moving to squeeze her breasts between his long fingers. His hips pressed against hers. He was massively hard. Were men supposed to get like this? Was she supposed to get this wet?

"Stop, please. Let me go. What do I have to do to stay away from you?"

"You don't like this?" He reached one hand through her linen, down her thigh, and easily slipped a finger in a long glide.

Iole nearly swooned. Never in her life had she imagined such a sensation. She wanted more. She didn't know what she wanted more of, but with an absolute certainty, she craved more.

"Yes!" The word was torn from her throat. Years of dutiful behavior had been erased in a touch. "Yes," she said.

He ran his hand over her cheek. "Iole, I must leave soon. I cannot stay much longer."

"No," she said, writhing for his touch, longing for fulfillment. "Stay longer. Please."

She couldn't see his face, but the warmth of his cheek permeated her stomach as he rested against her, running his fingertip along the line of her leg.

His fingers teasingly danced into her vee, over her nub. His fingers sent shocking jolts of desire through her blood. "We will be interrupted soon. Morning arrives."

"But how do I find you? Who are you?"

"Watch for me, Iole. Look for me. You know me."

"No, I don't . . ." She reached to caress his muscular arm, and—

"Lady. Lady!" Her attendant shook her gently. "It's time to wake, Lady."

I know you, Iole! the words echoed through her mind, heard only by herself.

To be known by one such as he—what power!

But fear suddenly snaked through her. A god had selected her; she could no longer deny it.

Mortal women fared poorly with gods. Were Persephone or Semele to be envied? No. Grimly she stood.

Iole needed to visit Hera's temple. She'd been plagued enough by her dreams.

5

Iole clutched Calandra's hand as they walked up the cobbled path toward the marble building. "Are you sure we should be here?" she asked.

"When Hera's priestesses tell you to talk to the oracle, you talk to the oracle."

Iole shivered remembering the priestess's words. After her last dream, she'd determinedly marched over to Hera's temple, Calandra in tow. Hera's acolytes conferred with bones and stars, convulsed and spat, and then they claimed that the Olympians would punish them for interfering in this particular affair.

According to Hera's priestesses, Iole was so embroiled in the Olympian's affairs that she was beyond their help.

The acolytes ordered that Iole seek the oracle's advice.

"But why is this happening to me? I'm nobody! I've never launched a war or killed a man. I'd be happy if only I could save some trees! What does Zeus or any of them care about trees?"

"Hush Sister, that's why we're here: to get some advice." Calandra pointed to the huge copper door glinting in the late afternoon sunlight. "We're here."

"I can't believe Father let us spend the night here. We've never slept away from home."

Calandra snorted. "The Pythia's his sister. Of course he'd let us. Besides, I told him how serious your dreams were."

"You didn't tell him—"

"Of course I didn't," Calandra scoffed. Then she took a softer tone. "I didn't tell him anything explicit. The phrase I used was 'recurrent dreams.' You know how he is about those."

Calandra was right. For three nights running their father had dreamed that his wife, their mother, had died, and by the fourth night, she was dead. Lord Aeson believed in the power of dreams.

The trouble was, Iole was starting to believe in them, too. She'd never heard of Hera's priestesses behaving as they had with her.

The doors loomed closer as Calandra nearly dragged Iole up the last elegant steps. As they approached, the copper doors silently slid open, welcoming and intimidating in equal measure. Iole wondered if she'd ever been so frightened. "I miss Mother," Iole said in a hushed voice as they walked through the doors.

"I do, too," Calandra said. Then she squeezed Iole's arm and added, "But I'm here for you."

An attendant held the door for them as they entered. The woman stood, eyes down, still as a statue. A narrow fillet around her head held kinky ebony hair in place. Her patrician nose gave her a noble appearance, despite her youth.

The attendant silently closed the doors as the sisters stood in the overwhelming room. The roof arched high above them, and the mosaic floor sprawled in swirls of cobalt and jade. A large fire burned in a brazier in the room's center, but the flames flickered in strange greens and purples.

Iole clutched Calandra's arm more tightly, wanting more than ever to return to her simple life.

The dark-haired attendant wordlessly approached the fire and pulled an ornate kettle from it. She poured liquid into a

goblet and handed it to Iole. "Drink it all and quickly," she ordered in a voice that sounded as thick as the smoke swirling
around her.

Iole glanced at Calandra, who nodded reassuringly.

Iole took the goblet, held her breath, and swallowed. It was
wine, disgusting and scalding hot. The aftertaste assaulted her
taste buds, reminding her of cat urine. Iole repressed a gagging
cough.

"Come with me," the attendant said.

"We want to see our aunt," Calandra said coolly. To Iole, her
voice sounded solid and steady. Iole clung to that strength, even
as the world took on a strange shimmer, even as the walls began
to sparkle as if covered in starshine.

The dark-haired attendant pointed the way as if she'd heard
nothing. Iole and Calandra looked at each other a moment.
Calandra shrugged, and then they followed.

"Not her," the attendant said, putting a restraining hand on
Calandra's breast. To Iole's eye, the touch lingered too long.

"I'm coming," Calandra began to insist, brushing the attendant's hand aside with an imperious gesture. Their father was
Lord Aeson, and no neophyte would keep her from her sister's
side.

"You are not, my lady. You cannot."

"Leave it be, Calandra," Iole said to her sister.

The strange sensation that her dream lover lurked here pervaded. The world seemed tinted in flickering golds and silvers.
Could he materialize from this haze? Could she be dreaming
while awake? "I'll go alone."

The dark-haired attendant nodded and led the way.

Some part of Iole's mind screamed that she should take care,
that danger lurked here. But the stronger part of her mind
could think only about her feet. The marble under her sandals
enthralled her, so cool and solid. And when the ground beneath
her evaporated, leaving her floating, she knew if she leapt she

could swim through the air. Iole considered trying it—swimming through the air—but she knew it would show poor breeding.

And then Iole caught a scent. Her dream lover, musky and masculine. An intensely familiar hunger tightened her belly.

"Please, my lady," the attendant said, nudging her gently. "He is not here. Not yet. Follow me."

Without realizing it, Iole had stopped walking and stood staring at the walls. She could almost see his handsome face in the shapes of the shadows. His face was handsome, wasn't it?

"Come," the attendant commanded again.

Obediently Iole followed as the woman led her through a maze of halls. When they came upon a scarlet door, Iole wanted to stop and admire the hue, the manner in which the late-afternoon light from the high-set windows played on the door's shadows.

Her dream lover would love this door, Iole felt certain. Iole knew if she called for him, he'd arrive. But the woman opened the door and indicated that Iole should enter.

The room held a large pallet, much larger than her bed at home, and muraled dolphins splashed across the walls, cavorting and caressing each other. A brazier burned under a clever flue, and here, flames flickered in natural colors.

Iole couldn't drag her attention away from the brazier. Why had she never noticed the depth of fire colors before now? Her lover's eyes flickered like these flames.

"Remove your clothing and lay on the bed," the attendant commanded, looking Iole in the eye. "The Pythia will be with us soon. We must hurry."

Was he coming here? Had these clever priestesses found a way to bring her dream world to life? Iole lost herself in the sea blue of the woman's eyes. She'd never seen her lover's eyes, but surely they were as beautiful as this woman's.

"Please, my lady. You must undress." The attendant untied her own chiton and let it slip to the floor. Nearly oblivious to the naked woman, Iole examined the discarded tunic, confused.

She could swim in the curves of the fabric on the floor. She could shrink and then slither through the valleys and tunnels like a snake.

And then Iole noticed the woman.

The firelight cast dancing shadows over her skin, making her breasts seem larger, then smaller, highlighting then obscuring the woman's nipples. The black nest between her thighs took on an auburn shade, then gold. Her nipples were tiny, smaller that Iole's own, and shockingly pink against the woman's ivory skin. Iole's fingers itched to touch them, to feel their waxy softness beneath the pad of her thumb. This attendant would be as real as her dream lover.

"What is your name?" Iole asked is a voice so thick she barely recognized it as her own.

"Hurry, lady!"

Iole did not want to hurry. Instead, she wanted to slowly undo the woman's fillet and run her fingers through her thick ebony hair. She wanted to touch the woman's face, and trace the aristocratic line of her nose. She wanted to lose herself in the woman's moon-pale skin. What would it feel like if she caressed between her—

The woman walked—no, glided—over to her, and Iole reached for her naked waist, mesmerized by the golden halo surrounding her. Gently, the woman brushed her hands away, and a small animal noise escaped Iole's throat. "Shh, lady. We must hurry."

The woman put her hands on Iole's hips and pulled her belt. Iole's linen chiton slid to the ground, and she stood as naked as the attendant.

The woman's lips were the most beautiful Iole had ever seen—curved and red. She wanted to trace their demarcation with her tongue, to taste each breath the woman drew. Something hot and wild exploded inside Iole, and she stepped toward her, intent on—

The scarlet door opened.

"My Lady Pythia," the attendant said quickly to the older woman, standing as straight as a wall, eyes on the floor. "My apologies. The wine affected her much more strongly than expected."

Iole stood speechless, wishing the acolyte wouldn't talk as if she weren't there.

Looking at the curve of the woman's bare hip, Iole wished the women wouldn't talk at all.

"Be easy, Tryn," the Pythia said, caressing the woman's breast with a craggy hand. Iole's mouth watered. "The god's hand is heavy upon this girl," the Pythia continued. "I made her wine appropriate for the evening."

"Yes, my lady. Thank goodness. I thought—"

"Additionally, Tryn, our purpose tonight is twofold."

"But I thought—"

"Yes," the Pythia cut off, "I know what you thought. I did, too. But by indoctrinating her into the ways of pleasure, we will discover her nighttime visitor as well. It may help her control the dreams."

"Does that mean—"

"Tryn," the Pythia said, reaching quickly toward her. Iole's aunt pinched Tryn's nipple between her fingertips. "Please quit interrupting me."

"Yes, my lady," Tryn gasped.

Iole watched the Pythia twist the girl's nipple, slowly, almost gently, as she spoke. A surprisingly kind smile graced her thin, wrinkled lips. "You interrupt incessantly, and I will not tell you again."

"I try—"

"Yes, I know you try. But you need something to remind you."

Iole watched Tryn's shoulders sag. "Yes, my lady."

The Pythia released Tryn's breast. "Bring me the crop, please—the bamboo one wrapped in leather."

Iole watched Tryn silently turn and retrieve the crop from a storage basket. As she bent over, Iole glimpsed a sheen glistening between the girl's thighs. With the wine's herbs humming through her veins, Iole imagined losing herself in the girl's wet warmth. The wet folds held all the world's secrets if Iole were brave enough to explore.

Sudden jealousy snaked through Iole. What power the Pythia had over this beautiful creature. And how she abused it!

Iole's knees quivered in desire. If she could save Tryn, perhaps the acolyte would be . . . grateful.

Tryn handed the whip to the Pythia.

"You know what to do," the Pythia said.

The dark-haired woman turned her back to the Pythia and put her hands on the wall. Iole felt her heart begin to wildly pound in strange anticipation. Iole wanted to stop the Pythia, but a secret part of her longed to see this beauty subjected to the Pythia's iron hand.

"Spread your legs, Tryn."

The priestess obeyed.

Hypnotized, Iole watch the Pythia lovingly run her palm over Tryn's buttocks, around her thighs. Her thumb brushed against Tryn's pink flower. Iole herself wanted to stroke the attendant, wanted to lick.

The words to stop the whipping formed in Iole's mouth, but she could not bring herself to say them.

The Pythia took a step back and lashed the girl's thighs, once. Then twice. Red welts rose up immediately, before Tryn could cry out.

The Pythia lightly caressed Tryn's welts, making a soothing sound when Tryn cried in pain.

"Stand, girl. Your punishment is complete."

Tryn straightened and faced her mistress. Though her eyes were downcast, Iole could see tears streaking down her cheeks. She wanted to kiss away the tears, the throbbing welts. "Thank you, my lady," Tryn said in a nearly inaudible whisper.

"Come here, Tryn."

Tryn stepped closer, keeping her eyes on the floor.

The Pythia took Tryn's lovely breast in her hand and gently caressed her. Iole watched Tryn melt into the Pythia's hand, sobbing now, silently. "You're a good girl."

A louder sob escaped her, and the Pythia hushed her with a slow, graceful kiss on her nipple. Iole watched the dark-haired girl arch her back, begging the wicked Pythia to take more of her breast.

"Perhaps now you will curb your enthusiasm."

"Yes," Tryn almost gasped. She lifted both breasts and offered them to the Pythia who hummed her approval.

Iole watched the older woman sample first one nipple and then the other, slowly, deliberately, as if she were ensuring the quality of some dessert before serving it to a queen.

"Tonight is not without reward for you," the Pythia said, stepping back from the girl.

Again, Iole wanted to shout "No! Don't stop!" As the Pythia subjected Tryn to her touch, Tryn's beauty blossomed, opened as it yielded. Iole wanted to watch the dance, wanted to see its completion.

Still, she stood in silence, watching. Only watching.

"You and Phaedra have tonight's pleasure, Tryn," the Pythia said, lightly running her craggy fingers over the younger woman's buttocks. "You may direct Phaedra while exploring Lady Iole's . . . condition."

Tryn and the Pythia paused to gaze in Iole's direction, and only then did Iole realize that she held her own nipples between her fingers. She was pinching them hard, and beneath her thumbs, they were rock hard.

"See how she calls her lover?" the Pythia asked. "Your job this evening—and Phaedra's—should be simple."

6

Iole looked at her fingertips, a pebbled nipple between each thumb and forefinger, and knew that modesty or embarrassment or shame should be burning through her.

Yet none of those emotions held her in thrall. Instead, empowerment coursed through her. She shifted her palms, lifting her breasts, cupping them, thrilled with the pleasure brought by these wild, new sensations.

"Yes," Tryn said, voice husky. "You are beautiful."

The Pythia had evaporated, leaving in her place a girl about Iole's age. Phaedra.

Phaedra's hair hung in thick straight sheaths that were nearly white next to Tryn's kinky jet lock, and Phaedra's tawny skin seemed nearly brown next to Tryn's ivory.

"Your waist, Lady Iole," Phaedra said, in a smoky whisper. Her pronunciation held a trace of something exotic. From Thera, perhaps? "You are so delicate and lovely."

The herbs coursing through her blood captured the phrase "delicate and lovely" and sent it to her head, to her nipples, to the apex of her thighs. Iole felt worthy of desire. Powerful with it. Helen of Troy would seem haggard next to her.

Iole slid her hands across her own breasts and stomach, over her waist. Tryn and Phaedra watched, rapt, and their luminous eyes electrified her. Iole luxuriated in her newfound power.

"Yes," Tryn breathed again, as Iole's hands danced over her thighs.

"May I," Phaedra asked, "touch you?" She ran her fingers over her own nipples, showing Iole exactly what she had in mind. "Or would you rather touch me?"

"Or me?" Tryn echoed.

Iole couldn't decide if she wanted first to taste Phaedra's brown nipples or Tryn's pink ones.

But the choice wasn't hers.

Even while Iole reached through the haze for Phaedra's breast, Tryn gently pushed Iole back to the pallet. Phaedra followed her lead. "Relax, lady," Phaedra bid her.

"I don't want to relax. I want—"

"Shhh," Tryn said calmly. "We know what you want. You won't leave here . . . hungry. Shh."

"But, I—"

Phaedra's lips descended on hers, silencing her words. The exhilarating sensation of Phaedra's lips against hers—soft, yielding lips rather than the demanding ones of her dream lover's—left her weak and quivering. And when Phaedra's tongue raced over Iole's, Iole realized that passivity wasn't the only response open to her.

Iole's tongue stroked Phaedra's, pressed and demanded. Phaedra's mouth molded to hers, telling Iole that Phaedra found her kisses delicious.

The heat between her legs, the silky river, demanded immediate attention, but Tryn and Phaedra together enforced a slower pace.

"Hold her wrists, Phaedra," Tryn commanded, and Phaedra quickly complied.

Tryn poured oil into her palm and rubbed her palms together, her eyes locked on Iole's. The scent of almond. The electrifying pressure of Tryn's hands over Iole's nipples. An animal noise escaped her throat.

Tryn pushed Iole's oiled breasts together, making Iole arch her back, begging for more. With her head gently spinning, Iole welcomed Phaedra's kiss while squirming under Tryn's touch, seeking a satisfaction she couldn't describe.

"Be easy, my lady. We will speak to he who haunts you," Tryn said.

Iole hungered, but it wasn't for food or ease. Phaedra's tongue laced her lips, and Iole lost herself, blossoming, opening. Tryn's dark head bobbed and Iole again thrust her breasts up, welcoming the priestess's hot kisses.

And Iole wanted more.

She shifted her legs apart. "Please," she murmured. "Please."

"Be easy, Lady Iole. These things must not be rushed. We have to invite your lover, make it impossible for him to stay away. We must discover why he has chosen you, what he wants."

"I know what he wants," Iole replied with an urgency that surprised her. "He wants this." With her words she grabbed a hand—whether Tryn's or Phaedra's she didn't know—and slid it between her thighs. Tryn's finger—no, Phaedra's—glided over her slippery nub, and Iole writhed in pleasure.

Iole heard wings flutter—in her mind? In the rafters? Iole couldn't say.

She didn't care.

Then she heard a dove's cry.

"What—"

The growing eruption drove all thought from her mind, all words from her mouth. She rubbed herself against Tryn's oiled fingers. She was so close, so close to . . . to . . . to something indescribable.

She heard the dove's wings again, and the beats of its wings matched the beats of her heart. Racing. Pounding.

"Yes," she said to the dove. "I hear you."

Behind her closed eyes, the world focused. Gone were the amorphous shapes, the red circles, the zigs and zags.

Instead Iole saw a firefly. A single one. Pulsing. Flashing. One became two. They flashed in counterpoint, first one and then the other.

The fireflies multiplied, filling the emerald trees. A symphony of sparks. Golden and indigo.

A slick glide. An electric bolt centered on her pulsing nub.

The sky darkened and their colors deepened. Crimson fireflies entered the winged dance. Iole reveled in their beauty. She wanted to embrace it.

Standing, she held out her arms, palms upturned. The magic seemed palpable.

The doves landed on her inner wrists, light and gentle as butterflies. Iole laughed. Blossoms sprang from the branches, pink and fragrant. The flowers opened and fell, showering her in their soft beauty.

She tossed the birds into the sky. Still the graceful beat of their wings matched her heartbeat.

Slowly, slowly her garment fell open, exposing her breasts to the air—and to him. She held her breath, anticipating his touch.

"You've come!" she cried. "I've craved you."

Her dream lover did not disappoint. He embraced her breasts lightly, tantalizingly.

"You've called," he replied. "I'll come whenever you call."

Iole pressed into his touch, loving the zing of pleasure elicited from the crush of her nipples against his chest.

"It thrills me that you've called," her lover said.

"But I called you to rid myself of you," she said, melting into his arms.

He didn't reply. He sucked in a nipple, hard, and she cried.

He sucked in the other. "Please," Iole begged. But whether she wanted him to stop or give her more, Iole didn't know.

The world twisted, and she found herself rolling in the softest, greenest moss, legs entwined around his. The gentle aroma of the crushed plants engulfed them.

His touch called to her, begged her to let go.

It was a call she couldn't ignore.

Iole lifted a breast and offered it to him. He groaned in appreciation and took it, sucking hard, first at one stiff nipple and then the other. While he sucked at one, she ran her forefinger over the other. He captured both fingertip and nipple in his mouth.

Iole felt her world spin again, and this time she knew it wasn't caused by wine or magic. It came from pure desire.

"Iole, tell me you don't want to be rid of me," he commanded. "Tell me instead that you can't live without me."

He didn't give her a chance to answer, skimming his hand from her breast to her thigh. There, he roughly spread her.

She knew now that being this swollen and slippery meant only one thing—she wanted him. Simple. There was nothing wrong with her, nothing that his touch couldn't repair.

He forcefully slid fingers inside her, not too far, but far enough to make her gasp in shock. He grabbed her nub, pressed his thumb hard over it.

Iole should run, she knew. Why didn't the priestesses save her? Where had they gone?

Another brutal stroke.

"Please," she said. Her voice sounded far away, as if it carried from far over the sea.

He spread her thighs farther. She spread them wider still.

"Tell me you want me to stay, Iole. Marry me."

He cupped her bottom in his hand, fingertip in the very place she'd never imagined a touch. The head of his penis slipped over her nub.

Iole knew at that moment that she stood on a precipice. If

she acquiesced, her life would take one path. If she refused, it would take another.

"Love me, Iole. For who I am." Penetration. Only a hair's breadth. But penetration nonetheless.

Her vagina accommodated that little bit, wanting more. Her anus, the same. Should she yield? Could she accept the changes brought about by giving this faceless man, this dream man, her maidenhead?

"You can save me, Iole. Love me, and you will save me."

His penis pressed against her, but the choice was fully hers. She knew he'd take nothing that wasn't offered.

"I don't know you," she said in anguish. "You don't know me!"

"But I know your dreams."

Iole did not respond.

"I know that you are kind and fair," he said, "that you are serious. I know that you long for knowledge, that knowledge makes you feel stronger. I know you love your parents, and that you only learned philosophy to please your father."

"But how—"

"I know that you love the warm breath of a horse on your face, on your neck, and that you long to save the woods in which you played as a child."

"But I know nothing of you!"

"You will be surprised at how much you know, beloved." He kissed her then, claiming her, promising to keep her. "I love you, Iole. I have loved you since I first laid eyes on you. Can you trust me? Can you love me?"

Iole knew the answer. "Yes," she said, yielding completely. He could have her. He could change her.

She would love him. She would love him forever.

Iole felt him draw back. She felt him prepare to go in. "Yes," she said, again. "I am yours."

"Do you love me, Iole?" he repeated, like he needed to hear the words again.

"I do." Iole arched her back to meet him, to give him what he asked. And then—

And then the priestesses were upon him, Tryn on one arm and Phaedra on the other. Two other attendants she'd never seen before helped, dropping a cloth over his head and binding his ankles and wrists.

"No!" Iole shouted. "I love him! He is mine!" A fifth attendant grabbed her wrists, prohibiting her movement.

"Iole!" he shouted. "Find me. I love you . . ."

The Pythia walked over to her, and sat in the moss next to her. The old crone put her arm around Iole's shoulder. "It is a trick, my love. The gods have many deceptions," she said, stroking her thigh.

"No!" Iole shouted again, pushing the harridan's hand away. "Get out! This is my dream!"

The Pythia shook her head with a disapproving look.

The world twisted again and Iole found herself back in the oracle's pallet, soft and comforting, although comfort was not what she wanted.

Iole tried to sit up but she was still tied. "Let me go back to him! Bring me back!" she shouted. Tryn and Phaedra were still there. Phaedra poured more cat-piss wine down her throat.

"Shh," Tryn said. "You're safe. He didn't hurt you."

"Of course he didn't hurt me," Iole sobbed. "He loves me."

"The gods don't love anyone," Phaedra said, patting her sweaty brow. "Not as we understand it."

"The Pythia will interview him. She'll find out what he wants," said Tryn.

Iole could do nothing but sob.

Phaedra and Tryn kissed her tears as they fell. Iole didn't fight either of them.

She didn't want to fight. She wanted her man, her dream lover, whoever he was. A sob ripped from her heart.

"I'm sorry, my lady," Phaedra said. "For your sorrow."

"His physique takes my breath away," said Tryn, tracing the track of Iole's tears with small kisses.

"His face . . . why can't I see his face?" Iole demanded.

"You are very lucky to have one such as he," Tryn said, and Phaedra nodded.

Iole lay silently, tears still streaking into the hair at her temples.

Tryn's kisses crept from Iole's cheeks to Phaedra's face. Iole blinked and through her tears saw that the two acolytes kissed each other above her.

The beauty of it distracted her from her loss.

Phaedra gently removed Tryn's fillet and loosened her hair. Her wild dark waves nearly obscured her pink nipples, which were hardened to pearls under the play of Phaedra's fingers.

The detached haze from which Iole watched melted as Tryn's fingers moved from Phaedra's face to her firm breasts. Iole too touched Phaedra's breasts. Her mouth longed for the soothing balm of Tryn's, and soon Iole lost herself in the woman's kiss.

When Phaedra nudged her thighs apart, Iole didn't stop her. And when she descended upon her, Iole spread herself wider— hot, moist, and open. Phaedra's clever tongue brought relief first and then a blossoming want for something more.

The first orgasm of her life ripped through her like a lightning storm, electrifying her to her very core. Her body was wracked with the pleasure of it, and the well-trained priestesses knew exactly where to push to maximize the longevity of the bliss. They knew exactly how long to wait before resuming their caresses.

But the orgasms didn't touch her heart.

Iole wouldn't change her mind.

She would find her dream lover. She would find him and save him.

7

Lord Echion looked at the Aegean Sea glittering in the late-morning sun, tossing diamond reflections onto the beach. Sunlight spiked off glossy equine coats and bridles, and silver sands muffled the thud of hooves as he and the ladies trotted through the wavelets breaking on the shore. The trill of song sparrows camouflaged in the emerald shrub roses made the outing seem magical, almost surreal.

Not that the party needed more allure. Echion appraised his companions and found them wanting for nothing. Both women glowed with beauty and health, hair shining as did the coats of their steeds. Even their slaves riding a discrete distance upshore were well mounted. He'd seen to that himself.

And both women sat their horses exceedingly well. The next meeting he had with Lord Aeson, he vowed to praise him for raising such well-rounded daughters, intelligent women who could ride as well as men.

Perhaps he'd make a more serious offer then, too. Did Iole understand the implications, the privilege, of being given his prized stallion as a mount?

"My lady, Ampyx favors you," Echion said to Iole. He didn't see the need to tell her that the stallion took care of all his riders, as long as he wasn't on the racetrack.

"You honor me by letting me ride your wonderful stallion this morning. I'd never have guessed from seeing him run that he was so sweet and responsive."

"And I bet this mare is the mother of champions," Lady Calandra said, expertly holding in her prancing mount.

"Her sorrel coat matches your own hair, Lady Calandra."

"The open stretch calls this mare's feet. Can we race them, Lord Echion?" Calandra asked.

A woman after his own heart. Still, Echion considered. These animals were bred for speed, not pleasure. "The thing is, ladies, once we let these horses run, we're committed to the race. They won't want to stop."

Calandra grinned mischievously, a delightful expression, and looked at her sister. "What say you, Iole? Are you ready to ride that champion?" Calandra dragged out the word "ride," leaving no doubt that she referred to something other than horses.

Echion watched Iole blush at Calandra's comment and bit back a laugh. What a serious girl his fiancée-to-be was. He had to have mercy on her. "Perhaps next time, Lady Calandra—"

"No," interrupted Iole with a determined expression. "Let's race." She looked up the sandy stretch and said, "To those palms?"

"As you wish, lady."

"At your word, Lord Echion."

"Are you ready?" he asked, and when both women nodded, he shouted, "Let's run!" and legged his horse into a slow gallop, letting the women take the lead.

Calandra didn't hesitate. She gave her mare her head and sat forward, urging speed with her seat.

Horse and rider took off in an amber blur. Echion knew the

mare could keep the lead for nearly half the beach if she were ridden right.

And it looked like Calandra could ride her well. She stayed above the withers, balanced perfectly to maximize the mare's speed. Sand flew as the mare's strides ate the beach.

Iole's approach with Ampyx was more cautious, but Echion didn't think less of her for it. A healthy respect for a winning stallion showed wisdom. Iole sat back on the horse, trying to keep some semblance of control. But that wouldn't work with Ampyx. He was bred to run, and run he would.

Keeping his horse behind the women, Echion watched Ampyx toss his head, warning Iole. "Let him go, Iole!" he shouted. "Fly with me!"

At his words, Echion saw Iole's face pale. Fear? He appreciated the courage it took to trust the powerful animal, to give him his head. But Iole did it. She let go.

Having been restrained and now released, Ampyx took off as if chased by bees. Echion watched Iole grab the stallion's mane and become part of the animal. Praise Zeus, the girl could ride. Ampyx wouldn't buck; he'd only run true. But he'd run very very fast.

Was she the kind of girl who loved this feeling—the uncontrolled power surging beneath her—or did fear make her hate it?

Somehow, the answer seemed very important to him.

He urged his gelding faster, not liking to leave too much distance between himself and Ampyx. This well-bred gelding couldn't touch his prized stallion, but he neatly closed much of the distance.

Echion spared a glance for Calandra as he passed her. With a huge grin on her face, she spurred her mare. But her urgings were of no use. The mare was exceedingly fast for short distances, but she couldn't stay the course.

He winked at her over his shoulder as he reined his horse toward Ampyx. Her Egyptian fiancé was in for a happy surprise. She'd make a delightful wife.

And so would Iole.

Echion wondered if Ampyx were showing off for her. The stallion ran farther and faster than he ever did in practice with him. After a few burning strides, Lady Calandra and the slaves were specks in the distance. Ampyx passed the finish-line palms and kept running. Echion watched Iole sit up and try to ease the horse back, but the stallion had other ideas. Snaking his head forward, he eked out more speed, more distance.

Echion fervently hoped Iole found this fun. She might never again talk to him, otherwise.

Iole and Ampyx rounded a turn, going out of view. Several heartbeats later, Echion made the same turn. He scanned the horizon, expecting to find a running dot, but they weren't there. Instead, Echion found the pair wading calmly in the surf. Ampyx pawed the waves as they lapped his chest. Iole was stroking his neck and crooning to him.

Echion snorted. The horse was eating her soft words as if they were sugared figs. Iole had won over both Ampyx and himself.

"He is spectacular, Lord Echion," Iole said as he approached. She panted with the ride's exertion. Her clear eyes sparkled with delight, her hair a chaos of spun gold.

Iole's beauty and delight nearly stopped his heart.

He knew what he had to do then. Echion dismounted and approached the pair. Patting Ampyx's shoulder, he took Iole's hand in his. He looked up at her, locking eyes. "Lady Iole, would you please be my bride?"

"Fly with me," he'd said. The words Echion shouted while racing across the shores echoed from the mouth of her dream lover. Echion must be the man from her dreams!

How did he get into her dreams? Why did he do it? Iole had

no idea. Maybe he'd gotten a god or goddess to intercede for him. Or maybe he was Zeus in disguise.

Maybe Echion was just magic.

Echion helped her dismount. The wet tumbling surf danced at their feet. She knew when he touched her, when she saw that look in his eye—he was going to kiss her. That knowledge filled her with . . . curiosity, some fear.

And much anticipation. This man was her dream lover! He must be.

When he kissed her, Iole braced herself for magic. She knew from her dreams how enchanting something as simple and timeless as a kiss could be.

Her time at the oracle had pounded that lesson home.

And then his lips touched hers. Echion's lips were warm, and he felt like he knew what he was doing—confident, bold. Lips touching lips seemed like a strange concept to Iole. Did he feel something . . . extraordinary? Was he going to want more?

Echion was gentle with her. Perhaps he sensed her insecurity. He didn't pull her too close. He didn't grab or grope. He simply kissed her, caressed her lips with his. After a few minutes, Iole felt encouraged. She'd kissed him back, tentatively at first and then more boldly.

When his tongue touched hers, sharp visions of her dreams barraged her mind—the way his kiss had taken her breath away, had made her feel weak and helpless. Her dream lover had made her feel like she'd die for his kiss.

Iole mentally checked herself. She felt fine, in full control of her emotions.

Not at all like she did in her dreams.

She peeked at him through her lashes, appreciating the shape of his cheeks, the strong line of his nose. Without pulling her closer, he continued his kiss. The silky soft exploration of his lips was . . . nice.

She broke it off, shyly, and looked at him. He placed his warm palm on her cheek and said, "Lady Iole, you are lovely."

She was lovely and he was nice. What more could a maid ask for?

When he'd proposed to her the answer seemed so obvious. He was gorgeous and rich. And he was her dream lover, wasn't he? Why else had he commanded, "Fly with me!"

Iole shook her head. She didn't know why she'd hedged, didn't know why she didn't say "yes" and jump into his arms. Calandra would have. Maybe it was Iole's natural caution.

Maybe it was the fact that Echion didn't have the copper-colored hair, the golden skin of her dream lover.

Maybe it was the fact that the kiss didn't live up to the dream's spell.

Cantering on horseback side by side on the beach, back toward Calandra and the attendants, Echion moved closer, took her hand in his, and kissed it. His kiss was warm and solid, but his horsemanship impressed her more. Not many men could rein in two loping horses so close together, especially if one were a stallion.

But she couldn't base a marriage decision on horsemanship.

Why not, when a stubborn part of her wanted to base it on an erotic dream?

But her dream wasn't a dream—not a real one! The priestesses had captured her dream lover, interrogated him. Fathered by Zeus and cursed by Hera, her dream lover could be saved only by the love of a maiden. Despite the priestess's spells Hera's geas held—he couldn't reveal his identity, couldn't reveal the nature of Hera's subterfuge.

If only Iole could see past Hera's evil magic, if only she could find him and love him, he would be freed and she would be loved. Truly loved.

"Ho, Lord Arcas!" Echion called, interrupting Iole's thoughts.

He legged his horse into a gallop toward Lady Calandra and her party.

Ignoring the men, Calandra rode toward her sister, grinning at her with a questioning expression. "Did you win?" she asked, suggestively.

Iole laughed quietly. "He proposed!"

"Oh, that's wonderful! We'll have an autumn wedding!"

"Shh! Calandra! I didn't give him an answer."

"Have you lost your senses? He's the most gorgeous man I've ever seen. I'd wed him in a heartbeat, and I've been doing my utmost to squash these growing pangs of jealousy. If you refuse him, I'm going to insist Father call it off with the Egyptian and marry him myself!"

Iole laughed. "Too bad only men can perform on stage. You've missed your calling in the dramatic arts!"

"I'm serious!"

"So am I. You know Father cannot possibly call it off with Egypt."

"But I don't want to go to Thebes! How can I live without you?"

"Shh, Calandra. It's our duty! It's for the good of the family."

"I know," Calandra said almost angrily. "But here you're offered the most perfect life and you're not leaping with happiness. Why didn't you—" Calandra gasped as an idea occurred to her. "He didn't force himself on you! I should never have left you alone with him!"

"No! No! He did nothing of the kind. It's just that . . ."

"What?" Calandra prompted.

"He kissed me. And—"

"He kissed you! That's it. I am going to disown you in a fit of jealousy!"

"But I didn't feel anything. I mean, shouldn't I have tingled or something when he kissed me?"

"I tingle just looking at him."

"Calandra!"

Calandra sighed, looking over her shoulder at the men. "So what are you going to do? Marry Lord Lump, the boar who followed us here uninvited?"

Iole looked at Lord Arcas. Even with his good eye facing them, he was hideous. "That seems equally unpromising," Iole said grudgingly.

"You know . . ." Calandra mused.

"What?"

"Didn't you say Echion used the words from your dreams?"

"Yes," Iole answered, slowly.

"I think Echion is your dream lover. Even with the lame kiss. Maybe that's part of the curse—maybe Hera hid the magic in his kiss."

"Is that possible?"

"With the Olympians, anything is possible."

Iole's heart sang at the possibility.

She kicked Ampyx into a gallop, aiming him toward Echion, and shouted over her shoulder to Calandra, "You're right, Sister! Plan that autumn ceremony!"

He shouldn't have come here, stalking her as if she were prey. But when his slave discovered Echion's plans for the day, Arcas decided to just happen upon them here at the beach. He hoped he could . . . what? Make Iole fall in love with him first? Arcas laughed at himself. Maybe he hoped only to forestall the inevitable.

Hera's curse was so strong. Even in Aphrodite's plane, where he'd been winning Iole's heart, he couldn't break the spell of silence placed upon him. Even through the haze of the priestesses' powers, he couldn't provide any clue to his identity, couldn't even say his own name.

Iole had said she loved him in her dream, that she would find him. Arcas clung to that hope.

Even as that hope dimmed.

Riding adjacent to him, Arcas examined Lord Echion. Arcas wasn't a jealous man by nature, but he'd pinned his dream on Lady Iole. Watching his competitor ride his Persian horse, Arcas fought the bile rising in the back of his throat.

How could he blame Iole for choosing Echion?

Echion's words—something about horses, the man thought of little else—rolled over his consciousness. It was her laugh that had his attention. Her laughter, billowing across the beach, caught in the ebbs and flows of the breeze and dispersed so all could luxuriate in the sound.

He scanned the horizon and saw her lying flat across the stallion's withers, which ran like the wind. Iole's honey-colored hair whipped behind her.

The time for self-pity had left with Aphrodite's kiss. Arcas couldn't let this gem slip away, not even to Echion and all his glory.

"Excuse me for a moment, Lord Echion," Arcas said abruptly. He reined his own roan toward Iole and legged her into a gallop.

"Lady Iole," Lord Arcas said, cantering toward her. "I would speak with you, if you please."

"But I—" she replied, looking around Arcas to find Echion. He'd obviously interrupted her plan. What was she so eager to tell Echion?

Arcas didn't want to know, didn't want to think about it.

"I need but a moment of your time, lady. Lord Echion will still be here when we finish."

"I'm sorry, Lord Arcas, but I don't want to keep our host waiting."

"Look there. Lady Calandra rides to him now. She is quite able to entertain him."

He watched her school her expression to something more patient, and then she said, "Very well, Lord Arcas. What is it?"

"Did you know that the forest where we used to play as children is just through that path?"

"Truly? I love that woods. I didn't know one could get there from here."

"Would you like to visit it?"

Arcas watched delight form in her expression. "I'd love to."
She shot another glance at Echion and said, "Do you think he'll
mind if I take Ampyx?"

"I'm sure he knows his horse is in good hands."

They rode in silence for a few moments while Arcas franti-
cally sought words that would create a bridge. She found them
first.

"I used to dream about these woods quite frequently."

"Did you?"

"In my dreams, I'm playing in the forest, capturing frogs
and snakes . . ."

"Making your poor tutor discover where each lived and
what each ate."

Iole laughed. "And he found out, too."

"If you used to dream about these woods, what do you
dream about now?" He felt the geas grab his throat as he asked
this, but it failed to choke him. Apparently the question was
just innocent enough to slip past Hera's curse.

Iole stopped her horse and looked at him, examining him as
if he were one of the frogs she used to catch. He could feel the
weight of her gaze on each of his bristly warts, on the flap of
skin covering his blind eye, on his hump. She blinked for a moment, as if clearing her vision, then she nudged her horse back
to a walk in silence.

Arcas was at a loss. What did she see? What did she think?
"Did I . . . offend you, my lady?"

"I dream of walking with my children through these woods.
I dream of showing them the same secrets my grandfather and
father showed me."

At that moment, the beach's scrub gave way to the beginning of the oak forest. A few thick trees towered above them,
dappling emerald shadows across Iole's face.

"Look," she commanded, pointing at a meadow of stumps.
The earth had been charred around them. No place for birds.

No homes for lizards. "They're all gone. Chopped. For warships and armies. For fortresses."

Arcas could only nod as he watched anger take hold of her.

"And you're just as bad. You sell weapons to the armies. So they can travel to distant lands and kill each other. I am tired of death and destruction!"

Arcas nodded again.

"Can you do nothing but nod?"

"I'd just reached adulthood when I realized that this forest was nearly gone," he answered. "Let's go this way." Arcas pointed to a northern path. "My father made his riches in weapons, and I was to take over his business."

Iole's steady gaze bore into him. He wished he knew what she thought, but he took comfort in the knowledge that she certainly wasn't focused on Echion.

"But—something happened." *Hera. His mother. The cliff.* "My father—" Arcas floundered. "After my mother died, my father allowed me freedom to do what I wished with our business."

"He allowed you?"

Arcas glanced at her. "That's not exactly right. His heart was broken and he had no interest in living. At first I tried to get him interested in the weapons. He had always loved to make swords, sometimes taking years to make one of perfection. But it didn't help. Then I tried jewelry. Wrought gold is tricky, taxing. But nothing helped."

"And then?" Iole asked.

Arcas pushed a branch from their path and said, "And then I realized that I couldn't help my father. I couldn't heal him. I had to heal myself, follow my own dreams."

"And what did you dream?"

"Like you, I dreamed of these woods." Arcas pushed more branches out of the way and allowed Iole to enter the meadow before them.

WINGED DREAMS / 137

This meadow was not filled with stumps. Instead, saplings graced the field. Oaks sprinkled with conifers. Myrtle bloomed throughout. The trees were young, it was true, but they were thick. And Iole saw no signs of destruction.

"This is lovely," Iole said. "But I don't understand."

"That glade to the east," Arcas said, pointing, "has a creek that runs year round. And a large lake lies not too far in that direction. If I squint I can see young Iole chasing her brother with a dead worm."

Iole pulled her horse to a stop again, breathing in the beauty. "But I don't understand," she repeated.

"I bought it, Lady Iole. Ten years ago I bought this land. I had the oaks replanted. The rest came up on its own. I keep the deer and boars culled to reasonable levels, and the meat helps pay for the upkeep. I also cull some of the timber, logging it selectively."

"You . . . you did this?" The hottest part of the day was upon them but birdsong filled the air, doves cooed from their bowers. A fragrant breeze hung in the air.

"Yes, my lady."

"Lord Arcas, I think this might be the most wonderful surprise of my life."

"And yet . . ." he prompted.

"And yet, I suspect another surprise." With that, she leaned across her horse and kissed Arcas full on the lips.

9

Even as the hair from his warty bristle jabbed her lip, Iole knew.

Lord Arcas was the man, her man.

In that moment—when she knew she embraced his vision, admired the way he approached life—she loved him.

The spontaneous kiss she gave the ugliest face she'd ever seen was filled with love.

By the time her lips fully kissed his, by the time she pressed warmly against him, the world spiraled, spun. Their horses melted from under them and cantered off toward the creek-filled glade, his mare's glossy roan coat the perfect foil to Ampyx's lanky bay. They nickered as they ran, and it sounded like laughter. Iole was certain that Ampyx winked at her.

Iole blinked, and she found her dream-lover's hand in her own as they looked down at a crushed moss bed, the same bed she'd seen in the dream while visiting the oracle.

Time took on a disjointed feel. Her life had rushed to this moment. Every breath groomed her for this heartbeat. And rather than rushing past, the heartbeat lasted an eternity. Iole watched a ladybug crawl up a branch while drinking in the warmth of her dream-lover's—Arcas's—palm in hers. An owl crossed the strange twilight sky and landed near her shoulder in the time it took Iole to register the texture of Arcas's hand, the strength of his grip in hers. Iole blinked and the sky had grown eerie, hewn in indigos and purples.

Iole looked at him, at his face. And saw.

She stared into the same amber beauty she'd seen at the chariot race. Hypnotic beauty, both eyes unimpeded now by Hera's touch. Both eyes fringed by thick lashes and tinged equally with pleasure and sorrow.

She sucked in an awed breath.

The owner of those extraordinary eyes was the most fero-ciously masculine man she'd ever seen. He made Echion seem like a boychild. A scar slashed his cheekbone from his right eyebrow to his chin, but it didn't diminish him. No, it gave him a fiercely capable look. He could protect her from anything.

His cheekbones were sharp, his jaw square. Iole ran her palm over that jaw. No warts, no hairs, and no bristles.

What remained could have delighted any sculptor, any artist. His lips. Phideas himself could have created these lips for the most gorgeous of his Parthenon statues.

Iole turned to face him, tracing her fingertips lightly over his bronze chest. Pure, raw muscle. Solid enough to be made of marble. He wore no clothing. Iole still had her linen chiton. As her fingers reached the perfect rows of strength cut into his stomach, she looked into his eyes and asked, "You look like Hercules. Is this really you? Do you really . . . look like this?"

"Hercules was—apparently—my half brother. And yes, this is what I truly look like." With that he claimed her mouth with ferocity, growling his need. Iole responded as she'd known she would, yielding to him, giving to him. She wove her hands into his hair, slanted her lips toward his.

This was him!

Iole rubbed herself against his erection, gasping and taking and giving. Her linen added to the friction, and her fingers dug into the hard roundness of his buttocks, quickening his rhythm.

This was him!

Their kiss slowed into something measured and tender. Knowing who he was, knowing and trusting him, this knowledge turned their kiss into something surreal.

More surreal than the fireflies and oddly colored skies. More surreal than the doves and the laughing horses. In his kiss, Iole could taste forever. She could taste her children and smell her grandchildren. In his kiss.

"You are so beautiful," she said brokenly.

"No, I—"

"You are. Your heart is beautiful. The forests you have saved and restored, they are beautiful."

Lord Arcas groaned as he melted into her. "Your words are a salve to my calloused heart."

Iole didn't answer as she kissed his brow, his temple, as she stroked his thick coppery hair. She ran her hand down his back, savoring the long muscled planes. "I said I'd find you. I almost didn't."

"Yet you did. You saved me." He pulled her close, pressing her breasts against his chest. Her nipples pearled, waiting for his touch. Waiting for his lips and fingers and tongue.

"We are both saved then, Lord Arcas."

With those words, Arcas sank to his knees and laid her carefully on the moss bed. He gently gripped her chin and met her gaze.

"We—no, you—have broken Hera's spell, but she is unlikely to acquiesce with grace. Do you understand me, sweet Iole? She is likely to torment me for days to come."

Something Iole couldn't read swam in his eyes. Hope? Fear? Dread? To her, it didn't matter. She loved him. "Make me yours forever, Lord Arcas. Let Hera be damned."

With that, the owl in the nearby tree squawked maniacally and flew toward them, talons extended. In a blink Arcas was on his feet, sword in hand. The weapon looked like the kind of sword Arcas's father would be proud of, elegantly straight and clean of line.

In this dreamscape, perfect swords must appear as needed, Iole thought.

"'Hera, be damned,' eh," the creature squealed as it flew toward Iole's eyes. Fear flooded through her. The hideous thing sprouted four more legs, each with blade-sharp talons. Even as Iole screamed in terror, the owl creature landed a talon on her bare arm. Blood welled and streamed.

Arcas sliced at the thing and hit only air.

"Ha!" the creature screamed. "Your mother was equally ineffectual! Did she teach you swordplay?" It launched itself again toward Iole.

"At least I have a mother!" Determination etched in the lines of his face, Arcas swung and lopped off the thing's wing. It sputtered to the ground, sprouting two more wings.

Iole screamed again. "It's Hera, Arcas! Owls belong to Hera!"

Arcas gave the owl beast no chance to learn to fly with additional wings. He smashed its head into the earth with his foot, grinding the bones with a satisfied grimace.

"So it is," he said, still smashing the creature underfoot. "Are you injured?" he asked, taking Iole in his arms.

"No . . ." But her bloodied forearm spoke for itself.

"It's my dreamworld," he said, running his palm over the sliced skin. The injury disappeared.

"You've killed it! No one bests Hera!" Iole said, collapsing into his embrace.

"I doubt she is dead, only delivered back to Zeus. Perhaps he'll chain her to Mount Olympus for a millennium or so."

How wonderful to be the one who snuggled this amazing man in bed each night, the one he pulled tightly to his side, his breath on the back of her neck, his whispers of love in her ears. How wonderful to walk through his enchanted woods with his enchanting children.

A sudden realization made Iole freeze. "Arcas?"

"Yes, my love."

"Zeus is your father?"

"Apparently, yes. Though I was raised by my mother's husband and knew not who I was until a few years ago."

"And you just killed the Hera owl?"

"Vanquished rather than killed, but yes."

"When a son of Zeus kills a god or goddess, he becomes a hero. You're a hero, Lord Arcas, well and true." She lay her head on his broad chest and said, almost to herself, "You're my hero."

A hero he may be, but her words rocked him to his core. His world did not become more steady. Her actions did not help.

With her petite fingertips, she brushed her chiton off. Her breasts were lush and lovely, and the sight of them made him tremble. She knew the worst of him, she'd loved him at his most grotesque, and now she offered herself to him. Willingly.

Arcas palmed one breast, and then the other, loving the way she closed her eyes and arched her back toward him. Her silent entreaty for more left him breathless.

He moved down her ripe body and sucked a nipple into the heat of his mouth. She gasped his name. It sounded like a prayer.

He sucked harder.

She stumbled then and he gathered her in his arms. Like a sheath of wheat. He gently set her in the soft moss, and as she twined her arms around his neck, his love for her overwhelmed him.

"I will protect you with my life. I will give up everything I have to keep you safe."

The love shining from the deep pools of her eyes gave him all the answer he needed.

Her knees clenched around his waist. Her hands gripped his hair. As if she owned him. And Arcas supposed she did. He continued to knead one glorious breast, stroking the pearled nipple between his finger while he sucked and licked the other. They were like the first strawberries of spring—pink and rosy, tiny and sweet.

His hand gravitated toward her belly, past her belly button. Arcas lightly traced his fingers until he found the silken heat of her. She arched toward him, wet and hot. Ready for him.

And finally, finally, Arcas could take her. In good conscience. She knew exactly what he was. Who he was. And she still loved him.

He wanted her beyond ready. He wanted her beyond hungry. Arcas wanted her to feel ravenous. He spread her legs and with the tip of his tongue, Arcas smoothed her wetness over her soft folds. He gently grazed the center of her desire.

"Yes," Iole said, pressing into him. "Yes. Touch me there."

He slowly sucked her into his mouth, inhaled her carefully but completely. When a small animal noise escaped her throat, he backed off. He didn't want her to come too quickly.

Arcas deliberately sank one finger inside of her, then another. "Do you know what comes next? Are you ready, my love?" Beads of sweat dropped down his brow. He nibbled her neck and then licked it as he thrust his fingers in a hypnotizing rhythm.

Iole cried out and lifted her hips. Arcas wanted her, no doubt, but this was not about him. Not yet. Arcas worked another finger inside of her. The tightness of her, her damp heat. By all the gods, he wanted her. Arcas pulled out his fingers and—

And she captured his throbbing member in her grasp. He could only lay helpless as she rolled him onto his back. Arcas knew then what she wanted, what she was going to do. The beads of sweat on his brow spread to cover his entire body in a fine sheen.

Iole's dark gold locks spilling across his abdomen, over his thighs, obscuring his shaft. Her tongue running the thick length of him, her mouth sucking him deeply inside her beautiful mouth. These images nearly made him come.

The reality of it did not disappoint him. Languidly sensual, she moved her mouth over his erection. He filled her completely. The eroticism of having his shaft buried in her mouth, her breast pushed against his thighs, nearly undid him.

"Enough," he said. He knew she could hear how desire had thickened his voice. He rolled her over and gazed down at her. "Now?" The word emerged frantic. Hoarse and eager. Arcas needed this woman more than life itself.

She nodded and spread her thighs, fitting his thick length against her, almost where it belonged.

They'd been here before, and he looked at her to see if she recognized it, the sweet precipice of penetration.

"No priestesses to capture you," she promised in a voice as husky as his. "This time, I'll keep you for myself."

"I am yours," he promised as his lips covered hers. Drinking hungrily, he impaled her. His eyes burned into hers, so aware of the pain she must be feeling. But she bore it bravely, closing her eyes for a slow heartbeat before recovering. And then she arched toward him, letting him know beyond a doubt that she wanted more.

"Don't stop," she murmured, grabbing his hips. She raised her own and buried him more deeply inside of her.

Arcas needed no further encouragement. He grabbed her soft buttocks and pumped into her. He pumped over and over and over.

"Arcas. Arcas. Arcas," her husky voice said with each

thrust. She wrapped her legs around his waist and clung to him like her life depended on it.

"Arcas," she nearly whispered. "I love you."

Then he cried out at the sheer pleasure of it, the heady bliss. He bellowed in triumph and release.

Unexpectedly, she came with him.

10

Arcas allowed himself a few more moments of quiet luxury, holding Iole in the protective shield of his embrace. The way she made him feel amazed him. Strong. Powerful. Her belief made it so. Her intoxicating scent mingled with crushed moss surrounded him. Her warmth pervaded his bones.

He knew she'd be here, Aphrodite. A part of him dreaded it. If he never saw another goddess or god or monster for as long as he lived, that'd be fine with him.

But conversely, he wanted to thank her. Her amulet had given him access to Iole's dream-self.

She arrived before he could stand, before he could dress. The coo of a dozen doves preceded her arrival. Iole shifted in his arms, and he carefully rolled her off him.

"My Lady Aphrodite," he said, standing naked before her. Her luxurious hair shone with an otherworldly luminescence.

"I see you have won your prize, my gorgeous one."

"With much thanks to you, my lady."

"Ah, your gratitude is appreciated." Aphrodite passed a gaze over the sleeping Iole, obviously replete. "Sometimes I envy you mortals your simplicity. You fuck. You reproduce. You sleep. You eat."

"You think we lack treachery?"

Aphrodite looked at the remains of the mutant owl. "On the contrary, I hope you are treacherous enough."

"Enough?"

"Chronos is my confidante."

"Meaning?"

"Sometimes I have access to the past and the future."

"You know the future," he said flatly.

"Well . . . it's never that certain, but yes."

"I don't like games, Goddess. What are you trying to tell me?"

Aphrodite approached him so closely he could smell her. Apple blossoms and spring rain. She rested her hand on his naked thigh and he instantly hardened. "My Trojan prince Anchises was both mortal and delightful, Lord Arcas. Would you care to replace him?" Now her fingertips ran over his chest, traced the muscles of his stomach."

"Aphrodite," he growled warningly.

She gave a playful moue, feigning hurt. "I know. I know. You love her."

"I love her completely."

Aphrodite sighed and said, "Lady Calandra's Egyptian lordling has backed out of his contract with Lord Aeson, although Aeson does not yet know it. She will be free to marry, which will make Lord Echion very happy. He will be like a brother to you."

Aphrodite waved her hand and the trees above them bloomed, then rained pink petals over his sleeping love. "I would tell her as soon as she wakes. From what I know of her, she will worry exceedingly about Echion's feelings, but there is no need. He and Calandra will be very happy."

"All well and good," Arcas said. "Now why must I be treacherous?"

A graceful flick of her wrist produced a long spear. "A gift," she said, "from Chronos."

Aphrodite handed him the iron weapon with a wicked blade. Green jewels encrusted the hilt.

Arcas hefted the dagger. "It is wonderfully balanced. Why have I a need of it?"

"Before it was slayed, the chimera produced a hatchling. Like its mother, it can only be killed by a hero, and then only with a goddess's help."

"Zeus is not known for keeping his cock in his chiton. Surely there are others."

"Ah, but Lord Arcas, I favor you."

Arcas crossed his arms, giving her a pointed look.

"Soon the chimera will grow large enough to attack Athens. Lord Aeson's home? Presumably your new home?"

"Fine, goddess. I'll do it."

Aphrodite smiled, and the sky cleared, taking on the blushing pinks of dawn. "Lord Arcas?"

"Yes, my goddess."

"You and Iole will also be exceedingly happy."

He grinned and replied, "I didn't need Chronos to tell me that."

"Very well," she said in a voice that faded as she evaporated.

"But thank you," he called into the empty air.

He heard her laughter and a last rejoinder, "Keep the amulet. It may help you in about seven years . . ."

Red Sport

1

She knew the beast lay within the labyrinthine cave, deep within the granite walls. As Larkspur stood in the mouth of the cave's hidden entry, the creature's dark presence made the hairs on the back of her neck stand erect.

She turned slowly, listening, careful not to touch the stony walls. Who knew the ways the beast could sense her, even at this distance?

Blinking, Larkspur realized she could see surprisingly well in the cave. An emerald glow flickered to her right. From the heart of the lair? From the dragon itself?

By the goddess, she wished she had more information. All she had was a name: Ekal. That, and a crushing sense of desperation.

Then she noticed something . . . unnatural about the light. The smoldering green radiance illuminated the path in a very particular way. While the lustrous peak of the high ceiling invited her eye, rough-hewn flagstone, shrouded in shadows, beckoned her feet. The effect welcomed the visitor to stare above while traipsing naively along the path.

But Larkspur wasn't an amateur.

She found the trap almost immediately. Without her training, without the glow, she'd never have seen it. At ankle height, a long taut filament reached across the pathway. Probably from a horse's tail.

She'd never have felt the hair against her booted foot, but brushing through the thing would have triggered cascading rocks or some other horrible catastrophe.

Larkspur silently stepped over the tripwire, balancing carefully on the balls of her feet. A rank beginner would congratulate herself and boldly continue down the path.

But a rank beginner would be dead. Larkspur found a second hair nearly immediately. And a few moments later she found a third.

Cautiously wiping beads of sweat from her brow, she steadied her shaking hands. By the goddess, nabbing the Jewel of Dragonkind from this lair was going to be difficult. Uncharacteristic nerves were making this far more difficult than she'd thought.

Larkspur paused to breathe, wishing that she didn't have to do this. Surely a better thief could have been found. Surely one with less at stake would approach this task with a calmer head.

The thief inhaled again, concentrating this time, letting years of training take the place of broiling emotions. She could do this. She had to.

The deep breath between parted lips let the thief catch stray fragrances. Any clue, any hint might give her an advantage in this mad quest. A name. Only a name? Had she ever embarked upon a quest so poorly informed?

She inhaled again, and the scent she found was strange, somehow masculine—pine trees and musk. Visions came to mind of young men practicing swordsmanship in the spring, their back muscles glistening under a blue sky. Or warriors swimming in a lake, water sluicing down the planes of their chests, across their stomachs.

The aroma was not at all what she thought a dragon would smell like.

Who enters my home uninvited? the voice thundered in her head.

Fighting the urge to put her hands to her temples, Larkspur froze. So he had a mindvoice.

Pus and piss, she'd already lost the advantage of surprise. Greenhaven's elders had been wrong in their confidence in her. Nearly any thief could have gotten farther than the entryway without alarming the dragon.

And did the mindvoice mean he could read her thoughts? The elders hadn't known.

I can smell you, Thief.

Goddess puke, maybe the monster *could* read her thoughts. Not good. Still, Larkspur did not answer—at least not aloud. How much Ekal knew was still open to debate.

If the beast understood her aim, he would kill her. Of that she had no doubt. No dragon could let the Jewel of Dragonkind leave its lair.

Her heart thudded at that thought, and she took a moment to master her fear, to slow the crazy beating. She could not allow panic to overwhelm her. She could not fail her people. She could not fail her sister.

Still, for the briefest moment Larkspur considered quitting— leaping over the horsehair triggers and dashing back into the sun- shine. Screw Greenhaven and its elders. Screw its young women. Screw doomed Phlox. Larkspur herself could live another day.

Instead, she marshaled her courage and took a soundless step along the path, having no other choice. Besides, maybe the dragon was just guessing.

Larkspur padded along the lambent trail, slowly at first, then picking up speed as her assurance grew. The dragon might have been able to smell her, but he wasn't stopping her—at least not yet. She'd see the day through, if fate would let her.

Fate had a different idea.

He grabbed her from behind before she'd registered his presence. His powerful hand clamped over her mouth with an iron grip. His other hand grasped her thigh, hard. He brushed her sex as he did so, and it sent an electric jolt strong enough to taste.

Lightning fast, she aimed a donkey kick at his groin and simultaneously sent an elbow into his solar plexus.

To no effect. Her heel met air as he stepped aside, and her elbow glanced off his chest. The hateful creature wore leather armor.

Brutally, he tightened his embrace. She couldn't move—Larkspur could barely breathe. Combat was impossible.

So Larkspur capitulated, collapsing into his arms. But all was not lost, not yet. A man didn't exist who wasn't distracted by a soft hip bumping over his cock. Melting into his arm, Larkspur cocked her hip and bumped. Gently. But strategically.

Her ploy worked. His cock, now hard as the granite walls around them, throbbed beneath her thigh. A slight shift of her weight, and he pushed against her mound. Believing her surrender, he relaxed his grip.

Larkspur pivoted and threw all of her weight into a rabbit punch, smashing into his neck.

Not fair and not pretty, but certainly effective. He fell into a heap at her feet.

Rubbing her sore wrist, Larkspur looked at the man, at a loss. What was she going to do with him? He presented a lot of problems.

First, he was huge, and potentially dangerous. Second, she didn't want to leave him loose. That punch had been loud enough to tell the dragon exactly where she was—where *they* were. She didn't want him to get roasted—at least not until she knew more about him.

Seeing only one option, Larkspur grabbed his ankles and

dragged him down the path, cringing as his head thumped over the flagstone. By the goddess, the man weighed as much as a horse.

I hear you, Thief, Ekal rumbled. His mindvoice sounded strangely groggy.

But what are you going to do about it, you big bulky thing, Larkspur thought to herself. Then she reconsidered the wisdom of such snide remarks. Maybe he could read her mind.

Larkspur pulled the prone man down the narrow path and into the next grotto. No dragon could fit here. She hauled him deep into the tiny cave, surrounding them both in pitch dark.

And then the darkness flickered. Larkspur realized that the man's clothing glowed with the same haunting green as the lair's heart. That was convenient—at least she could see.

But his glow suggested something else. Had he already stolen a dragon cloak of some sort?

And maybe he already had the Jewel!

Larkspur efficiently patted down his sides—velvet ribs, warm muscles, a tapering waist. No Jewel. She patted from his ankles to his hips. Naught. She skimmed over his cock, behind it, smiling as he grew hard from her hand. By the goddess, the man was big.

But he didn't have what she was looking for.

Her prisoner twitched. He'd be waking soon, and she had to make up her mind. Now.

The man was a thief—the cloak, his sneaky technique made that clear. The bounty on the Jewel was enough to tempt nearly anyone, and Larkspur couldn't let this man take the treasure. She needed the thing herself.

Despite the fact that master thieves were generally master assassins, she'd rather not kill the man unless necessary. So . . .

So she could tie him up and leave him until after she retrieved the Jewel. Or . . .

Or she could team up with him. He was good, definitely

blessed by the Goddess. She couldn't remember the last time anyone had successfully sneaked up on her, especially when she'd been alert. They could both bring the Jewel home. Together, they could both save Phlox and the other maids of Greenhaven.

She pulled a rope from her bag to tie him for parley. She'd invite him on her quest—if he would accept her terms.

But before she could inhale, he was on her. He tossed her to the ground with the precise efficiency of a herdsman tossing a calf. A heartbeat later, she was pinned on the ground under his massive thighs.

Panting for breath, Larkspur realized he was too huge—and wily—to best in a fair fight. She usually admired that in a man but not when crushed underneath him.

"Hey, stud." Larkspur spoke in a whisper, but the sound seemed to echo in the grotto, making her wince. Ekal's wrath was the last thing she needed now. "What do you have in mind?"

In the flickering light, he met her gaze. What she saw made her heart stop.

This thief was gorgeous. High cheekbones. An aquiline nose. Thick dark hair hanging in his wide-set eyes. His gaze was piercing, almost otherworldly, and his eyes were the most unusual shade of blue, robins' eggs with a handful of spring grass.

She opened her mouth to say something—anything—but he grabbed her waist with perfect deliberation, never breaking eye contact as he pulled her to her feet.

Larkspur realized then that the alluring musky pine scent belonged to him, not the dragon.

He pulled her closer. Against her will, she felt a surge as strong as the tides. Not many men had his perfect thief technique, and not many men looked this good. The combination was deadly. She wanted him to pull her closer still.

But the equinox was mere days away. Her sister . . . She had to run.

But smashing her way out of his massive arms might be difficult, if not impossible. And she doubted he'd fall for the same trick twice—he was carefully shielding his pelvis.

The smoldering look in this man's eye gave her another idea. When pleasant solutions to tricky problems appeared as if by magic, only the Goddess could be thanked. Maybe she could turn his craving to her advantage. In fact, maybe the quickest way to the Jewel was in his arms. Or his pants.

Larkspur turned the tiniest bit to press her ass into his palm. She brushed her breast against his arm.

He steered his cock clear of her hips, but with a subtle shift in his posture, he increased the pressure on her ass. She'd known men who took what they wanted without asking, and this giant was certainly big enough to follow that pattern, but the shy way he protected his cock even while so delicately caressing her ass melted her jaded heart.

This huge, skilled man was . . . endearing.

As sudden and surprising as flashfire, undeniable desire ripped through her.

Almost as if he could read her mind, he tightened his arms around her, and she sucked in her breath at his brawny strength. What was this hot, unpredictable passion that he awoke in her?

Goddess knew she'd seen men gazing at her hungrily, but he made her feel ripe enough to eat. For a heartbeat she fantasized that he was one of the fertility worshippers and that he'd roam her curves with his tongue and fingers. He'd savor the river between her thighs, and he'd be hers.

Knowing her yearning would be written in her face, she looked up at him. His reaction surprised her. She saw the oddest emotions there—fire, yes. But what else? Shock? Confusion?

No. She saw vulnerability.

He ran a finger slowly across her cheek. The deliberate caress nearly undid her. Larkspur forced herself to breathe.

A kiss would come next, she knew, a kiss that would both

satisfy and leave her wanting. She closed her eyes in expectation.

Instead he heaved her over his shoulder like a sack of grain. What the . . . ? Red-faced, Larkspur stifled a grunt and a curse.

But the need for silence pushed embarrassment into the background, cramming a realization down her throat: maybe the dragon didn't know two thieves crept through its den! Maybe the dragon only knew about her.

If that were true—if the beast were unaware of this massive man—he would make the perfect ally. They still had an element of surprise!

Her huge captor had Larkspur's wrists in one hand and ankles in another, and she realized she'd been wrong about at least one thing. This guy wasn't wearing armor; those were his chest muscles.

With some difficulty, she moved her head so that her lips brushed his ear. "Hey," Larkspur said in the softest of whispers. "Let's help each other."

No answer. No change. He simply continued along the path. He acted like a man with a plan. Even with her weight on his shoulders, he moved like a cat—silently, lithely. He simply padded toward the glow at the heart of the cave.

Impressive. She wasn't small.

Using her tongue, Larkspur shifted the slender thieves' pick she kept in the side of her mouth to the other side. Then she grabbed his earlobe in her teeth. She bit gently. She nibbled a little lower, tasting the salt on his neck. Yum.

The silent man faltered—only for a second, but unmistakably.

She had his interest.

Letting her voice go sultry, she tried again. "We can make each other happy, you know. We both have the skills we need to do this." Let him wonder exactly what she meant; either interpretation suited her.

Maybe both did.

When he turned off the path into one of the grottos, she wondered if she were playing with fire. Even with all her skills, this gigantic man could hurt her, kill her even.

Then she remembered his inquiring touch, his questioning expression. Whatever else he might do, this man would not hurt her.

The grotto into which he lugged her wasn't crammed with treasures. Instead, neatly organized books filled sprawling shelves. The spines were leather embossed with gold. Carpet-size maps spread across several tables. Several were rolled closed, but one lay opened to Greenhaven, Larkspur's home and home of this dragon's lair. A tapestry filled a generous wall. It depicted people reaping a garden harvest while a bluegreen dragon flew overhead. The farm folk looked protected by the dragon, not threatened by it.

This grotto was strange. Had he known this was here? How long had he been searching?

Larkspur eyed a huge bed with posters and a headboard of some dark wood. Ebony? A talented artisan had carved lizards of every sort into them. Tails and mouths twined around each other. Tongues slithered like tendrils. The artwork reminded her of . . .

She lost the thought when he tossed her on a claret-colored spread. The softest crushed velvet enveloped her. The bed had not been designed with mere sleep in mind.

When Larkspur spied handcuffs dangling from the headboard, she grinned.

This kind of trouble she could handle with her eyes closed.

2

_____

In her line of work, seduction sometimes served as a means to an end. Sometimes she tried to find other ways to steal her prize—old guys weren't generally as eager to believe their cocks over their common sense as the younger guys were.

But when the man who stood between her and her goal was good looking and amenable, her job could be fun.

Today might be a decadent treat, assuming this guy wasn't a brute.

Well, she'd keep his mind on other things.

Stretching seductively, Larkspur quietly pushed her satchel onto the floor where she could reach it later. She stretched again, arching her back to show off her breasts. Then she turned on her side, propping her head in her hand. She knew the position showed off the curve of her hip, inviting him. Larkspur dangled her thick black braid across her shoulder, its tassel ending where her nipple pressed against her shirt.

Let this intruder think she had straightforward sex on her mind.

Through lidded eyes, Larkspur observed the massive man

standing at her feet. The angle of his cheekbones gave him a slightly dangerous appearance, and his thick hair was so dark it almost glittered with iridescence, like a grackle's feathers.

But he stood looking like he didn't know what to do with his hands, hips, lips. His quizzical expression made Larkspur want to reassure him. She wanted to take his gargantuan hands into hers, smile into his eyes, and tell him everything would work out fine.

By the goddess, milkmaids in his hometown must have fought to roll in the hay with this guy—perilous and sweet in one package.

And yet . . . and yet the man's wide-eyed innocence spoke of a different life. Larkspur would bet that he'd never seen a woman in his bed before this.

Weird.

But she could definitely use his innocence to her advantage.

Larkspur crooked a finger at him and tried not to laugh aloud as his face turned bright red. *Careful,* she told herself. She didn't want to scare him off.

But his self-conscious demeanor did more than amuse her. It reassured her. No violent brute could possibly appear this adorable.

When he finally approached, his intent clear, she grinned—the mouse had taken the bait.

When he took her hands in his, she actually shivered, as if something enchanted had touched her.

A cleric once had given her a magic pebble that made empty bellies feel full when the correct words were uttered. Even when the spell hadn't been invoked, her palms had sensed the rock's potential. Tingling.

His touch made her feel just like the time she'd held that stone. He felt enchanted.

Looking much too forward to his embrace, to the weight of his body against hers, she wanted his warmth and strength to explore every bit of her flesh. Had she been craving this man for days? Her fingers itched to dance across his strong back, to feel the silky texture of his hair.

But he never gave Larkspur the opportunity. With super-natural speed, he captured her wrists and snaked them above her head. *Snick*. He locked her hands in the brass handcuffs. Larkspur didn't mind nearly as much as she should have.

Then again, a good thief rarely objected to a lock.

Perhaps she should have.

With no finesse at all, his strong fingers found the black laces of her bodice and tore them free. Larkspur swallowed a shiver of fear. Or was it excitement?

He shoved the garment aside her breasts so that it lay in a tangle around her neck and shoulders. Then he quickly flipped her onto her back. How could such a talented thief be so lack-ing in grace?

But his goal was clear. Larkspur's breasts lay free before him, nipples rock hard and erect.

He stopped to look, and she guessed he liked what he saw. She knew the claret-colored velvet complemented her black hair and coppery skin, and having her hands stretched above her head, full breasts bared, must please him.

His appreciative grin made her think she was right.

And that grin made her wet. There were times she loved her job.

His hands cupped her breasts, gently, as if weighing them or assessing them, and then he hesitated, looking at her question-ingly. Had the man never even seen a breast? Well, she smiled to herself, she'd be spoiling him for any others.

Her nipples burned for his touch, and she twisted to get them under his thumbs. By the goddess, she wanted him.

But he didn't seem to understand, at least not the fine details of pleasing. Nearly ignoring her nipples, his hands stroked from her breasts to her belly, finding and unhooking her pants. He pushed them down so that they slithered down her legs, and he set his palm against her soft vee. Then the man looked at her, as if asking, "What next?"

Larkspur certainly had an answer for him.

Bracing her feet against the bed, she pushed against his hand. When his fingers brushed against her clit, she shifted beneath him, getting his fingertips in exactly the right place. The expression on his face as he found the slippery wet spot made her want to laugh aloud.

But he didn't stay there, not long enough to satisfy. Larkspur suppressed a groan. He just didn't get it. In frustration she grabbed his shirt in her teeth and pulled, ripping the fabric and trapping one of his nipples in her teeth. This is what she wanted. Larkspur nipped insistently. For a heartbeat, his body froze. She bit harder. Then she sucked soothingly.

He jumped away as if on fire. The silent man stood then, moving himself out of her range. He eyed her, and to Larkspur, his appraising look seemed filled with wonder.

Come to my trap, mousie, she thought.

As if in response, the man deliberately removed his trousers and the tattered remains of his shirt. He was shaped like a warrior, chest and stomach armored in muscles. His arms were as thick as trees.

He moved as swiftly as an adder, pinning her hip under an immense hand. Larkspur couldn't move, could barely breathe.

Before she decided whether she was ready for him, he forced his cock into her. Roughly.

So much for foreplay. His technique reminded her of wild solstice couplings rather than something learned in a temple. He took what he wanted, but not cruelly. It seemed more like he just didn't know better.

Larkspur stifled a cry of pain and tried to twist her hips free of him. He definitely needed a tutor. A man as big as he needed to go slowly, but he seemed unaware of that fact. He drove into her.

Fear of the dragon kept her quiet. *Too fast!* she silently warned, slowing her hips to make the point.

He got it, and Larkspur breathed easier. Slowing his thrusts to match hers, she felt her muscles stretch to accommodate the biggest cock she'd ever imagined. The second thrust didn't actually hurt, not as wet as she was.

Larkspur relaxed into his rhythm, having no choice in the matter. He didn't seem to try to spare her. Again and again he pounded, so focused. She'd thought from his naïve expression when they'd started that he'd be a tender lover, but instead, he seemed completely unaware that sex could be mutually pleasurable.

Glancing at his face, Larkspur didn't see anger or the cold fury she associated with fucking. That wasn't his problem. Instead she saw only delight, intense and self absorbed.

This giant man with the face of a god was merely inexperienced.

He drove his cock into her. Each thrust hit that spot. Each thrust made her want to scream in pleasure. The carved lizards on the headboard began to dance with the growing stars behind her eyes. Eyes, teeth, tail spun in wild animation. Larkspur blinked and clenched her teeth to drive away the heat growing in her belly.

She would not come. Not yet.

The man, still silent, began an even faster and deeper plunging than before. Larkspur tried to resist, she tried to etch each individual lizard into her memory, but the wild thrusting within her, a thrusting that became increasingly intense, made her gasp with pleasure, despite herself.

Of their own accord, her hips flexed to meet his with each

plunge. She bit back a whimper, pressing her nose into the hollow of his neck as the electric flash of her orgasm crackled through her.

Still he thrust, the power of his iron-hard cock strong and wild. Larkspur was beyond herself now. Denying him was impossible. She met him stroke for stroke, and her belly quivered as the second orgasm laced through her body and mind, nearly blinding her. Still he pounded on, maintaining the same feral, unforgiving pace.

Through her mind passed the thought that the man was not human. Perhaps he was a demon who would completely consume her with sex. Still he drove into her, again and again, and her clit was now so sensitive that each thrust nearly made her scream—in pleasure and pain. She became a torch whose source of fuel lay in her cunt, the light and heat burning through her whole body.

Larkspur lay helpless as his assault continued, and amazingly, she could feel yet another, even more ferocious orgasm gather itself. Fear and anticipation filled her. He must come, too, for her plan to work, and sooner would be better than later.

She opened her legs wider, inviting him, begging him. Then a screaming orgasm tore through her like a cyclone.

Never had orgasms needed screaming as much as these did, but she didn't want to attract the dragon. Biting her lips to keep silent, she swallowed blood.

Then Larkspur felt her captor's body tighten, and she knew—the same storm that ripped through her was tearing through him. He bucked and writhed between her thighs, burying himself deeper than she thought possible. Her legs twined around his waist as spasm after unbelievable spasm of pleasure rippled through her body.

As his body collapsed over hers, Larkspur sighed in relief.

She knew her odds of success had greatly increased. Her spasms slowed in intensity and frequency, but each time she quivered, he did too.

At least some part of this giant man was now relaxed and satiated.

But she'd done something more than relax him. Had she . . . tamed him?

The giant sprawled across her, gazing at her face. He gently moved her dark hair from her cheek with the softest look in his eye. She'd met men who gloated at this point, mistakenly certain that their dazzling skills gave her every satisfaction.

This man, however, exuded contented appreciation. He unbraided her hair, wrapped a tendril around his finger and silently laughed when the kinky mass wildly spread across the bed. A handful of strands caught beneath his shoulder, making her wince in pain. He immediately freed and straightened her tresses, running his fingers through them as if each were made of the finest silk.

Then he moved to her skin, caressing her as if she were some exotic and precious creature. He explored her neck and shoulders and waist with thoughtful fingertips and warm palms.

Larkspur wanted to curl up in the safety of his arms and sleep.

But that wasn't possible. For her plan to work, she needed to get him off her.

Time for silent signals. With a big, noiseless yawn, Larkspur rolled him off. Then, with not-so-feigned fatigue, Larkspur curved her body around his. She draped a leg over his hip and pretended to sleep, burying her nose into the nape of his neck. Inhaling deeply, she wondered if she'd ever met a man who smelled as good as this one.

Moments later, she heard his breathing deepen. She jabbed him lightly. No response. She nudged him again while she studied his face. Nothing. He slept.

His thick black lashes, his aquiline nose. The man was gorgeous.

Quietly, she inched her face toward the handcuffs. With her tongue, she manipulated the lock-picking wire from the thieves' kit, and now, erect between her front teeth, the wire easily slid into the lock mechanism. She braced the handcuff against the headboard, stabilizing it, and angled the wire up and back. Once, she stabbed at it. Too high. She tried again. Almost there. And then on the third try, with a solid *click*, Larkspur knew she had it.

She carefully wiggled her wrist and relaxed slightly when the handcuff sprang open. The second mechanism unlocked just as easily. If she could make the four steps to the door, she'd be free of him.

Four steps seemed like infinity.

Larkspur carefully lifted the man's wrist, but he turned over and his eyelids fluttered. The goddess herself must have made this gorgeous man. And flashfire demons must have had a hand in him too, given the way he fucked.

Damn. He wasn't quite asleep enough for her plan.

Ignoring her thudding heart, she quickly put his hand back down on the bed.

After slowing her pulsing heartbeats, Larkspur nudged his wrists toward the headboard a hair's breadth at a time. She was almost to the cuff when he shifted again. This time he shoved his hands under her, pulling her possessively toward him.

This maneuver was going to require more patience than she'd thought.

Larkspur saw only one solution to this problem. Ah, the suffering she endured.

She put her hands above her head as if she were still cuffed, and she slid tightly next to him. She rubbed her breasts over his chest and moved until her ass was in his palm. She dared not kiss his mouth, not with her tools hidden there, but she nibbled his chest, licking his clavicle, nibbling his nipple.

Her bruised cunt was still wet and sensitive as she rubbed against his leg, and when he opened his eyes, looking at her quizzically, she wordlessly answered, "Yes."

Larkspur tried to set a more staid pace, a pace that wouldn't hurt her. She moved until her clit was under his fingers, but every time he tried to slip in, she pulled back. "Not yet," she said with her body, sliding her clit back under a fingertip.

She flexed her hip underneath him until she felt certain he had the message. Softly. Slowly. *That's exactly right.*

Larkspur felt the orgasm coming upon her like a spring rain, lightly and gently. Just before it peaked she slipped him inside. No pain this time, only exquisite pleasure.

Larkspur kept her orgasm simmering in the background as she rocked him, prolonging his pleasure, but as his thrusts became more urgent, she met him.

When the first shudder wracked his body, Larkspur let her own orgasm cascade. It washed over her, leaving her floating in his arms. As the last spasm shimmered through her, he held her tightly, as if cherishing her very being. And then he drifted blissfully off to sleep.

This time when his breathing deepened, she knew he'd sleep for quite a while. And he'd sleep deeply.

Larkspur told herself as she nudged first one wrist into the handcuff and then the second that she didn't feel one bit guilty about locking him up.

She picked up her pack and padded toward the grotto's entrance. Pausing a moment before she left, Larkspur stopped to admire the giant man tied to the bed.

Only then did she realize that the man's cloak didn't glow—it was his skin.

3

The flagstone path curved inward, its luminous ceiling still inviting the eye. Larkspur paused for a moment. No horsehairs. No traps.

According to the elders who'd provided the sparse information, the Jewel would be near the dragon, hidden in plain sight. In its claw, perhaps? At the top of its pile of loot?

Now that the rival thief was incapacitated, Larkspur could focus on her actual task: stealing from a dragon, a renowned fool's errand. The dragon, so eager to taunt her when she'd first arrived, was strangely silent. *The mindvoice*, Larkspur thought. Why hadn't she heard from the dragon lately? Had it gone to steal some sheep? Surely it wouldn't have left knowing a thief crept through its lair.

Her leather-clad feet slid quietly over the cool flagstone as she rounded a corner.

And then she found the creature.

The twisting trail opened into a large chamber, and the iridescent beast lay atop his mountain of booty. Shimmering green light bathed the chamber, and finally Larkspur understood its source: the dragon himself. The beast and the treasure all glowed with the light of a newly risen moon, with the green that had lit her way.

Larkspur froze, not wanting to exhale too loudly.

Rubies and agate and gold filigree made his nest. He lay amidst swords and scabbards and circlets and coins. Larkspur spied tiny animals carved of crystal and silver candelabras as tall as she. A woven blanket of some strange metallic purple material caught her eye. The blanket could have covered a warhorse.

But the aqua and turquoise shimmer of his scales outshone every item in his pile. As Ekal breathed, his scales winked like the first stars of the evening. The color of the heavens minutes after sunset, the dragon was the most beautiful creature Larkspur had ever seen.

She took a minute to study him. Ekal's closed eyelid shimmered like the cerulean of a summer day's sky, the color of a robin's egg.

In fact, the thief she'd left handcuffed to the bed had eyes of exactly the same color. That thought made her pulse quicken, and Larkspur forced herself to concentrate.

A dragon lay at her feet.

Tiny curls of smoke wafted from the dragon's nostrils, ebbing and flowing with each breath. The curls sunk to the ground, making it look like the great beast lay on a cloud.

Only then did Larkspur fully understand that the dragon slept.

Perhaps she had some respite. She inhaled deliberately, quietly, wishing she could contain the scent of sex wafting around her, wishing to be as silent as a winter morning.

She slowly turned her head, looking, seeking. Where was the Jewel? Where? She examined his talons—long, dark inky blue. With a flick, they could deal death. But no Jewel lay between them. Nor did it lie anywhere on his pile.

Aware of the painful ache between her thighs, Larkspur

took a silent step toward his other side, thinking the Jewel might be in his opposite hand.

Discomfort made her clumsy. Larkspur took the smallest misstep. When she scuffed the gold ring with her toe, it made a small sound, a hummingbird's sneeze.

The ring rolled along the path with as little noise as moth wings fluttering around a flame. Larkspur could see where it would land, what it would hit.

A large bronze shield stood propped against a steely armor suit. She could imagine the *ting* the ring would make when it collided with the shield.

She could imagine the *ting* signifying the end of her sister's life.

Time moved like honey in winter. Each revolution made by the ring as it rolled toward its goal took days. The ring needed a year to reach the shield. Two years.

But she stood powerless.

Torn, she needed to watch Ekal's eyelid, and she needed to see the ring crash. In those heartbeats, the faces of maidens slaughtered in Greenhaven flashed through her mind—her inability to save them. She saw her mother's face. Her sister's.

Disbelief washed over her, incredulity at being brought down by a stubbed toe, the ache of really good sex. A gold ring.

Ting.

The ring hit with a noise as loud as thunder. It may as well have. Larkspur's eyes chose to watch Ekal's, anticipating how magnificent the beast would look in flight, lunging toward her with death in his face and fire on his lips.

The ring spiraled wildly, wobbling crazily like a child's top. Gyrating, it tinged again, twice more. Each as loud as a shout.

Then all movement stopped.

Larkspur's hands flew toward her ears, expecting his booming intrusion into her thoughts, expecting his taunts to be the last thing she heard before she died, roasted in a column of flames.

But the dragon did not stir. His eyelid didn't flutter, didn't twitch. Ekal's silvery wings stayed unfurled, tucked lightly against his sides.

Larkspur's mind raced as curls of smoke slowly spiraled from his nostrils.

Nothing made sense. Nothing at all.

She stood, dumbfounded, staring blankly at the room bathed in emerald light.

And then . . . And then clues fell together like pieces of a child's puzzle. The clues painted a strange picture. The dragon's silence. The glow of the thief's skin. Perhaps even the missing Jewel of Dragonkind.

Larkspur picked up the nearest object, a golden helm, and chucked it with an easy underhand at the dragon.

The thing hit the dragon's blue-leathered flank, and with a twinkling sizzle, it bounced through and hit the floor. Though she still couldn't see through the apparition, Larkspur heard the helm roll across the rough flagstone with a clamoring noise, and stop.

The silence was deafening. But the dragon didn't move.

This time, she wasn't surprised.

The dragon wasn't real. At least this dazzling creature in front of her wasn't.

Larkspur paused for another moment, deciding. Then she turned on her heel and marched back up the path.

"Pus and piss," she muttered to herself, now unworried about the sound.

He lay where she'd left him, bathing in the warm green glow of his skin. She wondered if he resembled the bluegreen apparition she'd seen below when in dragon form.

"Stupid woman," she muttered to herself. She should have known, should have figured it sooner. No man, no human she'd ever met, could sneak up on her. Of all the clues, that's the one that bothered her the most. She should never have doubted her abilities as a master thief.

The man handcuffed to the ebony and crimson bed was a dragon in human form, and she should have recognized that fact instantly.

But enough of that. Taking her emotions firmly in hand, Larkspur realized that for the wrong reasons, she'd done the right thing. An opportunity lay before her. Literally.

Now that she'd chained the dragon to his bed, perhaps she could snatch the Jewel from him. If she could find it.

Two ways to approach her goal occurred to her. One method used carrots; the other used sticks.

Deciding which to implement was easy.

At the foot of the bed, she stood, legs spread in defiance. Larkspur deliberately shrugged out of her bodice. Larkspur realized she knew the man's name. "Ekal," she said, nearly whispering.

She watched his eyes open, and widen in appreciation. Somewhere in the realm a woman must exist who would not be flattered by that response, but Larkspur wasn't that person. His enthusiastic gaze sent a tide of desire through her blood.

"Ah," she said, using her normal voice for the first time since she'd entered the cave. "You're awake." With aplomb Larkspur unbuttoned her fly, shimmied her hips, and let her pants slink to her ankles.

Yes, the voice in her head said. *I'm very much awake.*

She placed her foot on the bed's footboard, giving him a teasing view of her shining sex, and began to unhook the boot buttons.

No, he said. *Leave them on.*

Larkspur chuckled, coolly. "Pretty sophisticated taste for a man—or dragon rather—who just lost his maidenhead."

Maidenhead, he snorted. *Thief, only human women are new to me.*

"Well, then, I guess I can excuse that poor display of foreplay."

What are you talking about?

She ignored him. "And if you're going to add humans to

your list of species with whom you've had sex, then I'm going to make sure you do it correctly."

Foreplay—

"Exactly," she answered, not giving him a chance to dominate the conversation. Dragons were known to be tricky.

Decisively, Larkspur spat her thief's kit into her pack. She'd need her mouth for this, and her tongue. "Your foreplay technique is as transparent as that fake dragon sitting on that fake gold."

The gold is real.

And then Larkspur spied the Jewel of Dragonkind, her salvation! Amid the landscape of carved reptiles cavorting across the ebony someone had embedded a round stone, only subtly different in texture in this light. In the emerald dragon glow, the green and red of the bloodstone nearly throbbed. The real Jewel of Dragonkind, hidden in plain sight as prophesized by the elders.

Afraid he could read her mind, Larkspur quickly covered her discovery with flippant words. "Are you implying that the dragon isn't real? How fake is the illusion? Is that what you really look like when you're in dragon form?"

Yes. I can most easily cast such a spell when I know what the illusion is supposed to look like.

"Oh, you're so very loquacious, now. So, is your man-shape some sort of illusion?"

No, I can take the form of any species—but only male.

"Well, your form is flawless. You're definitely male." All male. For sure. "It's your technique that's lacking."

No one has ever complained about my technique.

"I don't know what species you've, ah, covered in your exploration of the world, but you've learned nothing about foreplay."

Nothing! he objected. He tried to sit up but was jerked back by his trapped wrists. *I didn't notice you protesting.*

"As if you would have heard if I had," she said, and then she asked in her mind, *And can you read my mind?*

She stood, looking at him, waiting for an answer with a thudding heart.

You are staring at me, his voice rumbled in her thoughts. *Have my dragon horns appeared on my human face?*

"Can you read my mind?" she asked aloud this time.

Only with effort, and doing so without invitation is rude.

Larkspur sent a silent prayer of thanks to the Goddess. "Oh, you'd never be rude, I'm sure."

But if you purposely think a thought at me, I can hear it much more clearly than if you don't. Ekal paused and looked at her. Then he said, *And when people obsess about something, I can't help but overhear.*

How could she fail to obsess about . . . She stopped herself. Fear slithered through her mind, and she quickly squashed it, focusing instead on the obvious—sex.

She blasted Ekal with her feelings of dissatisfaction at their last encounter, letting him know that he'd ignored her needs. She let him know that she'd come despite his actions, not because of them.

Come here and I'll give you exactly what you need.

"You will," she agreed. "On my terms. This time you won't rush a single move. You'll go slowly, and appreciate the sensations. And you will do it right."

Standing naked, save her boots, Larkspur looked at her hardened nipples. She ran her fingertips lightly over them until they further peaked. "What does this mean?" she challenged him. Her wet sex could tell him, if he knew that signal.

I, uh—

"You don't know, do you?"

I want to know.

"That's a fine place to start."

For a moment, Larkspur bent over him, letting her breasts tease his lips. Then she sat back, placing a hand on either side of his face, a knee between his thighs. For a heartbeat she let her clit graze his thigh, but danger lay in that direction. She needed to stay in control.

Larkspur grazed her nipples over his muscular chest, trying to ignore how good he felt. Then, quick as lightning, she caught his nipple between her teeth. She bit down, but not too much, rolling her tongue over the now-hard bump.

Oh, he said in her head. He almost hummed.

Oh, indeed, she agreed to herself. Larkspur yearned to lose herself in the moment. In human form, Ekal offered nothing but temptation—exuberance, appreciation, and, perhaps most surprising to Larkspur, a kind eye.

"Now try me." Larkspur let him capture her nipple in his mouth.

I never knew. Dragons don't have this organ.

"Shut up. Lick. Suck. Don't talk."

Then his tongue found her nipple.

"The whole area is sensitive, dragon. Explore a little."

Like this then? He could talk and suck. Later she'd decide if that was a good thing.

Then he caught a nipple between his teeth, sending a finger of fear to her heart. He was so big, and he was a . . . dragon.

But his warm gentleness reassured her. In fact, maybe the possibility of pain—slight though she thought it was—turned her on. Maybe.

Ekal traced her areola with a hot tongue then rolled her rock-hard nipple between his teeth. "Ahhhh." The cry escaped her without warning. She choked it off, not wanting to distract him now that he was finally figuring things out. He licked her taut nipple gently at first, and then with more assurance, more pressure. He circled it with his tongue, and then he pulled her inside his hot mouth.

Too fast. She had to pull back.

But to reward him, she pressed her lips fully against his. He tentatively, almost awkwardly, returned the kiss.

Do I use the same technique here as I did with your breasts?

"You don't need to think so much, dragon. Let go a little bit." She slipped her tongue into his mouth, and she felt its intimacy for the first time. Again, an awareness of magical potential rippled through her. That must be her natural reaction to his dragon-ness. The mages should bottle this as an aphrodisiac.

Ekal got it. With deliberate slowness, his tongue caressed her. His lips ran over hers for the sheer pleasure. His kisses grew hot and tender. And under hers, his grew bolder.

She withdrew for a moment, just long enough to look closely at his face. Larkspur liked what she saw: Ekal was a slave to this passion. He wasn't thinking about roasting her.

He certainly wasn't thinking about the Jewel.

Wanting to keep him intensely distracted, she immediately took his lips again, harder and more possessively this time. Larkspur traced the inside of his upper lip.

And he followed her lead.

Her need to give instructions died as he took control. He touched her mouth with his tongue again, teasing and questing, until she parted her lips.

Rational thought fled as he took her mouth, deep and slow, covering her, his warm hand gripping her thigh as he tasted her. There was nothing tentative about him as he sucked the tip of her tongue, sliding, owning, dominating the kiss, leaving Larkspur breathless, clinging to his chest. By the goddess, the man learned fast.

His cock throbbed against her thigh, and she pressed against him. He made to embrace her but pulled against the handcuffs. His frustration came out in a grunt.

"Easy, dragon."

Apparently he took her at her word.

When he shimmered under her lips, under her leg, she thought of magic, that her heart knew something her brain had yet to register.

But when he momentarily disappeared and reappeared, she sat up. "How the—"

As his arms snaked around her neck, drawing her back toward him, she realized then that he was no longer handcuffed. Apparently dragons didn't need thieves' kits to escape; they shape-changed.

She wasn't sure she liked where this was going.

"Oh, no, big guy. You stay tied up for this lesson."

And he was in for one hell of a lesson.

4

Of all the men Larkspur had screwed—literally—in her line of work, Ekal was by far the most . . . distracting. She could become addicted to the enchantment of his touch. And that was a problem.

Looking at his throbbing cock, she thought, *A big problem.* She had to distract a dragon, not a man. Stark naked, slick with desire, Larkspur needed to nab the Jewel of Dragonkind right from under Ekal's nose.

And he could shift into deadly dragon shape in the blink of an eye. No ties could bind him.

No ties of rope or leather, at any rate. Larkspur had a different kind of bond in mind.

Freed, he wrapped his thick arms around her. The skin inside his massive forearms felt surprisingly soft against her waist and ribs.

"Uh-uh. No way," she said, extricating herself. Reluctantly. "If you want me to teach you the subtle art of human, um . . ." Larkspur foundered, at a loss for the right word. *Fucking?* Too crass. *Lovemaking?* "Love" couldn't fit into this relationship. Ever.

Bed sport? the dragon suggested.

"Mhmmm. That's right: bed sport." Larkspur wasn't exactly one of those temple virgins who indoctrinated the rich and lucky into adult pleasures, but she could surely show a willing and naïve dragon the finer points of passion. "If you want to learn human bed sport, you have to stay tied up."

Handcuffed?

"That's how they teach virgins in the temple," she said in an authoritative voice. Larkspur had no idea if that were true. "You need to submit to me." She pushed his wrists back above his head and said, "Completely."

Ekal shimmered out of sight, leaving her in complete darkness for a moment before he reappeared. With concerted effort, she kept her eyes away from the Jewel. When he came back, the steely bracelets held his massive wrists. An amazing trick. What was it like for him when he was . . . nowhere?

Assassin, I am yours to instruct now.

"I'm not an assassin. I'm a—" Larkspur suddenly thought better of pointing out what should have been obvious. Instead, she eyed what was obvious on him: his throbbing hard-on. To distract him, Larkspur went down, knowing it was a cheap trick.

But it worked.

Larkspur hooked an arm around his thigh and pulled him into her mouth. He was too big for her to take without swallowing, so she paced his introduction to fellatio. First, she licked, wide and slow, giving him time to feel each and every prickle of desire. Ignoring his humming moans, she flicked her tongue over the tiny opening and then over the sensitive spot behind the head.

Ekal's moans were nonstop, but Larkspur looked up to assure herself that he was enjoying himself. His eyes were rolled back in ecstasy. Perfect. Just the way she wanted him.

Relaxing the back of her tongue, Larkspur inhaled his entire cock, swallowing the head, gently and carefully.

Thief, he hummed. *If you don't stop . . .*

Larkspur wasn't going to stop. She released her throat's grip, bringing his head into her mouth. Sucking, she grabbed his balls, gently caressing them.

She'd planned a systematic introduction, a gradual buildup to the most delicious. An intense distraction. Instead, she was inhaling his huge cock like he was her last breath.

She was as bad as he was.

Larkspur slowed her pace. Enjoying the taste of him—fresh mown hay—she pulled back. She ran her tongue lightly over him, licking, teasing. Ekal moved his hips, trying to bury himself in her throat again, but Larkspur danced just out of reach.

She sucked harder, just a bit. The sound he made, the noise echoing through her mind, reminded her of feral wolves roaming in the woods, low and dangerous.

If she'd met this man in different circumstances, she would have fallen hard for him. Without a doubt. But she hadn't met him on another day in another place. Larkspur pushed regret to the back of her mind.

Without warning, she swallowed his cock again. She sucked him deep inside of her—for a second only. Under her body, his entire being tensed. She knew he was so ready. She'd show him a pleasure he hadn't even imagined.

Larkspur sucked again. Hard.

In a wild thrash, he came in her mouth, his body writhing crazily. His seed raced hotly over her tongue, over the back of her throat. Breaths crashed from his chest in short, hard puffs. For long minutes, he lay under her silent, wordless.

Satiated. At least for the moment.

Larkspur grinned to herself. She'd done her job well. Except that she burned for him, for his touch.

Ah thief, he sighed, rubbing the side of his face, surprisingly smooth, against her cheek. The caress was tender, sweet. *Dragons don't perform that.*

"That may be, dragon, but humans do."

Let me try it on you. His husky words were almost a command.

Larkspur studied him, pretending to consider the possibilities. He was stretched out, his hands locked on the headboard, framing the Jewel at which Larkspur tried not to stare. His muscled arms bulged as he held his powerful body taut. He presented a very tempting picture—just what she needed. In so many ways.

The need for the Jewel winked in her mind, and she quickly squashed the thought before Ekal could read it.

I'll go slowly. I promise. Ekal was staring at her with that famished look in his eyes, and Larkspur knew his patience was eroding.

So was hers.

"Not yet. I have more to show you." Larkspur wanted Ekal's eyes rolled back in his head in exhausted pleasure.

Releasing his still-pulsing cock, she worked kisses and caresses over his torso, stroking the topography of his muscles, savoring the warmth of his skin. Funny, she'd always assumed that dragons were cold blooded.

Larkspur leaned over him, running her breasts over his chest. Her nipples tightened, sending that electric jolt right through her cunt. Desire rippled through her, making her movements jerky as she tried to keep up with his mouth.

Despite the analytical part of her mind, Larkspur found herself losing focus. His tongue, his lips, they enchanted her. He beguiled her to surrender to him.

Show me where to lick, the voice said in her head.

"That's an idea," she said in a thick voice.

A good idea, Ekal added. *Stand up and show me.*

She stood, ignoring her wobbly knees.

Wait! Let me guess. What about where your boot meets your thigh?

"That would be a fine place to lick." She ran her fingertip suggestively around the curve of the boot's opening. "This is a soft place, ticklish even. Small kisses, even nibbling would be great."

And, of course your nipples.

"As you say, 'of course.' But you could start here." Her fingertip caressed her breast's underside. Slowly. Purposefully. "And you wouldn't want to ignore this spot." She drew a small arc above her breast. "You'd want to work closer and closer to your goal," Larkspur added, letting her finger dance nearer to her areola, "rather than jumping right in." With the last suggestion, she held her nipple gently between her thumb and forefinger.

Let me try.

"So impatient."

You're enjoying yourself, he accused.

"And the problem with that is . . . ?" she asked, still teasing her nipple with her finger. "Watch and learn."

Mmmm.

Larkspur took that as agreement. "Once you've gotten this far, you can't ignore the other." Larkspur took her other nipple in hand until both were erect in the green dragon glow. "Here," she offered, leaning into his face. "One small taste."

The slick glide of his tongue over her breast nearly undid her, and Larkspur jerked backed as if burned. She knew that losing herself in this man—in this dragon—would be nearly inevitable.

Where else would you like my tongue? Between your legs as you did to me?

"You mean here," Larkspur said. Her fingers confirmed what she already knew. She was ready for him, hot and swollen and wet.

Let me try, he asked again.

She couldn't lose her focus. Not now with the equinox looming so close.

"All right, dragon." She strode toward him, savoring her flood of anticipation as she closed the short distance between them. She put one knee in the crushed velvet next to his face, and he turned toward her. Overwhelmingly aware of his warm breath on her thigh, she straddled him.

The stroke of his tongue over her clit, the heat of his mouth as he sucked on her nub brought her close to coming. Her body trembled with the fierce need to move, to push into him, but Larkspur held her hips immobile.

After a moment that stretched into infinity, he gently rubbed his tongue over her nerve-filled nub. Ekal sucked again, insistently. But not painfully this time. His mouth tugged while his tongue explored. Stars sparkled behind Larkspur's eyes. They spun down her spine and directly to her cunt. She arched her back, pressing her clit into his mouth, begging him to fulfill her need.

Larkspur blinked. Her hands, braced on the headboard, were an ant's breadth from the Jewel.

The nearness of her goal made her freeze, and Ekal apparently took this for acquiescence. He slowed his mouth, deepened his kiss. With exquisite deliberation, he ran his tongue over her clit.

But she couldn't forget herself.

Another slick glide left her no choice. The orgasm tore through her.

Larkspur clasped the Jewel as shudders wracked her body. The Jewel popped from its bed.

The rational part of her brain, which was diminishing rapidly with each spasm, told her she had what she wanted—she could save Phlox. She should run, her brain insisted.

But her body had a different idea. She wanted his cock. She

wanted to be pounded by him. She wanted to be enveloped by his arms, his lips, his scent.

"I want you now, dragon."

Then I am yours.

The Jewel of Dragonkind grew heavy in her hand, and hot. At least that's what she thought. Shifting the Jewel to her left hand, she slid down.

The back of her hand brushed over his cock. Larkspur turned her wrist and softly gripped him. He hissed through his clenched teeth, letting her know her desire was reciprocated. Ekal was massively hard, and she pressed him against her belly, overwhelmed by the need to feel him deep inside her body.

She had to stop this. She needed to control the evil ravaging her hometown, but the thought seemed vague and powerless against the desire she'd built so skillfully in him—and herself.

She rubbed the head of his cock against her clit, barely controlling the shiver of pleasure rushing through her nerves. "Ekal," she moaned, not even wondering if he knew she had the Jewel.

Shh, he whispered in her head. *Just let me touch you. Let me free myself.*

"No!" Again, the Jewel nearly burned as it grew amazingly heavy.

Slow and seductive thoughts were long flown, but she couldn't release him. Larkspur thrust herself down on him, grinding her hips against his.

As you wish. His body bucked against Larkspur's, plunging so very very deep.

Larkspur writhed, unable to bear the strength of the pleasure roiling over her. "Ekal," she yelled, squeezing the Jewel in her palm, "come with me!"

And as the Jewel heated and grew heavy, he did, shuddering beneath her for long minutes.

* * *

In a sheen of sweat, Ekal and Larkspur lay together. His knee lay over her thigh, making her feel safe, protected. His gentle touch, the magic that emanated from him—she knew she should be basking in bliss.

Instead, Larkspur felt like crying.

Something between them felt real, worth nurturing. Her heart thought that magic could blossom here. The woman, the sister of Phlox, wanted to tell this man why she wanted the Jewel. He would help her, he'd be compelled to help—not because of the Jewel's power but because his soul was good. Her animal instincts told her that she could trust Ekal.

But the cool voice of Larkspur the thief overrode her. She couldn't afford to be fooled by a shared orgasm or two . . . or three. No dragon could relinquish the Jewel of Dragonkind, and she couldn't let Ekal stop her from taking it.

If Greenhaven's elders were correct, she could now control any dragon she met. The Jewel gave her the power to stop the carnage.

She needed to leave. Now.

Without treasure? Without gold and gems?

"I have what I need." The statement felt like a lie, and the sorrow she heard in her voice surprised her. Past successes brought her nothing but satisfaction. What was this?

Ekal shimmered into nothingness, and for a moment Larkspur thought he'd fled to his gold.

Ekal! she cried out with her mind.

He reappeared, freed of his handcuffs, now sitting next to her. *Thief.* He stated rather than accused.

"Yes," she said in a stark voice. Larkspur stood and shrugged back into clothes, buttoning the bodice awkwardly while holding the egg-sized Jewel. She risked a look at him, knowing she'd hate what she'd see on his face.

A raven lock hung almost in his eye, highlighting a disconcerting look of disappointment. "I'll give the Jewel back when I've finished with it—in three days. Surely I can borrow it for such a short time."

I need to warn you. The Jewel will not work for you—not on all dragons. Not on evil dragons.

"I need to save my sister, Ekal. The only way I can do that is with the Jewel."

But it will not work for you, not for you and Eraw.

"I have to do this," she said. Larkspur brandished the Jewel at him, knowing he'd be compelled to obey. "Let me pass. Please, don't stop me. I'm sorry for this, truly."

This time, Larkspur felt certain that the Jewel grew both heavier and hotter. At her command, the Jewel was ordering him to desist. He had no choice but to obey.

As you wish.

She pulled up her pants and put her satchel over her shoulder. "I'll bring it back after the equinox, Ekal."

Larkspur didn't spare herself. She looked right into his eyes. The deep reproach she saw there grabbed her heart, but so would Phlox's death if she didn't hurry.

Larkspur headed back to the sunshine, wondering why her heart felt like rain.

5

"Don't do it, Larkspur. Please," Jasper almost pleaded after he listened to her plan. He'd been waiting for her by the mouth of the cave, waiting while she nabbed the Jewel from the dragon.

Scowling, Larkspur ignored him, yanking the saddle from the small cave in which she'd stored it. She tossed it on her lanky mare, who tried to dance away, unused to such rough treatment. As Larkspur jerked the cinch tight, the mare tried again to skitter away, swishing her tail and giving her a baleful look as she did so.

"Not you, too," Larkspur muttered to the horse.

"Larkspur! I'm talking to you," Jasper shouted.

"I know. And I'm not talking to you." She flung the saddlebags behind the saddle.

"You'll get yourself killed!"

Larkspur stopped tying the saddlebags for a moment and looked at her little brother square on. His green eyes were hard with frustration. "And who will save Phlox if I don't?" she demanded.

"If *we* don't, you must mean. I'm here to help you."

"You're not a thief," Larkspur replied.

"And you can't use that Jewel," Jasper shot back. "That's what the elders said, and that's what the dragon said."

"Well, of course the dragon said that. He'd have to, wouldn't he."

"And the elders?" he challenged, arms crossed across his chest.

"They didn't say I couldn't use it." Larkspur sounded petulant, even to herself.

"You're right," Jasper said in a voice dripping with sarcasm. "They said your heart had to be aligned with that of the dragon's."

"That doesn't mean I can't use it."

"Do you think your heart is aligned with Eraw's?" They both knew the answer. Eraw had been viciously murdering maidens from Greenhaven for three seasons.

"Who knows what 'alignment of hearts' even means," Larkspur spat back. She pulled off the mare's hobbles and put on the bridle, careful even in her anger not to bang the steel bit against the mare's teeth.

"You do. You know what it means."

Exasperated, Larkspur sighed. "Jasper, what do you want me to do?"

"Give the Jewel to the elders, like we all planned."

"No one thought I'd have the Jewel this quickly. I—" She corrected herself. "We have two days. We can stop Eraw before the equinox, before he even gets to Greenhaven. We could save Phlox two days of dread."

She could also return to Ekal more quickly. But she didn't want to say that to Jasper.

"And what if you're not strong enough to stop Eraw by yourself?" Jasper asked. "Do you want to have a heart aligned with his? Do you want to be evil?"

"I have the Jewel," Larkspur said firmly. "I can stop him."

"We're talking in circles," Jasper answered. Larkspur saw worry laced around his eyes, but his anger seemed deflated.

"You're right. We are." Larkspur looked at him and shrugged. "I'm sorry, little brother. I don't mean to frustrate you."

He gave her a tired smile, and she realized he'd been camping roughly while she'd been enjoying satin sheets and the pleasure of Ekal's bed. A pang of guilt spiraled through her.

"I still have some of Mom's honey cakes, if you want some."

Jasper just shook his head.

Larkspur shrugged and pointed to his bay horse, still hobbled and eating thick green grass next to the stream. "Why don't you get your horse saddled?" She looked pointedly at the sky. "We can get to Eraw's cave before dark."

Jasper shook his head again. "I'm not going with you."

"What? Jasper—"

"When Mom loses both of her daughters to Eraw, someone is going to have to be at her side."

After Jasper had ridden away, Larkspur couldn't help but watch his receding figure. The great valley with its lovely brook seemed to swallow him up. He'd be back at home, eating fresh honey cakes with their mom, just as she reached Eraw's cave.

Fighting back tears, Larkspur sniffed. The late summer air smelled sharp and clean, like apples and cider. She couldn't help but compare it to Ekal's scent. Without her bidding, the memory sent a throb to her clit, softened something deep inside of her.

She'd disappointed Ekal by taking the Jewel. She'd disappointed Jasper by using it against their foe single-handedly.

But in two-day's time, Phlox would be stretched out on the terrible stone altar, and no one in the world was in a better position to save her than she was. No one else was as motivated.

What would happen if a human with an unaligned heart used the Jewel? Likely the black dragon would obey her just as Ekal had. If it hurt her head or heart to use the Jewel against an evil dragon, so be it. Her sister was worth the risk.

Still, she felt so alone in this task. She missed Ekal's bed, his arms.

She'd see him again, she reassured herself, when she returned the Jewel.

If she lived to return the Jewel, the cynical voice inside her head needled.

Larkspur deftly found a handhold then a foothold in the greasy darkness of the burrow. Unable to see, she concentrated on smell. Would this dragon smell piney like Ekal? Would he be sexy? Maybe all dragons were hunks.

No one could be as gorgeous as Ekal, her brain said. Her cunt agreed. So did her heart.

Sliding her palm down clammy stones, Larkspur considered. At least this time she knew to look for dragons disguised as humans.

Descending another body length, a sulfuric scent laced with methane assaulted Larkspur's nose. Definitely not Ekal's style. Was this cave volcanic? Was it active? The air certainly felt warm enough, and the temperature heated with every step down. Sweat trickled across Larkspur's forehead, down her neck.

Finally her feet hit flat ground. Relief was out of the question. This cave felt like the demons' depths, all cliffs and crags. She'd probably just found a ledge, maybe even a ledge disguised as a path. Once she stepped more confidently, the ground would drop from beneath her, plunging her to her death.

But tapping around, her feet found a solid path. It seemed solid in all directions.

So which direction to choose? In Ekal's cave, she'd followed the emerald glow, which had turned out to be the right decision—the radiance had come from the dragon himself.

Peering into the inky blue-black darkness, Larkspur squinted. Was that dragonglow to her left? Or was it a mirage?

She blinked a few times. Her hands and feet ached from the

rocky descent, and sweat still poured from her face, from under her arms. Even the spot behind her knees felt sweaty.

Worse, climbing down the spiraling, airless entry into Eraw's cave had left her confused, disoriented. A wave of sulfur washed over her, not helping a bit. And her feet still distrusted the path's solidity.

Finally Larkspur felt certain of something. A sickly yellow glow definitely pulsed to her left. The color reminded her of pre-gangrenous flesh. It held the unfulfilled promise of rot.

Larkspur hadn't appreciated how cozy Ekal's cave was until now.

Despite the weight of the Jewel in her satchel, a growing foreboding blossomed in the pit of her stomach. This place felt . . . evil. Maybe her impetuous decision wasn't the right one.

Larkspur shoved the worry aside. This place had to feel malevolent—Eraw had to be wicked. Dragons and people lived peaceably nearly everywhere. He'd gone rogue, torturing and killing young women. His malice must permeate the place.

She stopped again to search for traps. Touching nothing she looked through the ghastly light around her ankles and shins.

Here, the light looked like a bruise, not like Ekal's emerald glow, so clean and true. For a moment, Larkspur wished Ekal were at her side.

But he wasn't, and a dragon needed to be stopped. Larkspur searched for long moments but found no traps, no hair triggers.

And then Larkspur realized: no traps were needed in this cave. The malevolent dragon came directly to her.

Eraw stood before her, in human form. She'd never seen such cold, steely eyes. Her breath caught in her chest as if she'd fallen through ice and was drowning in the frigid waters. Stark dread slid up her spine even as Larkspur took measured breaths and regained control of her heartbeat.

The Jewel. She needed the Jewel. Unadulterated evil wafted from this monster. She'd order his heart to stop beating. She'd order him to close his eyes. Slowly she inched her arms toward her satchel.

"I knew you were coming," he said, using a human voice unlike Ekal. Could he, too, read her mind? Best to assume the worst.

Dagger. Dagger. Dagger. She filled her mind with images of the dagger, to replace any thoughts of the Jewel. Her fingers crept toward the . . . dagger . . . in her satchel.

"I was hoping to find you here, too," she answered in a steady voice. To eradicate you. To leave you as helpless as the young maidens of Greenhaven.

"Ah," he said in a voice as chilled as his gaze, "you've heard of my work there."

This dragon made no pretense; he blatantly read her mind. "Work," Larkspur derided, while cautiously opening her bag. "As if killing women bound to stone altars is work for a monstrously huge dragon."

"Perhaps the killing itself isn't so difficult, but arranging the sacrifices can be troublesome. Elders and mayors are never pleased."

Larkspur suspected he was trying to rattle her. This thief would not take the bait. Concentrating on her internal energy points, her blood pressure decreased, even as her fingertips sought their goal inside the bag. Dagger. Dagger. Dagger. "Your life is troublesome then?" she asked. "Not work?" *Dagger. Dagger. Dagger.*

There it was—

"Freeze," he commanded.

Larkspur could not move a muscle, couldn't blink. Couldn't breathe! Her fingers tingled. She'd pass out in—

"Breathe, Larkspur."

A rasping gasp escaped her lips.

"You will not touch that Jewel."

She tried. Every fiber of her being tried.

But even blinking was impossible. Pus and piss.

"Your dagger is in your boot, although your attempt at misleading was commendable, admirable even. Few with whom I deal have such presence of mind."

Fatherless abortion. That's what he was.

"Actually, my dear, my mother did not abort me, although she abandoned me quite early. Neither she nor her sisters believed me to be natural. Still, my parentage is quite noble. Did you know that your precious Ekal and I are half brothers?"

If she could have moved, Larkspur would have gawked. He must have read her mind. They didn't act alike or look alike. Both had dark hair, but the similarities ended there.

Eraw had a long narrow face and a hook nose. His hair hung dark and lank. But mostly—Larkspur knew this for certain— Ekal would never hurt her.

And she could see Eraw's love of pain in his eye. He'd relish her pain. He'd seek it. Larkspur saw her death in Eraw's eyes. Thank the goddess, her mother would still have Jasper.

Eraw embodied wickedness.

The monster strode to Larkspur's side and stroked her cheek, smiling cruelly. He ran a talonlike fingernail brutally under her eye, and Larkspur could see beads of blood appear, magnified by their proximity to her line of sight.

Eraw leaned in, so close that Larkspur could smell his breath, fresh as parsley, at odds with his rancid soul. Like a lizard capturing a cricket, his tongue flicked out and lapped the bloody beads into his mouth.

"What a delicious thief you are. What a delicious assassin."

With every scared fiber, Larkspur longed to flinch, to strike. She wanted to smash Eraw's hook nose into the back of his throat. But she couldn't move. The spell forbade her.

"My brother and I are different in many ways . . . as you shall see," Eraw said. "And while you scoffed at my work, I'll have you know that I've been very industrious."

Hording skulls instead of gold? Larkspur spat at him through her mind. *Was there some way to horde maidenheads collected in Greenhaven?*

"Such a cynical girl," Eraw chided. "While I admit to adoring gold as much as the next dragon, there is something I crave more: power. Each maiden who succumbed to my teeth and talons brought great dark energy to my chi. I want more."

What the—?

"See, my curious one, in my travels I obtained a book of great magic—dark enchantments. And it has instructed me as to the accumulation of power."

That explained his rogue behavior. Never had a dragon gone as renegade as this.

"And you've seen nothing yet. A few more maidens, a few more animals, and I shall become the most powerful wizard in the world."

Larkspur couldn't help her thoughts. Even as she knew she'd concede power to him, images of her sister tied to the gruesome stone altar flashed through her mind.

"And now I have my way to your fear." His yellow eyes crackled with glee. "See, the maiden—or animal—filled with terror contributes much more to my growing powers than does the calm one."

Ekal, Larkspur thought, helplessly. He had tried to warn her. So had Jasper. Why hadn't she listened to the words that might have saved her—and Phlox?

"My brother will not save you. Why would a dragon aid a human against another dragon?"

You have no idea what lies between him and me, she answered defiantly.

"But Larkspur, my dear, why would a dragon help a thief who'd just stolen the Jewel?"

To that, she had no answer. Eraw might be right.

Then foolish hope flooded through her. A sweet summer night more than ten years ago had seen the loss of her maidenhead. Perhaps she was of no use to Eraw.

"Don't be fooled by technicalities. I can smell you've lain with at least my brother, but I can still steal your sorrow-filled soul, with or without virginity. And after you've watched me rip the cunt from your beloved sister—Phlox?—you will be crazy with grief.

"Yours will be the soul that finally tips the balance. Your soul will make me the most powerful being in the land!"

_____

6

"You will follow me, now," Eraw commanded, and Larkspur's feet obeyed, although her mind screamed in objection.

Did Ekal, too, have the ability to compel? Had he simply not used it? Or was this a dark spell from Eraw's book?

"It is from the book, curious one. One of the first spells and one of the easiest. Of the hundreds of souls I have prepared, I needed only a mouse's soul to master this—the soul of a humble mouse. I use badger souls for some spells, and the souls of human virgins for others."

As graceful as a specter, the black dragon led her through the warren. He floated over the craggy granite floors. Like a dancer, his shoulder dodged the greasy-looking stalactites, his dark cloak billowing behind him.

Still, evil wafted in his wake.

The spell gave Larkspur just enough freedom to navigate the tunnels, to pulse hope through her heart. She could bob her head out of the way of the limestone icicles. Her feet followed his orders, but she could sidestep rocky outcrops.

Did that mean she could . . . ? But no. No matter how hard

she tried, she could not make her fingers reach the Jewel. She was his slave.

Glancing over his narrow shoulder, Eraw asked with a malicious grin, "Shall I have you torture your sister first, I wonder? That would most certainly add to your distress."

As the spell let her push against it to avoid banging her head on a rocky protrusion, Larkspur thought quickly. Perhaps she could grab her Jewel at the same time. Desperately she tried again to grasp it.

And again, she failed.

Tears of frustration dripped down her face, stinging her cheek when they reached the wound left by Eraw's fingernail. Larkspur was powerless to wipe them away.

More sweat beaded along her hairline, and she realized that the air had grown increasingly hot. Still a slave to her feet, she trailed the disgusting yellow glow of the monster ahead.

And the maze stunk, with more than the volcanic methane and sulfur she'd noted before. Now she detected rotting flesh. And . . . cooking meat?

"You shall see soon enough," he said in a tone that mocked in its reassurance. "But for now, shall we discuss methods for you to add to your sister's agony? You could blind her, for instance. Scalp her."

Images of her sister's cornflower eyes danced through her mind, her thick cinnamon hair. *Oh, goddess,* she prayed, *please help me.*

"And your mother? What of her? To lose both daughters. Surely that will cause her to grieve. Perhaps she herself will lose her desire to live. Will she lose her mind with sorrow? Pull out her hair? Cover herself in ashes, perhaps."

Larkspur all too easily envisioned the images Eraw painted for her. Anger expanded in her heart.

This monster, this abortion was ratcheting her passions with remarkable skill.

And that was the key. He *was* toying with her, trying to increase her emotional pain. By capitulating to despair, by increasing her desire to kill him, she increased his power.

Larkspur pushed her anguish into a deep recess of her mind. He might control her body, but she'd be damned if she let him have her mind.

"A courageous sentiment, my dear. I wish you well with it."

Abortion. Abortion. Abortion, she named him. She let the words reverberate through her mind.

"You are getting wearisome," Eraw said with an exaggerated sigh. "Perhaps this will give you something else to consider. It is just up ahead."

Eraw turned a tight corner, and Larkspur followed, forced to inhale his parsley-scented breath.

"Please note, to your left," Eraw pointed, billowing his long cape. "You'll see the source of the odor you noticed earlier. Unlike you, I find it quite pleasant—mouthwatering, in fact."

Larkspur noted a drying rack, natural flames flickering hungrily beneath it—reds, oranges, and yellows. Creatures were tied to the contraption, but at a distance from a fire.

Were the animals living, they'd be uncomfortably hot.

Each little creature had been slit from sternum to groin, and through the glittering shadows of the flames, Larkspur could see a glimmer of entrails. A muskrat's intestines were fully exposed. Maggots crawled in the warm, rotting flesh. Several mice and rats. A wolverine. A marmot. Defiled in death as they'd been noble in life.

"But Larkspur, my dear, they are not dead. Not yet."

With growing horror, she looked again at the creatures and saw what she'd failed to notice, avoided noticing. A fox's eyes flashed wildly. The muskrat's paws jittered and shook. A possum shifted its head, dripping saliva, which hissed in the flames.

Horror rocked her. Never in Larkspur's life had she seen—imagined—such brutality.

Ekal would never have had anything like this in his home. Larkspur remembered the tapestry in his bedroom. Ekal protected the weak. He didn't torture them. He couldn't.

Eraw hissed, sounding more reptilian than a true human could. "Ekal. Ekal. Ekal. My boring brother. Alwaysss brighter and more capable. Well, now we shall sssee, shan't we? Once I massster the final sspellsss, you shall sssee who iss more clever by far."

Apparently Larkspur had found the key to Eraw's private unhappiness. He was jealous of his brother.

Looking at the lank, greasy hair, Larkspur did not believe that this . . . thing . . . would ever match Ekal, not even in dragon form or human. No spell in the world could shape Eraw's black heart into one bearing the grace and dignity of Ekal's.

Eraw hissed again. "My brother is no match for me, especially now that you've deprived him of the only tool that might—might—have allowed him to dominate me."

Eraw turned, and patted the Jewel in Larkspur's bag with a terrible grin.

"But enough of my brother. Your sister, on the other hand. Your sister . . ." the man-shaped dragon suggested. "I believe she'd fit on the rack. Don't you think?"

Eraw shot her a questioning look, eyebrows raised in mock solicitation.

She would have thrown herself at him in a rage, if she could have.

With glittering eyes, Eraw continued, "And I could collect her tortured soul when I need to learn a particularly challenging spell, maybe after a year. Or two."

Larkspur drew in a ragged breath.

"That's what I do with these creatures, you know. I prepare them and then I harvest their souls."

Black repulsion filled her mind, and bile rose in her throat.

"Please, my dear, do not vomit."

Abortion. Abortion. Abortion.

"Perhaps I'll keep you until after I've mastered the final spells. Then I could oblige you to adore me the way you adore my odious brother."

Never, she spat in her mindvoice.

"My dear, 'never' is such a long time. I have so many tools available to me. With the ferret's soul I have, I could compel you to fellate me."

Larkspur let images of teeth and arterial blood flash through her mind. Detached penises and feral expressions.

"Now that's uncomely. With your sister's soul I could induce you to fellate me and love it."

Bleak despair filled her heart as she followed him through the stony corridors.

"Now Larkspur, my dearest, perhaps I am exhausting you with all of this talk. We are nearly to your chambers. I'm sure you will be quite comfortable. Ah, we've arrived."

With a graceful flourish, Eraw opened a door for her. "Please, after you."

Zombielike, Larkspur entered the room. She could imagine the Jewel's heat in her palm. She could imagine the short distance standing between the Jewel and freedom—and her sister.

It was the same distance as her doorstep from the moon.

"And you've done so much more than bring me your sister's doom," Eraw said with frightening warmth. "You've brought me my final tool. For when I gain my final spells, I shall use the Jewel of Dragonkind to rule the world as it has never been ruled before."

Larkspur forced calm into her mind, forced her breathing and heartbeat to slow.

"Ah, you have marvelous self-control, my dear. Causing that strength to crumble, to help you become a quivering worm at my feet, that will impel my power to the highest reaches."

In, Larkspur breathed. Out. In. Out. Do not give in.

"And you can rest here." Eraw gestured toward a granite wall. Manacles hung high and low. "Please, place yourself there."

Larkspur fought the command with all of her might. She imagined running toward the exit, running through the maze and into the late-summer afternoon.

To no avail.

"Now, now. You will rest easier if you simply obey."

Larkspur walked to the wall.

"Remove your clothing, please."

She did.

"Now, place your hands in the shackles. No need to lock them. My spell is stronger than any iron contraption—and imagine! All this power from a mere mouse! Think what I can do with the souls of other creatures."

Only a mouse. The phrase danced through her thoughts. She wouldn't need powerful magic to break through this. Perhaps a more humble approach would—She quickly squashed the idea, before the ghastly dragon could latch onto it.

"Larkspur dear, please look at the wall opposite."

A variety of instruments for striking and flogging, some with long lashes, others without, hung neatly. Eraw selected a particularly punishing-looking whip.

"The tip of this is made of finely honed steel. I'm told that when one is incised with this, one cannot feel it, sometimes not for full minutes after the cut. Perhaps I could cut off your breast and feed it to you before you realized it was missing."

Larkspur thought of the will of a mouse. Her mouse. She could envision each graceful whisker, each tapered toenail. She saw the mouse craftily avoiding a trap to get cheese.

Within the spell's confines, Larkspur gained control of her body. *Thu-thud. Thu-thud. Blood in. Blood out,* pumped her heart. Shadows of the mouse's life shifted into focus.

"Forget the mouse, my dear. Her soul is now mine. She cannot help you now."

In. Out. In. Out.

"And this." From its base, Eraw held up another crop. He pulled back and released the tip, which sprang sharply across and back. "I'm told that the merest flick from this can bruise down to the bone, although to be sure, I've never tried. Not yet."

The sickly glow that came from his skin reminded Larkspur of pus, putrid and yellow.

Mouse teeth were yellow. The mouse who had contributed to this depraved spell had been a momma. Eraw, in cat form, had caught her while she foraged for her nearly fledged babies. Her last thought before the dragon cat captured her soul was a fervent hope that her babies were strong enough to live without her. And that they were wise enough to leave the dragon's den.

Now, today, the momma mouse wanted the dragon's downfall. Even embroiled in Eraw's spell, she wanted those babies to live natural lives and come to natural ends. She'd do anything to prevent their souls from joining the dragon's wretched collection.

"I've always wondered what would happen if I let this crop bounce onto an eyeball." Eraw caressed her temple with the crop's bat. "I could try it on you. Your eye?"

Blood in. Blood out, Larkspur repeated.

"Ah! I could have you try it on your sister! Her . . . teeth? Her . . . clitoris?"

Blood in. Blood out.

"This one looks like a feather," his words intruded as he held up an implement for her to inspect. "But each—I don't know what you called these; tines, perhaps?—are barbed. They leave a serrated incision. I've tried this one, but not on a human. Not yet. The results were quite lovely."

Eraw ran the unbarbed end around Larkspur's bared breast.

Blood in. Blood out.

"Spread your legs, my dear."

Her controlled mind had no room for dread, even as she obeyed.

Blood in. Blood out. Mice had sharp teeth—sharp as knives. *Thu-thud.*

Thu-thud. Larkspur's internal focus was perfectly honed. Every beat of her heart was under precise control. Every chemical in her body—the adrenaline telling her to flee—was flawlessly monitored.

Mice had strong wills. Mice had sharp teeth. *Thu-thud.*

Eraw returned the serrated crop and selected a thick barbed rod. He ran it from her naked knee up to her thigh. Then he moved his body in right next to hers, pressed his thigh against her crotch. She could smell his parsley breath and feel the heat of his groin against her stomach.

"Larkspur," he said.

She knew that if she weren't absolutely centered right now, her blood would run cold.

Instead—*blood in. Blood out.*

"You're going to come when I shove this—"

She gave him no chance to finish.

Wham. Larkspur slammed her knee into his groin.

Eraw doubled over in pain, hoarsely shouting, "Stop! Freeze!" but to no avail. The spirit of the momma mouse was no longer in his control.

She was gone to wherever good mouse spirits go.

Larkspur smashed a rabbit punch into the side of his neck, sending him to the ground. Then she kicked his windpipe. Hard. She heard the ball of her foot solidly thump as his head whipped back.

He didn't move.

For good measure, she coiled her leg and kicked his nose with all of her might. In a normal man, shards of bone and hardened cartilage would have impaled his brain, killing him as dead as his virgins in Greenhaven.

But this was no normal man: this was a dragon. Larkspur knew her nemesis was not dead, that it was unlikely she could kill him. Not with her hands. Not with any of the terrible implements hanging on the wall.

With her eye on the prone figure, she dressed, quivering fingers fumbling with the buttons. *Flee*, her panicked brain said. And overwhelmed by terror, she did.

And she ran right into Ekal's broad chest, just as the Jewel of Dragonkind slid into her fingers.

7

Larkspur threw herself into his arms, absurdly glad for his solid breadth. *You're here!*

Thief, I couldn't let him hurt you.

You're here! she repeated, knowing her brush with terror made her slightly insane.

We've got only a little time. Come with me! he said, directing her toward the warren's exit.

But the Jewel! she said, hefting the weight of it in her palm as the clean scent of the cool evening air washed over them. *We can stop him! Lock him here for eternity!*

We cannot. We must leave. Eraw will wake at any moment. I can hear his mind squirming even now. Trust me, he suggested as he put his brawny arms around her.

And she did.

Ekal lightly linked his being with hers. Larkspur sensed if she resisted, even slightly, the link would break. But the clean quality of his soul delighted her, and her soul embraced his.

He provided a balm for all the horror wreaked by Eraw.

Connected to him, his joy at her presence imbued her.

Questions no longer remained, erased by certainty of his love for her.

Prepare yourself, he said as a strange tingling washed from her toes to her fingertips. *We will teleport.* His aura enveloped her, leaving her weightless. They became nothing—a breath of air, a wisp. For a moment, Larkspur and Ekal were everywhere. The heat of the rising sun, the tinkling of the brook, the smell of honey cakes baking in her mother's stone oven; Larkspur sensed all these for the briefest flutter.

And then her bones became solid once more.

Welcome back to my home, he said.

So that's what it's like to be nowhere, she marveled. *That's wonderful!*

You're wonderful, Ekal replied.

By the goddess, Ekal, you're in dragonform!

Yes, he said, curls of smoke spiraling from his aqua nostrils. *I am a dragon.*

But—but—

But what, Larkspur?

But you're gorgeous! Even more amazing than the doppelganger you have over your treasure.

The cobalt and turquoise shimmer of his scales outshone the hue in her memory, and now Larkspur noted rich indigo shadows where his thick legs met his torso. His scales twinkled like the spring raindrops as he breathed.

Ekal, Larkspur breathed, *your eyes . . .*

Tiny scales of the deepest indigo outlined his eyes, and his cerulean orbs swam with compassion and empathy, with kindness and might.

They're . . . stunning.

Thank you, thief. Why don't you climb onto my back?

His leathery scales were warm under her palms as she stepped onto him. She lay across his broad back, savoring the feeling of security and strength he gave her.

But Larkspur . . .

What is it?

I could have saved you from that, from Eraw's black soul. If I hadn't been prohibited by the Jewel, you would never have been in jeopardy.

That may be, but why didn't we stop him? she asked. *I knocked him cold. I could have compelled him to stay there for the rest of his life!*

The great aquamarine beast paused. Dragons were renowned for their affection for treasure. Was he missing the Jewel already? Did he long to feel it under his claw? Under his chin? "I would have given the Jewel back," she said. "You could have sat on it the rest of your life."

Thief, you misunderstand. I cannot let you even borrow it. He blinked, giving Larkspur a moment to appreciate the beautiful texture of the scales curling around his eye.

If she wanted to walk out of there with the bloodstone, she could, Larkspur knew. The thing had warmed and pulsed with power at her touch when she'd commanded Ekal in bed. Larkspur knew she could compel Ekal right here and now to obey her every command.

But she didn't want to do that.

Instead, she said, *Ekal, I don't want to belabor the obvious, but I don't think you can stop me.*

You need my help, thief of my heart. You cannot hold the Jewel in your hand, murmur Eraw's name, and expect him to fall at your feet.

But it worked that way with you.

I am not evil, and you are not evil. The Jewel works easily when the bearer and subject are of the same heart.

The elders' words came back to her. *That's what they meant, the elders. 'Hearts must be aligned.'*

Yes. For a human to compel a dragon with the Jewel of Dragonkind, they must be of the same heart.

I could become evil to save Phlox, she said, knowing the statement was false even as the words fell from her mind.

Larkspur, he said with sorrow in his tone. Compassion. *You cannot use the Jewel on Eraw, even if you take it from me again.*

No Jewel? Her sister, tattered and dead, other maidens whose fates would follow—these images made Larkspur want to cry. And the thought of Eraw ruling the world was a dark one, indeed.

But I will help you, nonetheless.

Hope leapt in her heart. *You can help me?*

We will use it together. I've been waiting for centuries to stop him, but I've been unable to do so alone.

I don't understand.

I've seen your true self, Larkspur. I've seen your loathing of suffering. You are unlike any dragon—except me. Our hearts are aligned, Thief, and they are aligned perfectly. I knew it the minute you stepped foot in my cave.

How can we save her?

Humans must be of like hearts to compel dragons with the Jewel, but dragons cannot use it against each other. Not alone.

So we can stop him? We can rid the world of him? Together?

We must. If we don't, Eraw's actions will first bring the wrath of people down upon all dragons. It's happened before. Arrows, assassins, weapon-bearing posses . . . After a dragon has gone rogue, this rains down upon us—all of us.

I won't let that happen. She thought of the elders. *I know people of influence.*

But that's not the only problem, is it? he asked. *Once he's hoarded power the way our kind amasses treasure, even I can't imagine the dark turn history will take.*

Larkspur thought of warriors hacking at Ekal's iridescent scales and said, *I've become fond of your skin.*

Which brings me to my price.

Price?

Be prepared to jump, please.

Ekal shimmered into man form. Larkspur landed on her feet.

"Larkspur." His voice did something physical to her. It seized hold of her as strongly as any wizard's spell, echoing with power, sounding as gritty and smooth as volcanic ash and gold dust. "Thief." The sound of his voice was a gift to her.

With the tip of his tongue he painted faint halos of saliva around Larkspur's mouth, licking the salt off her cheeks and turning her head to taste her earlobe.

Larkspur's head swam under the sorcery of his tongue. She became balmy with desire, yielding fully to the hands now touching her, the fingers fanning out over her breasts, slinking down to seek the throbbing presence of her sex.

With amazing strength, he tossed her on the bed. In the nest of crushed velvet, on her back, Larkspur opened her eyes to see his shadow standing over her, shedding his cloak, his shirt, his trousers. She turned onto her side and quickly removed her own clothing.

Ekal drew her legs up, and she planted her feet firmly on the bed, arms spread. Ekal put his hands on the inside of Larkspur's thighs and parted them until her knees were tilted at angles. He uncloaked her cunt, displayed her labia to the cool air, to his eyes.

"You look like a lustrous bloom in my dragonglow," he said to her.

Larkspur had no reply. She drew Ekal down into her arms, their mouths blending, tongues flowing in concert to music only they could hear.

Exhilaration coursed through her as his finger winnowed in the vestibule of her cunt, then forged deeper into the slippery channel. His thumb pressed into the resilience of her asshole.

They began to embrace and kiss like a possessed succubus and her willing victim, writhing about on the crushed velvet bed. Larkspur knew only motion, exquisite and flowing, that gradually became a mounting promise of orgasm. Both bodies merged and fused, sex to mouth, mouth to sex, both of them urging come from each other's sex.

Finally, her cunt exhausted, her lips and tongue strained, Larkspur opened her eyes and saw him adoring her with his eyes.

"The human form is a good one," he said.

"My love," she heard herself whisper into his ear. His fingers caressed her body, touching her throat, her breasts. His fingers rippled her taut nipples, trailed over her stomach and into the soft, dark hair above her sex. As Ekal stroked her arms, her legs, her lightly sweated hair, Larkspur drifted into somnolence. The flow of his delicate stroke, the whispered words she could almost hear in the depths of her mind and body, accompanied her. Finally, shadows gently enclosed her.

8

The power of Ekal's wings surged beneath her, and the wind whipped her hair. Ignoring watering eyes, Larkspur looked at the land below: Greenhaven, the cliffs, the waterfall and river, fields filled with long windrows of hay. Livestock and houses looked like toys.

From Ekal's perspective, Larkspur realized that her world seemed so small.

And yet Larkspur felt as strong as the mountains.

Together we are as strong as the mountains, Ekal said, eavesdropping on her thoughts. *Forces have finally come together to conquer the evil that's been growing for centuries.*

Larkspur thought of the animals who'd suffered so cruelly, the young women in her village who'd been sacrificed to Eraw's rapacious hunger. She thought of all the families who'd lost their livelihood to his devouring appetite, her sister's pain and the hole her death would leave in her heart. Once he consumed Greenhaven, neighboring Ysidra would be next. Town by town, the country would turn black.

Riding Ekal's broad back, the future suddenly seemed less bleak. Their aligned hearts could make things right.

Ekal, what will happen to Eraw when we bring out the Jewel?

You will see.

She almost believed she heard dread in his tone.

But he knows I have the Jewel. Maybe he'll be too afraid to come out today.

He is strong and knows no fear. Likely Eraw believes you compelled me to help you with the Jewel.

But I'd never . . . I didn't . . .

I know that, but he does not. He'll underestimate our strength.

Ekal banked steeply, and Larkspur craned to look over his cerulean shoulder. What she saw made her shudder. Phlox lay chained to the rock altar. Her arms were above her, and her legs were chained apart. She writhed. Spying the girl's flame-red hair, Larkspur's heart clenched. She doubted Phlox had even kissed a farm boy yet. Phlox was too young to die.

Larkspur scanned the sky. If left free, the monster lizard would fly in and rape the girl. He'd fly by again, eviscerating her, thereby gaining horrible power to cast dark spells.

Phlox would miss her indoctrination into the pleasing ways of womanhood by the trained priests in the temple. She'd miss the pleasure of rocking her children to sleep. Instead, she'd die naked in front of all who loved her, her intestines mangled, roasting in the hot sun, her torn and bloodied cunt exposed for all to see.

Get ready, Ekal said.

Should I—

Pull out the Jewel. He must obey the bearer.

Hardly needing to accommodate the beating wings of Ekal's smooth flight, Larkspur extracted the Jewel from the pocket in her bodice.

Listen carefully, thief of my heart. By now Eraw has dreadful power. His thoughts, even his words will be dangerous to you.

I'm listening. What do you want me to do?

Do you trust me? Even if you did not bear the Jewel, would you trust me?

Yes, she answered simply.

The words that can stop him must come from you, but I fear your will—by itself—is not strong enough to withstand him.

Sweat broke across her brow, despite the cold wind that cloaked them at that altitude.

What would you have me do?

Turn yourself over to me. Seek shelter in my mind. Let your mind—your will—become one with mine. Together we are strong enough to stop him.

Larkspur swallowed. *You can—you can do this?*

Yes. He paused for a moment before adding, *Can you?*

Larkspur looked across the achingly blue sky. Death didn't feel imminent.

But years of training taught her better. Tomorrow was never promised; the next heartbeat was never promised. She decided she trusted Ekal with her life.

Ekal? she asked. *I can do it.*

Yield to me.

I did that this morning, Larkspur said wistfully.

Think of that moment.

She thought of it: giving in to his hands, the instant when her brain switched from feeling his hand on her to being subject to his hands. She focused on that ethereal flash when no matter what he asked, she'd yield willingly, she'd crave to surrender.

Larkspur surrendered her will to Ekal, gave him her thoughts, her very being. *Yes,* she said, *I am yours.*

And then her world shimmered, shifted.

Good, Ekal hummed. *You're here.*

She was in his head, his body. Literally. She felt the play of his wings in the wind as if she had leathery sheets rather than hands and arms—no, she felt more like she had both arms and wings. Both Ekal's senses and hers registered in her brain.

Relax more, he said.

Larkspur breathed deeply as both the woman and the dragon. And then . . .

New emotions tumbled over her. A great desire to fuck her, to be fucked washed over her. An image of a green field next to a large placid lake flashed through her mind. Fat sheep grazed in the clover. Larkspur knew she'd never seen it herself.

She'd never wanted to eat a raw sheep either.

She felt a great urge to return to her lair, to guard her treasure. Through his heart, Larkspur hated the idea of leaving the gold and gems. She knew then how much he loved her hair, how he saw the long black tresses as the ultimate luxury—better than satin, better than velvet. An image of her own breast flashed through his mind, and she knew how much he wanted to bite it. Firmly. Only a little painfully.

She could feel him sifting through her thoughts, too. He chuckled at how her mouth watered when she inhaled his scent, how he smelled like pine to her.

And then she caught a new smell, a smell her human nose could not have detected.

Eraw comes, they said together.

Sunlight glittered sharply off the black dragon's scales. Larkspur needed to squint her human eyes. The grace of his wings reminded Larkspur of a huge black lion she'd once seen racing through the swamps with lethal precision. Eraw verged toward them, savage and eerily beautiful, like that big cat.

You've become a pussy, Eraw said to Ekal. Through her dragon ears, his voice sounded cracked and blistered, like riverbank mud pounded dry by fierce sunlight for weeks on end.

You always underestimated women, Ekal replied.

You've heard what I do to cunts.

Through her dragon eyes, Larkspur saw that not only were Eraw's scales black, a murky aura of light surrounded him even in the bright daylight. A vile pus-colored cloud edged him, evidencing his abilities to work dark magic.

You must change your ways, Eraw, Ekal and Larkspur said, needing to give him even a slim chance to reform.

You'll see what I do to the cunt the village offers, brother. Eraw spat a huge plume of fire at them and said, *Then you'll see what I do with you. And that cunt on your back.*

As they banked to keep the brunt of the blast from vulnerable human skin, she marveled at the power and agility of her dragon body. They feinted to the left, then plunged right, spewing a long fiery flame of their own.

The column hit Eraw straight on, but the pus-colored aura coalesced, interfered. None of the flame touched him. Eraw turned immediately toward the village, toward his waiting victim.

With this last cunt, the dark wisdom of ages will be mine! Eraw screamed as he folded his wings tightly against his body, barreling toward Phlox's prone form.

Through dragon ears, Larkspur heard villagers cry and shriek. She could even hear Jasper.

Oh, Phlox! Ekal, we must stop him now!

Stop! The next words came from Larkspur's mouth but from Ekal's will. *We have the Jewel of Dragonkind. You are commanded to cease your flight.*

Nooooo! Eraw shouted. Ekal and Larkspur felt the Jewel curl a mental hook into the mind of the black dragon.

Inside the bloodstone, the Jewel's red bas-relief began to glow against its green background while Ekal and Larkspur held it aloft. Souls were captured inside the Jewel of Dragonkind, dragonsouls! Between Larkspur and Ekal, their dragonsense ached for the very essence of dragonkind imprisoned within the Jewel.

I will not yield! Eraw howled defiantly.

You have no choice! Larkspur and Ekal commanded. *You must stop.*

The dragonsouls trapped in the Jewel greedily reached to Eraw, compelling him to obey their order. The hooks sunk deeper even as Eraw threw spell after spell toward the souls trapped in the Jewel.

Larkspur and Ekal continued to hold the Jewel aloft, even as it burned their human palm and fatigued the human arm. As the souls within the Jewel struggled with Eraw's soul, power pulsed from the bloodstone.

Human eyes looked away, unable to bear the intensity of the light.

Eraw threw a lightning-fast spell at the souls within the Jewel, rocking Larkspur and Ekal with his horrific power.

But the Jewel absorbed it, sunk their hooks more deeply into Eraw.

With a terrible screech that sent rocks tumbling down the adjacent mountainside, Eraw resisted. *Noo!* The air crackled as the black dragon marshaled his power for a resisting attack.

And fear assaulted Ekal and Larkspur. Did the accumulated knowledge within the Jewel exceed his dark learnings?

Eraw blasted his spell at the Jewel, which bucked in Ekal's human hand. Despite the raging heat blistering through the bloodstone, despite the fat blisters growing on his human palm, Ekal and Larkspur kept the Jewel of Dragonkind aloft.

For long seconds, the Jewel had no answer to Eraw's power. But then the trapped dragonsouls responded with a horrendous power of their own. As if on silky spider threads, invisible hooks flew out from the Jewel, wrapping thickly around Eraw's mind, the black coal of his heart.

His freedom was draining from him, adding to the power of the captured souls.

You will not win, Eraw shouted, exhaustion heavy in his voice. *You will not win everything!*

Through Ekal, Larkspur could sense Eraw's final efforts. Through a sheer force of will, he made the tiniest adjustments to his body. He may have been losing, but Larkspur felt his determination to wreak as much devastation and unhappiness as he could in his final breaths.

Eraw pinned his wings tightly against his body, and shot a long tendril of fire toward Phlox's feet. Eraw's mouth was open, ready. If he could gain access to her soul, he might yet dominate the Jewel of Dragonkind and make its strength his.

Larkspur and Ekal's dragonsense felt the final vile spell Eraw threw at the Jewel. All the suffering endured at Eraw's talons and teeth went into the spell. The horror of each sacrificed virgin, the suffering of each tortured animal—these gave him terrible strength.

The glow from the Jewel expanded with a final pulse in response. The Larkspur/Ekal amalgam sensed the Jewel would capture him or burst as the Jewel's sphere swelled toward Eraw's aura.

Eraw directed his sickly aura toward the Jewel's with a terrible shriek, a shriek ripped right into the brain of both dragon and woman.

But the Jewel's power only increased. Larkspur/Ekal registered the hundreds—perhaps thousands—of dragonsouls that had been captured by the bloodstone Jewel. Each one beckoned Eraw, demanded that he accompany them. More invisible hooks flew from the bloodstone.

Eraw shrieked again, causing another rockslide on the granite-covered mountain, but he was powerless to resist. He'd cast his last spell.

Finally.

The Jewel drained the aura from him, sucked it inside the bloodstone with the other dragon souls. Eraw's soul was forever captured within the Jewel of Dragonkind. The world was forever free of his wrath.

But Phlox was not.

This is for you, Larkspur! Eraw shrieked with his final breath.

Without his soul, Eraw's lifeless body sped mindlessly toward Phlox. His body shot in a deadly trajectory.

His torpedo body would hit Larkspur's sister in nine heartbeats. Eight.

We've got to block him! the human side of the pair cried, as villagers scattered. The dragon side responded. They had no time to roast the beast from the sky. Their two bodies were the only weapon they had.

You can stay with us, what was left of the individual Ekal offered. *I can do no less than love us.*

Become . . . one? the human part asked.

Yes, they answered.

As one, they thought of the beauty and strength of the human body riding on the dragon back, and they held that thought in their mind as they blasted toward Eraw's shell.

With grim determination Larkspur and Ekal pulled what remained of Larkspur's soul and mind into Ekal's consciousness heartbeats before impact.

When Larkspur and Ekal hit the black dragon's carcass with their own, Eraw's soulless corpse exploded into a cascade of ashy particles. Silvery sparks so bright they flashed in the clear sunshine danced where the monster had been, and the air crackled with energy. Through dragon eyes, Larkspur could see the ash land on the houses below.

But Larkspur's soulless body had all of her reflexes and instincts, honed by years of intense training as a thief.

When Larkspur and Ekal collided with Eraw, her human body catapulted from the dragon's back. Mindless fingers clutched for horns or wings and found air. Eyes spied the ground and huge granite boulders, spied haystacks, spied the fast-running river directly beneath.

When her body hit the deep blue water, it did so with exact precision, the perfect swan dive. Larkspur saw it with her dragon eyes, with Ekal's eyes.

Thief of my heart, she heard in her head. *Wake up. Please.* Did he sound worried?

She coughed and sputtered as Jasper unceremoniously dragged her onto shore. "Goddess puke, sister," he said. "You weigh as much as your stubborn mare."

Only then did the thief realize that she and Elak were no longer united in one body. Her body must have survived the crash.

Was that relief washing through her, or dismay?

Where are you? she asked her dragon.

At the sound of her mindvoice, Ekal's overwhelming happiness poured through his veins. Larkspur realized—he loved her! She could do no less. Larkspur let him bathe in her love for him.

I'm with your mother and sister at your home, he replied. *Are you unharmed?*

"I'm fine," she said to both Jasper and Ekal. "And I am not that heavy, Jasper. I'm just wet."

Wet? the dragon asked. She could practically see the wicked grin on his face.

"Okay, my petite sister," Jasper teased. "Can you walk then?"

Larkspur rose on wobbly legs, lake water sluicing down her face, and nodded. "Let's go home."

Her mother met her at the door with dry clothes and a big towel. Seeing her chattering teeth, her mother said, "There's a big pot of tea sitting on the stove. Let me pour some for you." She pushed her daughter down the hall toward the kitchen.

"Ekal?" Larkspur asked through blue lips.

"He's filling up the kitchen with those broad shoulders," her mother said with a wink.

Entering the room, warm with the scent of tea and cooking, Larkspur saw her mother's point. Her dragon dwarfed the pine chairs and took up all the space that two men would use.

He stood when she came in and wrapped his arms around her. *Thief*, he said for her mind only. *I thought I lost all of you—your soul and your body.*

I am here. How could I die knowing you were there for me?

"Let her sit," her mother chided, apparently unworried by the hulking dragonman in her kitchen. She attacked her daughter's long, dark hair with the towel and a brush.

Her sister sat rubbing her chafed and bloodied wrists. Seeing Phlox so pale and weak wrenched Larkspur's heart. "So," she said to Phlox, "Do I still owe you for that green velvet gown my dog ate last season, or can we call it even?"

"You still owe me for the shoes," Phlox said.

The thief smiled and relaxed, bathed in the love of her family. And her dragon.

"That dive was amazing, sister," Phlox said.

"All those summers at the lake were good for something. Who would have guessed that a swan dive would save my life?"

Her mother placed a plate of honey cakes in the table's center. The cakes were warm from the stone oven, and the sweet fragrance hung in the air.

Grabbing the top cake, Jasper said, "It wasn't a swan dive, sister. You became a dragon."

"Became . . . a dragon?"

"We all saw it," agreed Phlox, her voice still shaky. "You had wings and everything."

Larkspur looked at Ekal in his gorgeous human form and said, "Anything is possible, isn't it."

Ekal, she urged, *faster*. The wind whipped through her hair. Her heart felt hugely expectant, absurdly happy. Clasping the dragon with her thighs, she held out her arms to embrace the wind, the sunshine, all of life's possibilities. Larkspur knew she was grinning like a lunatic.

Ekal.

Yes, thief of my heart.

This is wonderful—you are wonderful. She ran her hand down his iridescent neck, admiring its cobalt luster.

Your soul is wonderful. So is your cunt, he replied.

Uncouth thing, she chuckled. *You better not talk that way to the women in town or in court.*

Why not? he asked. *It works so well with you.*

She heard teasing in his tone.

Watch yourself, dragon. Crude charm doesn't always work. Oh no?

Could a dragon be arch, she wondered.

I'm going to tie you to that bed and spread your legs and run my hands and tongue over your neck and breasts and thighs and nipples. And only when you're begging me to fuck you will I touch your cunt and then I'm going to—

The river between her thighs threatened to drown her. *Ekal,* she groaned. *Stop.*

I can smell you. You want me.

I do, Larkspur replied.

You can have me. I can have you.

What are you talking about, my winged friend?

I can fly and fuck.

I'm pretty sure that that feature never made it into the legends of dragons.

Take off your pants.

But—

Now. He dipped threateningly.

At his mercy, she obeyed. He soared for a moment, steady and true, giving her an opportunity to remove the offending article. *Okay, dragon. Now what?*

See that nub right in front of you?

It's awfully big to be called a "nub."
You know what to do with it.
But—
Yes?
But what's it feel like for you? I may be a thief and occasionally an assassin, but I'm not selfish.
Ah, the human sense of empathy is something we dragons could learn from.

Larkspur slid her palm over the so-called nub, which was actually more than her hand-length in size and nearly as thick as her wrist. Unlike the rest of his leathery skin, this was smooth and pliant. With its blunt end, it looked—and felt—a lot like a penis, albeit a large, blue one.

Mhhm, Ekal hummed. *Don't stop. Please.*

She grinned, rubbing her clit against it. *I think I might like this.*

Ekal responded with a moment of freefall.

Larkspur put her arms behind her to brace herself. She rubbed harder. *Do dragons do this to each other, Ekal? Can a dragoness do this to you?* Larkspur moved, pushing the dragon inside her—deep inside her. Vast and lush, her cunt welcomed him like a member of her own species.

For a second, Ekal dropped like a rock, and Larkspur laughed, rocking against him with the rhythm of his beating wings. *Are you sure you can fuck and fly, big guy?*

Ekal snorted and climbed back up to his preferred altitude.

Can you fly a little faster? Please? Larkspur could hear panting in her urgent request, and when he accommodated her with a choppy beat of his wings, she came almost immediately.

By the goddess, Ekal, you make me feel like the luckiest thief in the world.

Walk on the wild side with WOLF TALES II,
a sizzling new paranormal from Kate Douglas.
Available now from Aphrodisia . . .

The hand cupping Tia's breast was warm and rough, both palm and fingertips callused. Her nipple rose to a painful, unbelievably sensitive peak, pinched between a blunt thumb and forefinger. Her vagina actually pulsed with each beat of her heart as a moist tongue followed a line from her breastbone to her navel, then dipped inside and swirled. She shivered, caught in that sensual state between sleep and wakefulness, her arousal growing with each gentle caress.

Lapping slowly, surely, the long, slick, and very mobile tongue now swept the crease of her buttocks then delved between her sensitive labia and licked deeply into her pussy. She caught back a cry as the fiery trail swept upward, barely teasing at her clit before sliding once more across her lower belly.

Spreading her legs even wider, slipping lower in her seat, she raised one eyelid to get a better view of her lover.

Time stood still—painfully, irrevocably still.

A wolf stared back at her, amber eyes glowing, tongue still lapping slowly at her belly, his ivory canines curved like sharpened sabers. He looked up and slowly licked his muzzle, wrapping that long, rough tongue almost all the way around.

The scream caught in her throat.

A soothing voice clicked into Tia's consciousness and shattered the image crouched between her knees.

"We've started our descent into San Francisco International Airport and are currently flying at 27,500 feet. If you're on the left side of the plane you should be able to look out your window and see Half Dome in Yosemite, sticking up like a . . ."

Tia gasped. Her lungs pumped like a bellows and her skin flushed from hot to cold. She blinked rapidly, noted that the older man next to her still snored, blissfully asleep. Quickly scooting back in her seat, Tia sat upright and smoothed her wrinkled denim skirt. Her breath escaped in a long sigh. For extra measure, she fastened her seat belt, pulled it firmly across her middle, and prayed the moisture between her legs hadn't soaked through the denim.

Damn the dreams. Until last week, she hadn't had any this explicit in almost three months. Why now? Tia glanced once more at the man sleeping next to her and flushed, her skin once again going hot and cold all over. What if he'd awakened? What if someone had seen her, sprawled out, legs spread wide, lips parted, and breasts heaving?

She cupped her forehead in the palm of her hand and shuddered. Damn, this had better be the right choice, this move back to San Francisco. Somehow she needed to understand the dreams, the explicit, sensual dreams that had finally broken the link between her and Shannon, Tia's dearest friend in the world.

Her friend and her lover. She'd been with Shannon for ten years, ever since they were teenagers heading off to boarding school together, their hormones in high gear and their need for one another overwhelming. It had been so good then, so perfect, both emotionally and physically.

Tia sighed. She missed the intensity of their teenage affair, the forbidden nature of love with another female, the heart-stopping, lung-bursting climaxes they'd managed to wring out of one another. So good at first. So fulfilling, for a time, at least; then slowly, surely, Tia had acknowledged something important was missing.

So had Shannon. The last five years their relationship had merely been a safety net for both of them. A safety net held together by friendship and, only rarely, sexual love.

Even Shannon admitted to occasional sex with a man, something Tia enjoyed as well, but it had never been enough. Not with one man, not even with multiple partners. The sense of something else, something more powerful, more sensual, lured her out of every relationship, away from any commitment.

Away from Shannon.

The dreams hadn't helped. Explicit, arousing, forbidden dreams. Always the wolf, amber eyes glowing, teeth sharp and glistening, the rough, mobile tongue lapping, licking . . . Tia blinked away the image and scrubbed at her wrists and forearms. Why, when she remembered the dreams, did her skin crawl? She hated it, the itchy, agitating sense of something just beneath the surface. Sometimes she wondered if she were losing her mind, descending into some unexplainable madness.

The plane jerked a bit as it descended. The FASTEN SEAT BELT sign blinked overhead. An attendant leaned close, awakened the man sleeping next to Tia, and asked him to fasten his belt. She smiled at Tia and moved on to the next sleeping passenger.

Tia shook off the strange sensations, and her thoughts returned to Shannon. If her father had only known how close the girls were when they'd asked to go away to boarding school together, he might have forbidden it. Obviously, he didn't have a clue. In fact, the poor man had been so relieved when Tia left, it was almost embarrassing.

It couldn't have been easy for him, raising a daughter without her mother there for guidance. Coping with hormones and emotions completely foreign to him, not to mention the issues that occasionally arose because of her biracial status. Maybe Tia and Shannon wouldn't have become lovers if they'd had mothers, but Shannon's mom had died of cancer when Shannon was only five. That shared loss had drawn the girls together.

Tia's mother had been murdered. To this day she didn't know all the details, only that her father had never even talked of remarrying. He'd loved her mother beyond all women.

He'd loved Tia as if she were a princess, put her on a pedestal. *More like a perch,* she thought, *locked securely in a gilded cage.* Rationally, she knew he'd wanted to protect her, but he'd merely driven Tia away.

What would it be like now, to live in the same city, to see her father whenever she wanted, to finally learn more about his life? She'd have a chance, maybe, to learn the details of her mother's murder. More important, she'd have the freedom her adult status now gave her to search for answers.

Tia sighed. She wished she remembered her mother more clearly, but the image she carried of Camille's smile was the face in the snapshots, the pictures both Tia and her father treasured.

Ulrich had always had presence, as far as Tia was concerned. She wondered how he did now that he was partially retired. From his letters and calls and their infrequent visits, Tia knew he was still active and involved, busy with his detective agency. He'd always had a lot of friends.

Lucien Stone's image popped into Tia's mind. *Luc.* She hadn't seen him since the summer before she and Shannon went off to Briarwood, but he and her father had always been close. He was probably married by now with a couple of kids, but he'd filled her fantasies for years. When Shannon made love to her, it was Luc's mouth tasting, licking, driving her over the edge. When Shannon had used a vibrator or dildo between Tia's legs, Tia had been filled by Luc.

She stared out the window, watching the multicolored squares in San Francisco Bay as they glided down over the salt beds, and tried to picture Lucien Stone with ten years added to his stern yet boyish good looks.

By the time the plane landed and Tia unbuckled her seat belt, she had an image in her mind of a potbellied, middle-age man with thinning hair.

When she reached for her carry-on luggage in the overhead rack, Tia added bad teeth and an earring. She was grinning as she walked down the enclosed ramp to the gate, the image of an older Lucien Stone taking on cartoon properties in her over-active imagination.

She was still smiling when she arrived at the luggage carousel. Her father waited there, just as overwhelming and handsome as when she'd last seen him, his skin ruddy from wind and sun, his hair a thick shock of white badly in need of a trim. Ulrich pulled her into a hug, his big arms and broad chest erasing every mis-giving Tia had felt about coming home.

He smelled just the same as always, a combination of Dial soap and Colgate shaving cream. Tia took deep breaths, just to absorb his beloved scent.

"Sweetie, you are absolutely gorgeous."

Her father stood back for a better look, his big hands clasped tightly to her shoulders. "I've missed you. I'm glad you're home."

Tia's eyes filled with tears. She wanted nothing more than to throw herself back into her father's arms and tell him how lonely she'd been, how much she'd wanted to come home. How terri-bly glad she was to be back. "It's good to be here, Daddy."

"Was the trip okay?" He reached for the bag she grabbed off the carousel, set it on the floor, and then snatched another she pointed to.

"Yeah. Just long. I . . ." No. It couldn't be. Not Luc? A chill raced along her spine, a sense of awareness that left her weak-kneed and shivering.

"Hello, Tia."

"Luc? Good lord! I haven't seen you since . . ."

"Since you were a skinny little sixteen-year-old with braces on your teeth." Smiling, Luc stepped forward and drew her into a friendly, brotherly hug.

At least, Tia assumed it was meant to be brotherly. Where her father's hug had been home and comfort, Luc's was bed and beyond. His big hands stroked her spine, the briefest of contacts that left her feeling naked and wanting. His lips brushed her cheek and she fought the urge to lean closer for more. She breathed deeply of his scent. He was spice and fresh air, deep woods and dark rivers . . . intoxicating and addictive.

When he released her—was it only seconds later?—Tia clamped her jaws together to keep her teeth from chattering. "Luc, you look . . . you haven't . . ." Her voice drifted off and she realized she was staring at him.

He grinned, obviously aware of her discomfort. His teeth were perfectly straight and very white. His nose wasn't nearly as straight, but the bump on the bridge where he'd probably broken it at some time during the past ten years only made him look stronger, more masculine.

Tia blinked. The dream she'd had earlier on the plane materialized in all its sensual detail. Damn, Lucien Stone looked exactly like that hungry wolf with his deep-set amber eyes and feral grin. It was much too easy to picture him kneeling between her thighs, his tongue lapping away at her cream.

Tia gulped, no ladylike swallow at all, but Luc ignored her *faux pas* and instead reached past her to pick up the last two of her large bags off the carousel. He slung one over his shoulder and gripped the other easily in his left hand, then grabbed the two smaller ones in his right. Ulrich took Tia's carry-on bag from her and led the way to the parking garage.

Tia followed quietly, her inner thighs sliding moistly, one against the other, with each step. The two men were discussing something, but the words merely sailed past her without sense. Awareness of Luc screamed a steady beat inside her brain, echoed in the rhythmic clenching between her legs. Her chest felt tight and her skin itchy and she'd never been this aware of another human being in her life.

Tia didn't think to question how Luc had identified her mismatched set of bags out of all the others on the luggage carousel until he shoved them into the trunk and shut the lid.

Somehow he'd found them without her help. But how? Tia turned to ask, but Luc opened the door and gestured with his hand. She smiled as he seated her in the front. Ulrich stepped back on the curb when Luc moved around to the driver's side and climbed into the Mercedes.

Frowning, Tia lowered the window. "Dad? Aren't you coming with us?"

Ulrich smiled, leaned close, and kissed Tia's cheek. "I've got a meeting in Burlingame so I'll catch a cab. Luc will get you settled, then I want him to bring you over for dinner this evening. Is that okay with you?"

Tia nodded, blinking nervously. Like she had a choice? Why did this feel planned, as though the two men followed a script? She glanced once more at her father and realized he was looking steadily at Luc. If she didn't know better, Tia would have thought Ulrich and Luc communicated without speaking. She turned to Luc, noticed his slight nod, and when she looked back at her father it was to see his broad shoulders and back as he walked purposefully out of the parking garage without another word.

And here's an advance look at at Jami Alden's
DELICIOUS,
coming soon from Aphrodisia . . .

Suddenly a large, proprietary hand slid around Kit's hip to flatten across her stomach. She didn't even have to turn around to know it was Jake. Even in the crowded dance club, she could pick up his scent, soapy clean with a hint of his own special musk. Without a word he pulled her back against him. The rigid length of his erection grinding rhythmically against her ass let her know her dance floor antics had been effective.

What she hadn't counted on was her own swift response. Sure, he'd gotten the best of her in the wine cellar, but she'd written it off as a result of not having had sex since her last "friend with benefits" had done the unthinkable and actually wanted an exclusive relationship. She'd had to cut all ties and hadn't found a suitable replacement in the last six months.

Tonight, she'd only meant to tease and torment Jake, give him a taste of what he wanted but couldn't have. Now she wasn't so sure he'd be able to stick with that game plan. The memory of her gut wrenching orgasm pulsed through her, her nerve endings dancing along her skin with no more than his hand caressing her stomach and his cock grinding against her rear. His broad palm slid up until his long fingers brushed the undersides of her breasts, barely covered by the thin silk of her top.

She was vaguely aware of Sabrina raising a knowing eyebrow as she moved over to dance with one of the other groomsmen.

Without thinking she raised one arm, hooking it around his neck as she pressed back against the hard wall of his chest. Hot breath caressed her neck before his teeth latched gently on her earlobe. The throbbing beat of the music echoed between her legs, and she knew she wouldn't be able to hold him off, not when he was so good at noticing and exploiting her weakness.

"Let's go," he whispered gruffly, taking her hand and tugging her towards the edge of the floor.

She wasn't *that* easy. "What makes you thing I want to go anywhere with you?" she replied, breaking his hold and shimmying away.

A mocking smile curved his full, sensuous mouth. "Wasn't that what your little show was all about? Driving me crazy until I take you home and prove to you exactly how good it could be between us?" To emphasize his point, he shoved his thigh between hers until the firm muscles pressed deliciously against her already wet sex. "What happened earlier was just a taste, Kit. Don't lie and tell me you don't want the whole feast."

She moaned as his mouth pressed hot and wet against her throat, wishing she had it in her to be a vindictive tease and leave him unsatisfied, aching for her body.

But her body wouldn't let her play games, and she was too smart to pass up an opportunity for what she instinctively knew would be the best sex of her life. Jake was right. She wanted him. Wanted to feel his hands and mouth all over her bare skin. Wanted to see if his cock was as long and thick and hard as she remembered. Wanted to see if he'd finally learned how to use it.

And why not? She was practical, modern woman who believed in casual sex as long as her pleasure was assured and no strings were attached. What could be more string free than a hot vacation fling with a guy who lived on the opposite side of the country? And this time she'd have the satisfaction of leaving *him* without so much as a goodbye.

Decision made, she grabbed his hand and led him towards the door. "Let's hope you haven't oversold yourself, cowboy."

"Baby, I'm gonna give you the ride of your life."

Outside, downtown Cabo San Lucas rang with the sounds of traffic and boisterous tourists. Jake hustled her into a taxi van's back row and in rapid Spanish he gave the driver the villa's address and negotiated a rate.

Hidden by several rows of seats, Kit had no modesty when he pulled her into his arms, capturing her mouth in a rough, lusty kiss. Opening wide, she sucked him hard, sliding her tongue against his, exploring the hot moist recesses of his mouth. Her breath tightened in quick pants as he tugged her blouse aside and settled a hand over her bare breast, kneading, plumping the soft flesh before grazing his thumb over the rock hard tip.

Muffled sounds of pleasure stuck in her throat. She couldn't ever remember being so aroused, dying to feel his naked skin against her own, wanting to absorb every hard inch of him inside her. She unbuttoned his shirt with shaky hands, exploring the rippling muscles of his chest and abs. He was leaner now than he'd been at twenty-two, not as bulked up as he'd been when he played football for the UCLA. The sprinkling of dark hair had grown thicker as well, teasing and tickling her fingers, reminding her that the muscles that shifted and bulged under her hands belonged to a man, not a boy.

Speaking of which . . .

She nipped at his bottom lip and slid her hand lower, over his fly until her palm pressed flat against a rock hard column of flesh. The taxi took a sharp curve, sending them sliding across the bench seat until Kit lay halfway across Jake's chest. He took the opportunity to reach under her skirt and cup the bare cheeks of her ass, while she seized the chance to unzip his fly and reach greedily inside the waistband of his boxers.

Hot pulsing flesh filled her hand to overflowing. Her fingers closed around him, measuring him from root to tip and they exchanged soft groans in each others mouths. He was huge, long and so thick her fingers barely closed around him. It had hurt like a beast when he'd taken her virginity. But now she couldn't wait to feel his enormous cock sliding inside her stretching her walls, driving harder and deeper than any man ever had.

She traced her thumb over the ripe head, spreading the slippery beads of moisture forming at the tip. Her own sex wept in response. Unable to control herself, she reached down and pulled up her skirt, climbing fully onto his lap. She couldn't wait, her pussy aching for his invasion. God this was going to be good.

If anyone had told her twelve years ago that someday she'd be having sex with Jake Donovan in a Mexican taxicab, she would have called that person insane.

Pulling her thong aside, she slid herself over him, teasing his cock with the hot kiss of her body, letting the bulbous head slip and slide along her drenched slit. She eased over him until she held the very tip of him inside . . .

The taxi jerked abruptly to a stop, and Kit dazedly realized they'd reached the villa. With quick, efficient motions Jake straightened her skirt and shifted her off him, then gingerly tucked his mammoth erection back into his pants. With one last, hard kiss he helped her down from the van and paid the driver as though he hadn't been millimeters away from ramming nine thick inches into her pussy in the back of the man's cab.

Kit waited impatiently by the door, pretending not to see the driver's leer. Like they were the first couple to engage in hot and heavy foreplay. Jake strode over, pinning her against the door as he reached for the knob and turned.

And turned again. He swore softly.

"What is it?" Kit was busy licking and nibbling her way down the strip of flesh exposed by Jake's still unbuttoned shirt. He tasted insanely good, salty and warm.

"I don't suppose you have a key?"

She groaned and leaned her head back against the door. "I didn't take one." There were only four keys to the villa, and when they went out they all made sure they had designated male and female keyholders. Unfortunately tonight, Kit wasn't one of them, and apparently, neither was Jake. "What time does the housekeeper leave?"

Jake looked at his watch. "Two hours ago."

He bent over and picked up the welcome mat, then inspected all the potted plants placed around the entry for a hidden key. Watching the way his ass muscles flexed against the soft khaki fabric of his slacks, Kit knew she was mere seconds away from pushing him down and having him right here on the slate tiled patio.

He straightened, running a frustrated hand through his thick dark hair. Eyes glittering with frustrated lust, he muttered, "There has to be a way in here."

"Through the back," Kit said. All they had to do was scale the wall that surrounded the villa. The house had several sets of sliding glass doors leading out to the huge patio and pool area. One of them was bound to be unlocked.

With a little grunting and shoving, Jake managed to boost Kit over the six-foot wall before hoisting himself over. Holding hands and giggling like idiots, they ran across the patio. But Jake stopped her before she reached the first set of doors.

"Doesn't that look inviting?"

She turned to find him looking at the pool. Wisps of steam rose in curly tendrils off the surface. The patio lights were off, the only illumination generated from the nearly full moon bouncing its silver light off the dark water. A smile curved her mouth and renewed heat pulsed low in her belly. "I could get into a little water play."

He pulled her to the side of the pool and quickly stripped off her top. Kit arched her back and moaned up to the sky as he paused to suck each nipple as it peaked in the cool night air. Her legs trembled at the hot, wet pull of his lips, her vagina fluttering and contracting as it arched for more direct attention.

His hands settled at the snap of her skirt. "I like this thing," he said as he slid the zipper inch by agonizing inch. "Kinda reminds me of those sexy little shorts you wore that first time—"

Her whole body tensed. She didn't want to think of that night right now, didn't want to think about the last time she let uncontrollable desire get the best of her. Her fingers pressed against his lips. "I'd rather not revisit unpleasant memories."

She caught the quick hint of a frown across his features but he hid it quickly as he slid her skirt and thong off, leaving them to pool around her feet.

"In that case," he said as his shirt slid off his massive shoulders, "I better get down on creating some new ones."

Damn, the woman knew how to hold a grudge. But the sting Jake felt at Kit's reminder of just how unpleasant she found the memories of their first time quickly faded at the sight of her in the moonlight, fully nude except for her stiletto-heeled sandals.

With her long legs and soft curves, sex radiated from her pores like a perfume, sending pulses of electricity straight to his groin. His cock was so hard he actually hurt.

In the clear moonlight he could make out the sculpted lines of her cheekbones, the dark sweep of lashes over her blue eyes, the full curve of her lips. Her dark hair swung forward over her shoulders, playing peekaboo with the tight, dark nipples.

His hands followed his gaze, tracing the taut, smooth plane

of her abdomen, coming to rest just above what he'd felt before but hadn't seen. Her pubic hair was a dark, neatly trimmed patch over plump, smooth lips. Her breath caught as he combed his fingertips through the silky tuft of hair, inching his way down but not touching the hot silky flesh that lay below.

He was afraid if he touched her he wouldn't be able to stop himself from pushing her onto a nearby lounge chair and shoving his cock as hard and high in her as he could possibly go. His hands trembled at the remembered feel of her soft pussy lips closing over him, stretching over the broad head of his penis as she straddled him in the cab. If the driver hadn't stopped, he knew he would have lost control, would have fucked her hard and fast until he exploded inside her, ruining his chances of proving he'd learned anything about self control in the past ten years.

So instead of dipping his fingers into the juicy folds of her sex, he knelt in front of her and removed her lethal looking sandals before shedding his slacks and underwear. Taking her hand, he led her into the pool.

He pulled her against him until her breasts nuzzled his chest like warm little peaches, reveling in the sensation of cool water and warm skin. He kissed her, tongue plunging rough and deep, just the way he wanted to drive inside her. He couldn't believe after all these years he was here with her again, touching her, tasting her. She tasted so good, like vodka and sin, her wet mouth open and eager under his. One taste and he regressed back to that horny twenty-two year old, shaking with lust and overwhelmed by the reality of touching the woman who had fueled his most carnal fantasies.

Greedily his hands roamed her skin, fingers sinking into giving flesh as he kneaded and caressed. He wished he had a lifetime to spend exploring every sweet inch of her. Kit gave as good as she got, her hands sliding cool and wet down his back, legs floating up to wrap around his waist. He threw his head

244 / *Jami Alden*

back, clenching his jaw hard enough to crack a molar. Hot, slick flesh teased the length of his cock, plump lips spreading to cradle him as she rocked her hips and groaned. He backed her up against the smooth tiles that lined the sides of the pool. One thrust, and he could be inside her.

"No," he panted, "Not yet."

Water closed over his head as he sank to his knees, drowning out everything but the taste and feel of her. Eyes closed, he spread her pussy lips with his thumbs, nuzzling between her legs until he felt the tense bud of her clit against his face. Cool water and hot flesh filled his mouth as he pulled her clit between his lips, sucking and flicking until her hips twitched and he heard the muffled sounds of her moans distorted by the water. A loud buzz hummed in his ears, and occurred to him that he might pass out soon from lack of air.

Surfacing, he sucked in a deep breath and lifted her hips onto the tiled ledge. She drew her knees up, rested her heels on the edge to give him unimpeded access to her perfect pink cunt. He parted the smooth lips with his thumbs, lapped roughly at the hard knot of flesh, circling it with his tongue, sucking it hard between his lips as her pelvis rocked and bucked against his face. Every sigh, every moan, every guttural purr she uttered made his dick throb until he was so hard he feared he might burst out of his skin.

"Oh, God, oh, Jake," she moaned. Another rush of liquid heat bathed his tongue and he knew she was close. The first faint flutters of her orgasm gripped his fingers as he slid inside, clamping down harder as the full force of climax hit her.

Kit stared up at the bright night sky as the last pulses shuddered through her. Taking several deep, fortifying breaths she risked a look at Jake. His dark head was still between her thighs as he rained soft, soothing kisses on the smooth inner curves. Tender kisses. Loving kisses, even.

Oh, Christ, she might be in really big trouble.

She could never remember responding to a lover like she did to Jake. Then again, she'd never had a lover treat her like Jake did, either.

Her last partner was exactly the type she liked. She told him what she wanted and he listened, bringing her efficiently to satisfaction before finding his own.

But he hadn't looked at her like she was the most beautiful woman he'd ever seen. He hadn't run his hands over her skin like he wanted to memorize every inch of her. He hadn't buried his head between her legs and licked and savored her pussy like it was the most succulent, exquisite fruit he'd ever tasted.

And he sure as hell had never made her come so hard that her vision blurred and her body felt like it was wracked by thousands of tiny electrical currents.

She heard the sound of water splashing, and her stomach muscles jerked as Jake held his dripping body over hers. Bracing himself with his hands, he came down over her and kissed her with the tenderness that almost made her want to cry.

Crap. What was wrong with her? This was Jake, the man who'd so rudely introduced her to the world of slam bam thank you ma'am. To give him credit he'd prove—twice now—that he could make her come. Really, really hard. But still. It was just an orgasm.

The smartest move would be to get up and leave before she fell victim to this weird hormonal anomaly. But her brain had ceded all control to the area between her legs that still throbbed and ached to feel all of Jake buried deep inside her.

And to think men got a bad rap for being controlled by their dicks.

She draped a lazy hand around his neck and slid her fingers into the wet silk of his hair. Then he was gone, water splashing as he levered himself out of the pool. She could barely summon the energy to turn her head to watch him dig around the pockets of his pants.

Moonlight cast silvery shadows on the muscles of his back and shoulders, illuminating the drops of water cascading down his long strong legs. A renewed jolt of energy rushed through her as he turned, his cock jutting out in stark relief. Though she couldn't see his eyes, she could feel him watching her as he rolled on a condom with slow deliberation. Stroking himself, reminding her that in a few moments the whole of that outrageously hard length would be buried deep inside her.

She rolled to her knees as he walked toward her, reaching for him as he got close. He brushed her hands away, slipping back into the water and pulling her in with him. The cool tile was hard on her back as he pulled her close for a rough kiss. He lifted her leg over his hip, burrowing the tip of his erection against her. "I can't be gentle," he murmured. "I've waited too many years to have you again."

Waited years? What did he mean by –

The thought was abruptly cut off by the sudden, swift presence of him shoving inside her. Even though she was wetter, readier, than she'd ever been, the sheer size of him caught her off guard. Stretching tight slick flesh, pressing deep, and just when she thought she couldn't take any more he drove in another inch.

Her mouth opened wide on a silent scream of pleasured pain, her startled gasps swallowed by his mouth as he pumped inside her with his cock and his tongue. Towering over her by several inches, he surrounded her, dominated her. She'd never felt so invaded, so claimed. She wasn't sure she liked it. But her body did.

She felt herself easing, softening around him, relaxing to take him deep with every surge of his hips. "Oh Kit," he groaned, the helpless note in his voice perfectly matching the way she felt. Suddenly he pulled out, ignoring her embarrassing wail of protest as he spun her around to face the edge of the pool.

Gripping her hips so hard it should have hurt, he thrust in from behind, whispering all the while how beautiful she was, how hot and tight her pussy felt around him. Whispers that faded into groans as his hands reached around to cup her breasts, pinching her nipples hard enough to make her yell as she pulsed and clenched around him. His hips pumped faster now, short shallow strokes interspersed with long deep plunges as he gasped and heaved behind her.

Bracing her hands on the tile wall, Kit pushed against him, working herself on his swollen shaft, pushing him so deep she felt him at the base of her spine. Her climax hovered around the edges of every stroke, knotting and tightening low in her belly. Suddenly he stiffened behind, a low roar bellowing from his chest as he jerked heavily inside her.